A SHARED MOMENT OF LAUGHTER— AND PASSION . . .

He moved up to straddle her thighs with his knees. "C'mon, Button. Tell me the truth." He grabbed her hands and held her arms captive behind her back. Still soaking wet, he rubbed his freshly shaven jaw against her cheek, across her lightly freckled nose . . . "Admit it, Button. Tell me ya were watchin'." With intent to torment her further, he nipped at her neck, then snaked his fingers around to her ribs and began to tickle her mercilessly.

"All right! I admit it!" she shrieked, laughter bubbling up from deep within her. Leaning her head back, she screeched at the ceiling, "I was watching you bathe!"

She pushed against his chest, kicking her feet all the while. "There! Are you happy? Now let me go." She lunged her body against his.

A button on her shirt popped off. The fabric fell open.

In that movement, he caught sight of the soft mound of pale flesh rising just above her camisole. He could feel the warm surge of her rapid breathing . . . His gaze slipped lower to where his hand rested beneath the underswell of her breast.

She gasped . . .

DIAMOND WILDFLOWER ROMANCE

*A breathtaking line of searing romance novels . . .
where destiny meets desire in the
untamed fury of the American West.*

Diamond Books by Deborah James

GOLDEN FURY
BELOVED WARRIOR
WARRIOR'S TOUCH
TENDER OUTLAW

Tender Outlaw

Deborah James

DIAMOND BOOKS, NEW YORK

If you purchased this book without a cover, you should be aware that this book is stolen property. It was reported as "unsold and destroyed" to the publisher, and neither the author nor the publisher has received any payment for this "stripped book."

This book is a Diamond original edition,
and has never been previously published.

TENDER OUTLAW

A Diamond Book/published by arrangement with
the author

PRINTING HISTORY
Diamond edition/September 1994

All rights reserved.
Copyright © 1994 by Debbie Bailey.
This book may not be reproduced in whole or in part,
by mimeograph or any other means, without permission.
For information address: The Berkley Publishing Group,
200 Madison Avenue, New York, NY 10016.

ISBN: 0-7865-0043-3

Diamond Books are published by The Berkley Publishing Group,
200 Madison Avenue, New York, NY 10016.
DIAMOND and the "D" design
are trademarks belonging to Charter Communications, Inc.

PRINTED IN THE UNITED STATES OF AMERICA

10 9 8 7 6 5 4 3 2 1

To my daughter Michelle, whose robust spirit, oft-times high-browed pride, yet compassionate heart have made me hold my breath, laugh, and cringe more than a few times in fear of what she'll do next.

Even so, your zest for life generates more pride in this mother's heart than words can ever convey. You *are* the essence of Chloe . . .
I hope you like her.

Tender Outlaw

ONE

Nevada
Early Summer—1878

WHAT WAS THAT OLD ADAGE? SOMETHING ABOUT GOD looking after little children and fools? Chloe Summerhorn swallowed hard, her heart pounding above the thundering hoofbeats of the horses that pulled the Concord coach over a narrow bridge. She peered out the window and over the wooden trestle suspending the stage some thousand feet above the crystalline water of Lake Tahoe.

Which was she? Fool or child? After stealing away from Boston's very posh Miss Hannah Hauser's Young Ladies' School of Social Prominence, as Chloe had just done, one might find it difficult to answer that question.

She had never really seemed to fit at the school, with all its rules. She had constantly slipped out in her men's jeans for a secret horseback ride—usually getting caught in the end.

And now she had run away into the night to marry a man she had not seen since childhood. She shivered and prayed that God held the saying close to heart.

"Geeyup there, Duncan." The inebriated driver cracked his whip over the team's heads.

The stage teetered dangerously close to the massive support timbers.

Chloe's eyes flew wide, and she gripped the edge of the window. Staring down at the glistening water, she held her breath and sent a silent plea heavenward. What about drunkards? She squeezed her eyes closed. Oh, Lord, could you please include just this one on your *looking after* list as well?

What had she been thinking when she allowed herself to board the stage in Carson City this morning and head out to her final destination of Glenbrook, Nevada? She had been able to tell, even at such an early hour, that the stage driver had been drinking heavily. She should have waited for a later coach, but she had been too excited at the prospect of seeing her fiancé, Shea Taggert.

She had endured eleven long years of only being able to correspond with him through her letters laced with romance and visions of the home they would share. She had been infatuated with Shea since she was a little girl. And now that she was a grown woman, she found the many miles and years that had stretched between them had only served to bring them closer together—much to her father's chagrin. The *passing fancy*, as Seth Summerhorn had called it, had flourished into love. She was so close to Shea now she could not wait even one more day to see him again.

The coach rocked, and Chloe flew back against the seat. Her head slammed against the padded leather, knocking her oh-so-smart and very refined hat lopsided across her brow.

"That's quite a differ'nt sorta rig ya got perched up there today, Miss Summerhorn." One of her fellow passengers, a rather rough-and-ready young man, grinned at her from beneath the ragged brim of his oversize hat. "Nothin' like the simple foo-fa-ras ya been wearin'. I s'ppose this'uns special—for yer intended. Somethin' . . . well, I s'ppose you'd just have t' call that tiny li'l thing—uh—"

Straightening from his slouched position, he unfolded his arms and pushed the hefty brim of his own hat higher on his forehead. He smoothed his thick black mustache down around his mouth to his chin, his dark gaze shimmering mischievously.

Rolling her eyes with a suitable display of aggravation, Chloe bristled. Was there no end to this insufferable man's rudeness? Whatever his intentions at conversation today, she would let him know she did not find him any more charming now than when he had first boarded the train in Wyoming a week earlier and introduced himself as Tyree Cameron.

She had tried to be friendly when he had approached her with his less-than-amusing company. But after discovering that they were headed in the same general location, he had taken it upon himself to stay only too available to her. He had even gone so far as to take what she had considered simple, polite conversation for something more.

His attention had frightened her at first. But, as she had been taught, Chloe was not to be unnerved—at least, not for long. She had quickly put a halt to his advances with a well-placed jab of her hat pin to his side. Discreetly, of course. But he had not remained daunted for long.

Not even her disclosure of her intended marriage had appeared to dissuade him. In fact, the mention of her fiancé had only seemed to draw him closer.

Setting herself in an upright position again, she adjusted the stylish suit-turban to its earlier jaunty tilt atop her head.

She stole a glance at the woman dressed in a plain brown traveling suit seated beside her, then peered back at her own attire. Self-consciously, she traced her fingers over the fashionable French twist at the back of her head, then allowed herself a moment to toy with the golden ringlets dangling to her shoulder from one side of the coif.

Maybe she was just a tad overdressed out here, but that did not mean she should have to endure anyone's insults. No. She straightened her posture. She would ignore the man's remarks. Instead, she focused on bracing herself against the continual rocking of the stage.

Mr. Cameron's grin broadened. It appeared he had no intention of being brushed off quite so readily. He slapped the top of his Levi's-clad thighs just as the coach bounced again with a loud creak of its springs. "Well, I guess I'd just have t' call it nothin' short o' *fashionable*. Yes'm, fashionable, that's what it is." He nodded as if expecting her to be pleased with his choice of words.

Good Lord. He was still going on about her hat? Glancing up at him, she was not completely certain he had meant his statement as a compliment. More than likely, he was taunting her for her *snooty sophisticated ways*, as she had overheard him calling them to one of the other passengers during their journey.

A twinge of annoyance plucked at her already sensitive nerves, which were nearly frayed from the less-than-genteel traveling accommodations.

She eyed his own enormous hat with equal scrutiny. Its dirty, sweat-stained crown formed a most unusual high ridge in the center of what once must have been a gleaming shade of white wool. Now it was a mixture of mottled shades of grungy grays and blotchy browns.

Chloe arched a brow and looked down at the layer of dust growing thicker by the second on her traveling suit. She swiped at the dirty film with an air of nonchalance. "Well, since you brought it up, Mr. Cameron, I must say how inordinately snappy I find that remarkable piece of millinery work you're wearing."

Tyree Cameron pulled a face as if he were sipping sour lemonade. "Huh?"

Chloe hid an amused giggle with a forced purse of her lips. She cleared her throat. "I believe out here you call it a *stertor*." Pleased with her educated use of proper English, she flitted a glance to the faces of the two passengers sitting beside her—a boy of about six and his mother—each wearing the same puzzled expression as Mr. Cameron.

Still smirking, she coughed to keep from tittering out loud. Since she had began her trip two weeks earlier, she had found herself relying on her little game even more so than when she was in school. It had always kept her occupied, and helped to alleviate some of the insecurity she felt when confronted with unfamiliar circumstances.

She found that her practice of using sophisticated words could be quite a remarkable tool when confronted with an uncomfortable situation. And her proper education gave her substantial leverage against her feelings of inadequacy in such cases. It made her feel slightly superior to speak over the heads of her fellow travelers. For although Chloe was of the ripe old age of twenty, she had never really experienced much.

She had only been taught how to properly establish herself in the presence of life—not how to actually involve herself in it. The fact being, Chloe Summerhorn simply had been tutored to be a spectator, not a player.

The game was her defense against the realities of the outside world, and her only successful way to feel confident in public. And it had worked . . . so far.

Looking up, she caught the eye of an older gentleman, one Mr. Angus Gentry, sitting next to Mr. Cameron. He smiled cunningly, then gestured toward the huge hat with a flip of his hand. His silver-blue eyes remained fixed on Chloe. "She means yer hat, boy," he said with a heavy Texas drawl. His lips spread wide beneath a thick, drooping mustache, displaying a row of unusually well-kept teeth.

Mr. Cameron plucked his hat from atop his head, turned it from side to side, then plopped it down on his knee. "Oh, yeah, o' course," he said in a perturbed tone. He had probably hoped his little quip would see Chloe flustered, but by all calculations this round of the game was hers.

Folding his arms across his chest, the elderly gentleman nodded toward the younger man, but aimed his conversation at Chloe. "It's called a Montana Peak, ma'am. Bein' an Eastern woman like yourself, you prob'ly don't get much call fer seein' such rugged and *practical* apparel as ours. And . . . I believe what you meant to call it was a Stetson." He touched the brim of his own hat with a finger. "Like mine, here. And . . . if I'm not mistaken, a stertor is somethin' like a snore, ain't it?"

Chloe felt the sting of his ridicule. Every now and again, she had the unfortunate habit of using the wrong word. Invariably, it always seemed to happen at the most inopportune time. Her cheeks flamed hot with embarrassment.

"But that's to be expected I guess." He paused for a moment before continuing. "You see, ma'am, it's different out here. Folks just talk plain, and they work hard for their money. They can't afford to be wastin' their breath on a bunch of smooth-tongued words, or squanderin' their hard-earned wherewithal on fancy clothes, expensive gewgaws, and reckless jaunts back and forth across the countryside."

Smooth-tongued words? Wherewithal? Chloe snapped her head up and glared at him. What was he insinuating? Who had invited him in on the game?

"No disrespect intended, ma'am." Mr. Gentry lifted a brow, subtly yet most assuredly marking his conquest. "I didn't mean you, of course. I understand that you've come from a fine upstandin' ladies' school, and that you're on your way to meet your husband-to-be."

The man had expertly planted his insults where they would be felt the hardest—deeply imbedded in her pride. "Yes," she said, stiffening her spine as if she had not felt a single stab. "I most assuredly am." She started to look out the window, but could not resist the urge to set the old man straight. He was not about to best her—at least not without a fight. "And as for my wardrobe, let me simply say that my father bought everything I own, and he is every bit as *hard-*

working as anyone—more so than others." She eyed him none-too-discreetly. "Small as it may be, he has his own ranch in northern California. He earns a living—enough to send me to a very respected school, and I don't think you could call that *squandering* his money on *reckless jaunts*."

"Beg pardon, ma'am." Mr. Gentry pursed his lips, causing his thick mustache to twitch like a tweaked guitar string. He almost appeared as if he were truly sorry—almost, but not quite. "It's just that a lady alone, dressed like you are and unescorted, well, I—" He dipped his head again. "S'cuse me for buttin' in where I hadn't oughta be."

She had won! Again, the game was hers... or was it? Mr. Gentry's apology only made Chloe feel even more deceitful than when she had left Miss Hauser's. But then the old gentleman knew nothing of her daring adventure. The man did not know that Seth Summerhorn was unaware of her defiance. Or that she *was* misspending her father's money. In fact, her father was so set against Shea that if he had had any hint of what she was going to do, he would probably have hired a detective to watch her full-time.

Her eyes flew wide with the thought. She shot a nervous glance out the window before stealing another look at Angus Gentry. Could it be? She studied him a full second, trying to recall where she had first met up with him on her travels. It had been *at least* four or five days into her trip. No. She shook the absurd thought from her mind. No one knew of her plans except Shea.

Still, she could not help but wonder at the elderly man's reason for *buttin' in*, as he had called it. She lowered her gaze, and folded her gloved hands. He had properly chastised her—and quite smartly, too.

She glared out the window at the sheer cliff passing by her. And just who instructed the instructresses at Miss Hauser's? Right now, she would like nothing better than to throttle them all for their ignorance. But then, how were any of them to know about Western witticism? She tightened her mouth into a pout. Once she had settled into married life with Shea, she would have to write the school and inform them of their need for tutors trained in Western culture.

The jolt of the horses' gallop subdued as the dense forest swallowed up the coach and team in its tall stand of virgin timber. And, after a time, Chloe relaxed again, allowing herself to enjoy the wonder of this lush countryside.

Brilliant with sunshine, the cloudless sky domed the scenery in a translucent shade of blue. Clear and sparkling like iridescent glass, the lake was not to be outshined. Winking through the trees, its seemingly boundless sapphire and emerald surface appeared to challenge the heavens in a competition of tranquil beauty.

Chloe took a deep breath and inhaled the clean, crisp scent of pine sailing down off white-capped peaks still blanketed with snow. This was nothing like the crowded, dirty streets back East. The traffic of countless carriages, carts, and wagons milling through the city was not unlike a battle scene. And the people—so many—everywhere.

Funny. She thought back to the constant din of clattering hooves and loud voices, and the stagnant air that filled what until now she had called home. She had almost forgotten how spectacular and untouched by the frantic madness of urban hustle and bustle the world outside of Boston still remained.

Closing her eyes, she lifted her face to the warmth of the sunlight and smiled. Shea could not have picked a more glorious place for them to begin their life together. She leaned back and tried to picture what he might look like. After so many years he must surely have grown into a handsome man. He had always been such an adorable little boy.

She remembered the wicked glimmer of amusement just below the surface of his mischievous hazel eyes. It always seemed to lie in wait for just the right moment. Usually it was when he was in the midst of some roguish prank aimed at her. She had never truly minded any of his antics. To be honest, she had enjoyed the attention. She chuckled softly, basking in the innocent sweetness of her childhood memories.

Would he be the same now? Her heart fluttered at the thought of him holding her and loving her. She felt her body warm slightly, as it always did when her musings turned on a more wayward course—and they always did when she thought of Shea these days, it seemed.

She glanced up and searched the faces of her fellow passengers.

Each appeared absorbed in the splendor of the scenery and their individual thoughts.

Good. No one had taken any notice of her. Looking back out the window, she returned to the privacy of her imagination. Would Shea's hands be pleasantly rough against the softness of her skin? Would she fill the air with tortured moans of passion beneath his kisses as she had read in the romantic escapades in *Harper's Monthly*?

She and Shea were no longer children of ten and nine with games of pretend as they were when she had been sent away to school. These things would most certainly occur now that they were really going to be married.

And what about their wedding? How would Shea react to her arrival? She had waited until the last possible moment to telegraph him of her decision to leave school. She was not about to give him the chance to thwart her plans. And if the lackluster words written in his ever-decreasing letters were any description of his somber personality of late, it was almost a certainty he would have tried to stop her. As it was, she was not entirely positive she would be well received—at least, not at first.

She could not help but wonder why his usual, lengthy love letters had slowly dwindled to short, barely entertaining notes. Had he simply lost interest in her? Chloe gave herself a mental shake. Surely not. It had to be this new job he had written her about. He was just working too hard, and too many hours. He had told of how the job afforded him little time to even sleep, let alone find snatches of time for any sort of pleasure.

But that would end shortly—she would see to it. After all, he was the foreman of the gainful and distinguished Lightning Tree Logging Company.

Why she had just read in the Carson newspaper that the new owner, William Sharon, had become the personal financier for a smaller logging company when their payroll had been stolen. The Lightning Tree must certainly be a reputable business to have such funds. Shea had done well to secure such an advantageous position in such a short period of time.

Now maybe Daddy will think less harshly of him. She tipped her head pensively. It really did not matter, though. After she and Shea were married, her father would have to accept him. He would simply have no choice.

An uproarious ruckus sounded in the distance off to the other side of the coach.

Startled, Chloe squinted into the glaring light.

Riding pell-mell from the cover of the trees came four masked men wielding pistols. They skidded their mounts up to the rumbling stage, firing a volley of shots into the air.

When a besotted command to *whoa* came from the driver, the team abruptly halted and the coach trembled to a sudden stop.

Chloe would have been thrown into the lap of the young man across from her, but an instinctive hand to the window secured her with only a painful jolt forward. Pulling herself upright again, she peered at her companions.

All appeared well, yet they seemed just as stunned by the incident as she.

Without hesitation, both Mr. Cameron and Mr. Gentry drew rather formidable-looking guns from the holsters strapped to their legs.

"You ladies all right?" the old gentleman asked in a subdued tone.

Blinking, Chloe nodded. She pushed her toppled hat back up on her head with a huff. "What on—"

"Shh!" Mr. Cameron touched the barrel of his Colt to his lips, his other hand held up in an obvious gesture for continued silence.

Nonplussed, Chloe shot him an irritated glare.

"You there . . . in the coach," a man's commanding

voice boomed over the winded snorts of the horses. "Get out and stretch for the trees."

On the edge of true fright, Chloe tried to take advantage of the moment and collect her splintered wits. Afraid to even shift her gaze outside the interior of the stage, she swallowed. "Who are those men . . . and what do they want?" she whispered.

A movement blocked the window light.

"No need to be afraid, lady." A sharp click followed the deeply masculine voice.

Stunned, Chloe watched as the two men in front of her slowly lowered their guns.

Their faces drew taut.

Hesitating, she cautiously followed their line of vision. Fear unlike anything Chloe had ever felt before strangled a convulsive gasp.

Above a dirty yellow-and-red bandanna, two large and horrid lashless eyes stared out at her from beneath a shabby hat. "Ya just do like yer told and ever'body'll be just fine."

Chloe felt as if her heart had just lodged in her throat. Her gaze fell to the threatening gun pointed just inside the window. Heaven help them . . . the stage was being held up.

The bandit jerked open the door, then wagged his gun at them. "C'mon, now. Be smart, and all o' ya git outa the coach real slow an' easy like." He gestured to the men. "You two, drop them shootin' irons out the door here. We don't want any itchy fingers throwin' lead, now, do we?"

Both men tossed their weapons on the ground at the outlaw's feet.

Mr. Gentry was the first to depart the stage.

Mr. Cameron hesitated a moment, then leaned forward ever so slightly. "Do as they say," he murmured. "Everything'll be all right if we just do like they say."

"That's right, kid." The highwayman's overly large eyes narrowed into taunting slits. "You see that them womenfolk do right, hear?" Reaching inside, he gripped the young man's shoulder and pulled him outside.

Mr. Cameron collided with Mr. Gentry.

"Watch 'em!" The burly bandit extended his hand toward the youngster. "C'mere, boy."

"Mama!" The child wheeled around in his mother's arms, his face embedded against her breasts, his arms clasped tightly around her waist.

Instantly, Chloe looked to the outlaw. She was afraid of what he might do. She tried to keep from shaking, but she could not stop.

"Ah, c'mon, little guy." The masked man sounded as if he was the one who was being wronged. He leaned nearer and winked, lowering his voice on his next words. "I ain't gonna hurtcha." He tugged playfully on the child's shirt. "We're jist gonna play a little game."

After a moment, the boy glanced up. He appeared both skeptical and hopeful. He blinked away an undropped tear, then sucked in a shuddering sniffle.

Now that he had moved closer, Chloe could see the seasoned age in the outlaw's leathery face.

He appeared to have softened in the presence of the child. "C'mon, now. You don't wanna spoil all the fun, do ya?"

Instantly, the boy perked up. He glanced at his mother, as if to ask her permission to play along.

The woman shifted her gaze from her son to the

threatening man, and back to the child. She squeezed his hand tightly and nodded, a nervous smile masking her features.

It was a valiant display of courage, but Chloe could see the unquestionable fear that reigned in the older woman's eyes.

"What the hell are you doin' in there?" Another man, visibly younger around the eyes and apparently the leader by his authoritative tone, stepped into view. He, too, wore a bandanna over the lower half of his face. "We ain't got time for socializin'. Get the women out."

"You heard the boss, ladies." The first bandit moved aside so the women could disembark.

Once Chloe and the mother and child had taken their leave of the coach, they were quickly ushered a good distance away. Immediately, she saw the other two outlaws and the double-barreled shotguns, one pointed at the driver, the other aimed at the men passengers.

The second robber took off his hat and gestured toward the forest with a flourishing wave. "Have the driver unhitch the team," he yelled, then he leapt into the stage.

From out of the stand of trees another rider, also disguised by a bandanna, rode up to the others.

"You men lookin' for somethin' special?" Mr. Gentry asked. He did not appear too upset by the incident, though he kept his hands extended quite high.

"The strongbox of money" came the answer from the older bandit.

"Hell, man." Mr. Gentry gave a snort most ungentlemanly. "There ain't no strongbox on that stage. Just trunks of female whatnot and two saddles. I heard the payroll's comin' in a special Wells Fargo coach."

"Yeah, sure." Leather-Face chuckled. He shot a glance back over his shoulder. "It in there?"

"Yup. Pretty clever, too," the leader called out. "The passengers were sittin' on it."

"Well, I'll be a shifty son-of-a-sidewinder!" Mr. Gentry remarked.

The old bandit lifted his weapon as if it were a glass of champagne and he were making a toast. "Keepin' it warm for us and ya didn't even know it." His eyes squinted with what must have been a most exuberant grin beneath his bandanna.

Even though the older outlaw had lessened the severity of his manner, Chloe was still frightened. But she just couldn't resist stretching her taut muscles. Being jostled and cramped inside a rocking interior with four other people for the last three hours had left her achy and sore.

"Where the hell's that nitro?" the leader shouted from the stage.

"Nitro?" Mr. Gentry's eyes widened and his face paled.

Chloe froze midaction. "Nitroglycerin?" She had learned of the new liquid explosive from her science courses in school—knew, too, of its volatile nature. Cautiously, she lowered her arms and darted a wary gaze toward the rider who was removing a small box strapped to the horn of his saddle. "That's three times more powerful than gunpowder."

"Do tell?" The wrinkled-eyed bandit shifted nervously from one foot to the other. "Got to use it, though. That strongbox's said to be padded with three layers of tungsten steel and welded into the floor. Plain ol' dynamite ain't gonna do the trick."

Mr. Cameron snickered. "So you're gonna blow up the money, too? That's smart."

The bandit turned his weapon on the younger man. "The boss knows what he's doin' rightly enough. You just don't worry 'bout it." He lifted his brows, causing the brim of his hat to bounce upward. "Butcha oughta be worrin' 'bout yer own self though, don't ya think?"

Chloe held her breath. She had no wish to see any true violence. "Please, Mr. Cameron. There's no need to provoke them. Remember your own words. Just do like they say."

"Yes, Mr. Cameron." The crisp, antagonistic voice of the leader startled Chloe.

She had been so shocked by the information about the nitroglycerin and concerned for Mr. Cameron's well-being that she had not heard the man's approach.

Though the features beneath his eyes was concealed, Chloe felt quite certain the leader of these outlaws was smiling at her. The fact that he and his cohorts were masked only served to summon up her natural curiosity.

"You ready in there?" He tossed the words over his shoulder, yet his cat eyes remained fixed on Chloe.

"Yeah" came the man's voice who had delivered the explosive. The smaller-framed bandit stepped lightly from the coach to the ground, then he dashed over to where the two stood holding the shotguns. With a fling of his wrist, he motioned for the outlaws and the driver to move off to a safe distance.

"Now, if you'll all be so kind as to step back a space or two."

Without hesitation, the other passengers and the older bandit hurried off some thirty feet.

Chloe remained where she stood. She suddenly realized just exactly what damage this holdup meant to her personally. Primed as dangerously as any explosive, anger suddenly coursed through her veins. "Excuse me." She stiffened her spine and glared at the leader.

"Ma'am, I really don't think—"

"I don't give a ten-horned toad what you think." All of her proper, ladylike training always seemed to abandon Chloe when her temper rose. No matter how hard she tried to keep the inbred, unyielding disposition that had been handed down to her from her father from surfacing, it continually thwarted her more genteel education.

She took a breath, trying desperately to hang tight to her more lofty tutelage. "It's quite evident that you intend to get your money. And, as I've noticed your use of nitroglycerin, I would also surmise that you intend on blowing up the stage as well?"

The bandit appeared puzzled at her question. Still, he nodded.

Chloe gripped the sides of her skirts. She planned to enlist the aid of her game against the outlaws. Her knowledge of words was her only defense—or in this case, attack. She cleared her throat. "Well then, let me advise you that my repository, which is on the upper deck there, will in all probability be destroyed. It contains all that I own in this world, not to mention my trousseau. And, while its demise will neither benefit nor injure you in the least, these possessions are irreplaceable to me."

"Repository? Trusso?" The outlaw quirked a brow,

puzzled. He scanned the half-masked faces of his men. "Any of you know what the hell this female's rattlin' on about?"

Shrugging and murmuring amongst themselves, all four members shook their heads.

"It means she's gettin' married," Mr. Cameron interjected. "The lady's come all the way out from Boston to marry her beau. Her weddin' dress is up there with her things."

The outlaw's eyes cut into her with the fierceness of his stare.

Chloe held herself rigid against the discomfort of his silent scrutiny. He appeared angry. But why? What was her impending marriage to him? He did not know her.

Suddenly, the severity of his gaze softened. "And this beau of yours, does he know you're coming?" His tone sounded almost amused.

"Yes," she admonished with a haughty lift of her chin. "Of course he does."

The echo of her last words hung on a long, awkward pause.

His stare appeared to taunt her—as if for some reason he did not believe her.

It made her even angrier. How dare he question her honesty. Even in voiceless mockery—he still taunted her. She would not allow this to continue longer. "Please." She nearly bit the end of her tongue off with forced politeness. "If you must blow up the entirety of the coach to obtain your ill-gotten riches, will you be so kind as to take my trunk down first?"

His eyes crinkled at the corners and his bandanna puffed in and out with his light laughter. "Oh, so it's your trunk you're worried about." He suddenly bent at the waist as if he were a dignified butler. "Well, then by all means, ma'am, it will be my greatest pleasure to serve you." Without so much as another glance her way, he sauntered toward the stage.

Enraged beyond belief, Chloe hurried after him. She was not about to let his insolence go unpunished. Miss Hauser's proper ladylike training be damned! It was her father's English, hell-bent stubbornness she clung to now. She waited as he carefully climbed atop the coach.

"Which one is it?"

"The large one on the opposite side." Her fear slightly lessened by her anger, Chloe followed him around to the back end. She would wait until he had unloaded her trunk before unleashing the full force of her ire.

After untying the straps securing the luggage, the outlaw pulled the huge trunk from its place. Apparently unaware that she had followed him, he kept his back to her, shoving the heavy baggage across the top, little by little.

Eyeing him with growing fascination, Chloe was impressed with his display of strength. It had taken two men his size, spewing a considerable amount of curses, to hoist the burden up and onto the roof of the stage.

He pushed again, and it caught on something, halting with a jerk. It must have taken him by surprise, because he stumbled and fell across the trunk lid. His bandanna slipped, exposing his face.

Chloe sucked in a breath. His rugged, unshaven features were those of a very determined, attractive man.

He froze. His gaze shot out to the others. Still, he

must not have known Chloe could see him. He must have thought she had remained on the side of the coach in view of his men. He snatched the bandanna back up to its original position.

Chloe hurried around just in time for him to pull the trunk over the edge of the roof and onto the driver's seat.

He motioned for two of his men to come to his aid. After handing over the sizeable luggage, the leader jumped down beside her. The corners of his eyes lifted in an obvious smile. "Now," he said with controlled yet labored breath. "If there's nothin' else I can get for you . . . ?"

So taken aback by her momentary glimpse of the outlaw, Chloe had forgotten her earlier rage. She smiled thinly. "No. That's all, thank you."

Taking her elbow, the leader hurried her over to where the others waited.

"If you're done with your lordly duties, do you think we can get on with this robbery?" The smaller man who had set the explosive voiced his impatience. "There'll be another stage along any time now."

"Ma'am." The leader ushered Chloe back a step. "Wouldn't want you to get injured before that intended of yours got an eyeful of what he's gettin'." He swept a capricious gaze over her form, before returning to her face.

Any other time Chloe's anger would have been incited by the boldness of the man's insinuation.

But unlike earlier, there was no taunting in his remark. He appeared to be genuinely impressed by his appraisal of her—was it actual admiration she saw sparkling in his eyes?

Strangely delighted that he had found her attractive, she felt her face warm, and she smiled self-consciously. But the moment was short-lived.

In the next instant, the outlaw's gaze narrowed. He pierced her with a bold, rakish stare that left nothing to the imagination about his thoughts.

Chloe Summerhorn had been duped! Her mouth fell agape. There was nothing honorable about this rogue. He was a bandit—a thief, nothing more. She had lost yet another round of the private game she thrust upon others, and found herself fully immersed in a new and unpredictable contest—a very frightening game without any rules, and with no Miss Hauser to intervene. The West was definitely the vulgar, wild and woolly place she had heard it was.

Lifting his Colt, the leader took aim at the stage. He glanced at her one last time. Then, as if he had not insulted her enough, he gave her a most suggestive wink.

Charged with renewed fury, Chloe's temper won out over her naïveté. Her face flamed red-hot. "You licentious, villainous—"

The gun fired. The bandit's eyes twinkled.

And her barb-edged words died, strangled in the ear-shattering blast of the exploding stage.

Two

STANDING OUTSIDE THE STAGE DEPOT, CHLOE WATCHED as for the second time that day her trunk was hoisted down from atop a Concord coach. Never again, she mentally promised herself, would she *ever* be inclined to travel by such a reckless and reproachable means of transportation.

Western culture certainly left a lot to be desired. She would have to find out the name of the owner of the stage line and inform him of her ordeal. It was another letter to be written, but one of the utmost importance. Something simply had to be done to protect the passengers from such untoward mishaps as had befallen her and her traveling companions.

The planked walk trembled beneath her feet with the vibration made by the huge trunk thudding to the ground.

"Be careful with that," she commanded sharply. She glared up at the porters. Diplomacy be damned. She had endured enough discord and embarrassment this day. With the holdup, the boorish bandit and his devil-may-care attitude, *and* having to wait well over an hour for another coach to come to their rescue, she had lost all pretense of amiability. She and her possessions had finally made it to Glenbrook with only a fragment of her pride frayed around the edges. She was not about to have her personal dainties spilled out onto the street for public display now.

"So now, tell me again, Hank. How come only the lady's baggage was taken down before them outlaws blew up the stage?" A youth with blond fuzz for a beard jumped down from the roof of the coach, one eye squinting against the late-afternoon sun. He frowned at the stage driver. "I don't understand why they'd save hers and nobody else's."

The once-inebriated coachman tugged at his gloves. "'Cuz she asked 'em to, I reckon," he answered in a low, surly tone. He did not appear to be the slightest bit pleased by the young man's persistent questions. He glared up beneath the bent and ragged brim of his hat. "And I'll thank ya to call me Mr. Monk, *boy*."

"Polite outlaws? Ain't never heard such a thing." Apparently oblivious to Chloe's nearness, and ignoring the driver's harsh tone, the youth shook his head, then laughed out loud. "Hell, Hank—uh—*Mr. Monk*, if they was so accommodatin' and all, why didn't ya just ask them to wait an' rob the next stage 'stead o' yers?"

"Ya know, *boy*, this isn't the first time such a thing's happened to me."

"It ain't?" The youth sobered.

"Nah," The driver shook his head. "Here we was, just 'bout dusk. Steep hills all around us," he drawled in a serious, thoughtful manner. "Purtiest trap as could be sprung."

"What happened?"

Chloe found herself being drawn into the intrigue of the story, too. She leaned forward.

"Well, now, I'll tell ya. There was bullets from the

guns them bandits was shootin' 'round our heads. I told Bill, that's my messenger, to keep on firin' so's I can unloose the horses. He did, and when I got back to him, we held off those desperados for nigh on two hours."

Chloe was so caught up in the story, she had to struggle for a breath.

"All the time, though, our ammunition's gittin' lower and lower. We tried to save our shots until we was sure of a good hit, and by this time we'd already kilt us a passel—'bout sixteen, I reckon—maybe seventeen." He shrugged. "I don't recall zackly. Anyhows, we finally run clean outa shot."

"And did ya escape?" the boy asked breathlessly.

Chloe swallowed, waiting for the reply herself. For a moment, she thought she detected a glimmer of moisture in the driver's eyes.

"Nah," he replied in a voice choked with emotion. "They buried us under a tall yeller pine over yonder." He pointed toward a rising peak in the distance. "If ya look real hard, ya can still see our graves to this very day."

The youth followed the man's directions.

Chloe, too, peered up into the forested mountain. Then, she caught herself. Her gaze fell to the driver's smug grin. He had been lying. Lying! Rage instantly overtook her senses. She stiffened. She had been duped again. Itching to wield her hat pin in defense of her own naïveté, she reached up and retrieved the slender weapon from her bonnet.

"Whoa, there." Mr. Cameron came up from behind her, then jumped to one side. Grabbing his ribs as if it were him she was about to subdue, he raised a palm to her in mock terror. "Who you plannin' ta skewer now?"

Chloe flinched. Her face warmed. She had not known anyone was watching her. Looking down at the metal pin, she smiled in spite of her embarrassment. She could not let him know she had been just as taken in by the tale as the boy. Gathering her composure, her gaze returned to the man in front of her.

Clean-shaven and freshly dressed in unsoiled clothing, he now appeared more presentable than he had on their travels together. Odd. She had not noticed how attractive he could be. Even his hair had been combed neatly beneath the enormous brim of that—what had Mr. Gentry called it—Mountain Peak? No, that was not it. She grinned at the thought of her accidental humor. No matter. It looked like a mountain peak to her.

"Forgive me, Mr. Cameron. I didn't mean to startle you." She replaced the pin as best she could without the aid of a mirror.

"Ol' Hank's quite a storyteller, ain't he?"

His question did not chafe Chloe as much as his animated tone. She knew he had witnessed the entire scene. She took a deep breath and drew herself up, ready to do battle again. "I really don't know what you're talking—"

"Say," Mr. Cameron interrupted. "Where's that fiancé of yers?"

Chloe blinked. She had almost forgotten. She had been waiting inside the depot for nearly an hour, and had become quite irritated with Shea's delay. Now, after standing outside for nearly a quarter of an hour, and with Mr. Cameron's question, her displeasure peaked again.

She glanced up to one end of the walk and searched the area beneath the sign that read LAKE BIGLER TOLL ROAD.

Workers, dandies, and skirted ladies shuffled in and out of the various shops and hostelries lining the street, but not one of them looked familiar. Still hesitating to answer Mr. Cameron, Chloe peered down the opposite end of the street. Again, except for the handsome porticoed doors of the Glen Brook House a few buildings down, the same scene appeared before her.

Her shoulders slumped. Where was Shea, indeed? True, she had not waited for a reply to her telegram, but surely he would not have been so angered by her impending arrival that he would not meet her ... would he?

"Miss Summerhorn?"

Tyree Cameron's voice drew her from her thoughts. Facing him, she lifted her chin and smiled exuberantly. "It seems my fiancé has been detained by his work." She turned her head and focused her gaze up the street as if interested in some goings-on at one of the many hotels. "He's foreman at the renowned Lightning Tree Logging Company, you know."

"Really? I don't believe I've ever heard of it."

Chloe saw him grin out of the corner of her eye. He may have looked different, but his exhausting wit remained just as vexing. She exhaled with forced tolerance. "Yes, well, you will, Mr. Cameron." She cut him a quick glance before returning her attention to her trunk. "Rest assured, if you remain in Glenbrook long, you will."

Then without so much as a congenial good-bye, she gripped the sides of her skirt and wheeled away from him. With quick strides, she moved to confront the porters. "Excuse me," she said in her most commanding tone.

The men jumped up straight as if at attention.

"Yes'm?" The older man whipped off his hat.

Chloe pretended not to be amused by his exaggerated look of surrender. "Do either of you know where a Mr. Taggert of the Lightning Tree Logging Company dwells?" She offered the question in a louder than usual voice. She had to let Mr. Cameron see that her fiancé was so well known that even common laborers such as these would know of him.

By their expressions, both men appeared puzzled.

"No, ma'am, can't say as I—" The older man's voice whooshed out of him.

"You ain't talkin' 'bout *Shea* Taggert, are ya?" The younger man's face brightened a bit.

Mr. Cameron's chuckle attacked Chloe's senses from behind. She held herself rigid against his mirth. She had not counted on these hirelings knowing her Shea quite so intimately. Ignoring Tyree Cameron, she nodded at the youth. "Yes, Mr. Shea Taggert. I should like to know the whereabouts of his home."

He pointed to the north. "It's a white house just yonder inside that stand of timber."

Chloe followed his direction with a squinting gaze. All she could see was the long string of buildings lining the front of the lake. She shaded her eyes and peered harder.

"Ya can't see it from here, but it's there all right."

Bristling, Chloe glared at the young man.

He beamed a brassy-toothed grin at her. "Just ask anybody. It's easy enough to find."

Chloe tugged down the edge of her shirtwaist.

"Well, then, if it's so *easy*, do you think the two of you could manage to transfer my accoutrement to Mr. Taggert's stately abode?"

The youth glanced at his friend and frowned. "What'd she say?"

Mr. Cameron stepped up beside her. "The lady's from Boston, boys. I've been travelin' with her for a few days, and I've discovered Eastern folks just don't talk plain like we do."

"Mr. Cameron, I assure you I can handle this my—"

"I think she wants you to take her trunk over to her intended's house."

"Intended? The blond man's brows shot upward. "You mean yer Shea's darlin'?"

Chloe blanched. She had been called a lot of things, but *darlin'* had never been one of them. The youth had a way of making what she felt quite sure was an endearment sound like an insult. "I'm his fiancé," she corrected. "Now. Are you able to—"

"Oh, yes'm." Looking her up and down in a most unappreciated manner, he flashed her another grin. "We'll be happy to bring it to Mr. Taggert's—uh—abode."

After what seemed like an endless walk through the beribboned business district, and an intolerable amount of ogling from the townspeople, Chloe finally managed to make her way to the stand of pines to which she had been directed. She stood at the gate of the picket fencing and looked back at the town.

Everywhere people were getting ready for the Fourth of July. Gay bands of red, white, and blue were even now being strung across the faces of the buildings. Signs had been posted announcing some big debate for congressmen. Yet, even with all the business going on, everyone had taken a minute to stare at her. It made her quite uncomfortable.

It was only too apparent what had happened. The porters certainly had not wasted any time in announcing to the entire community just who and what Chloe was to Shea. Everyone had greeted her with a courteous dip of the head, but Chloe had not missed the critical, sidelong glances cast her way. And by the snatches of murmured conversation she had overheard as she passed, all appeared extremely interested in why she had arrived unescorted, and moreover, why no one had met her at the stage depot.

This, too, weighed heavily on Chloe. She would have to ask Shea the reason for his absence. Turning back to the house, she allowed herself a moment to take in the quality of the home that she would soon share with Shea as his wife.

With pride-filled eyes, she scanned the ornate trim edging the roof of the gable protruding just above what looked to be the parlor. Cornice work? Here? Her heart swelled. It appeared as if Shea had spared no expense in creating their dream home. Painted white and adorned in dark green, it was just as they had planned in their youth and in the letters they had exchanged over the years.

Happy tears threatened her composure. Shea had not forgotten even the smallest detail. Until now, she had only imagined the beautiful little home the two of them had designed in their dreams, but to see it actually standing before her— Her breath shuddered out of her. A rush of pure love for the man flooded her body.

Her gaze slid to the single window at the front of

the upstairs. A network of sheer curtains hid the interior from view. She felt a swelling in her throat. Nottingham lace, just like Aunt Dudee's room back home.

She had almost forgotten how much she had loved to lie flat on her aunt's bed back home and watch the breeze rustle the silk filigree. She inhaled deeply, and for a second she thought she could smell the delicate white rose fragrance that had always enveloped the only mother she could ever remember. She sighed. How much she missed Aunt Dudee.

She shook her head. She would not allow a single moment of melancholy to set in—not today—she was too excited. Pushing open the gate, she hurried inside the yard and up the steps of the porch. She smiled. A swing—he had even remembered that. He must have been planning on her joining him here all along.

That was it. Of course Shea had wanted her here with him. The fact that he had not met her at the depot was merely an oversight. With all of the many stages running in and out of Glenbrook, how could he know for certain which one she would take, or when she would arrive, for that matter?

Everything had worked out for the best. Now she would have the pleasure of surprising him. Hurrying on tiptoe, she dashed up to the front door. Using its etched-art glass, she checked her reflection for any muss in her coiffure or attire. Only a few wisps of tawny hair strayed out from under her suit-turban. Her cheeks had a bit more color from the heat than she would have liked, but all in all she had managed to remain at least somewhat presentable. It would have to do.

Squaring her shoulders she knocked on the wood frame surrounding the glass. She took a breath and held it. What would Shea look like after so many years? Would he be handsome? And what would he think of her? Would he still smile at her that same curious way he'd had when they were children?

Footsteps sounded, growing louder as they neared. Her heart pounded harder against her breast.

The door swung open, and a woman's round face framed by the blackest, most finespun hair emerged into view.

Chloe's eyes flew open wide.

Petite to the point of being positively tiny, a serene-eyed Oriental woman stared out at her. Her thin black brows lifted. "I help you, Meesie?"

So taken aback with the young woman's exotic beauty, Chloe could not even speak. So ... this was the reason behind Shea's dwindling and despondent love letters. Several emotions hit her at once. Deep, abiding pain. Humiliation. Embarrassment. And beneath them all, flaming hotter by the moment, anger—seething, raging anger. How could she have been so naïve? She should have known Shea would not wait for her.

"You lost, Meesie?" Crescent-shaped, the woman's dark eyes appeared concerned and puzzled. "You in need o' help, Meesie?"

Still unable to speak, Chloe swallowed hard. Shea had fallen in love with another woman. She squeezed her eyes closed momentarily. This could not be true. Staring at the little woman, she again took in the splendor of the house around her. No. This could *not* be true. This was definitely the home Shea had promised Chloe.

Securing herself with this knowledge, she drew herself up as tall as possible. Chloe would find out who this woman was and why she was in *her* home.

"Chloe? Child ..."

No—it could not be. Shocked beyond belief, Chloe shifted her gaze to stare straight into the endearing blue gaze of her Aunt Dudee.

"So you came anyway? I knew you would. Why didn't you wire us of your arrival time from Carson City?"

Of its own accord, Chloe's mouth fell agape. It *was* Aunt Dudee—here—in Shea's house.

The stout woman threw open her arms as she rushed down the remaining stairs to the vestibule.

The Oriental woman sidestepped out of the way.

"Aunt Dudee?" Chloe questioned her eyes again. But how could this be?

Clutching Chloe to her more than ample breast, Aunt Dudee squeezed tightly.

Every time her aunt hugged her, Chloe felt quite certain she understood what it must be like for a pillow to be crushed. The scent of white roses combined with the light odor of the woman's usual hard-earned perspiration assured her this was definitely Aunt Dudee. If she had any doubt before, she did not now.

"What time did you get in, child?" Clasping Chloe in a one-armed embrace, the robust woman ushered her inside with customary vigor.

Still in shock, Chloe was barely aware of the first question before her aunt bombarded her with another.

"Did someone escort you to the house? Don't tell me you found us all by yourself? But of course you did—you're an educated Boston lady now, aren't you? Oh, but look at you. You're as red as a ripe tomato. Do you want something to drink? Of course you do." She turned to the Oriental woman. "Ushi, would you be so kind as to get my niece a cool glass of lemonade?"

Chloe glanced over her shoulder, then returned her gaze to her apple-cheeked aunt. Her eyes must have asked the question she had not as yet been able to voice.

"Oh, that's Ushi, Shea's housekeeper. Pretty little thing, hmm?" Aunt Dudee leaned nearer, her temple touching Chloe's. "She's one of many China girls that came into San Francisco on a wave of emigrants from the Orient."

"Shea's housekeeper?" Barely aware of her aunt's acknowledgment, Chloe stared after the servant. She had been wrong to think such awful things about Shea and the young woman. How could she have allowed her insecurities to attack her confidence so bitterly?

"Yes, poor thing," Aunt Dudee continued, almost without a breath. Moving into the parlor, she pulled Chloe down to sit on the brocaded velour divan. "It seems her mother obtained the job with Shea on his arrival here, but the woman fell ill with influenza about six months ago and died. The girl's only other family—two brothers—found work on the railroad, but Ushi has lost touch with them. Now she's alone, poor thing. Shea felt sorry for her and kept her on as a replacement for her mother."

Never did it cease to amaze Chloe how Aunt Dudee could summarize so much vital information in one sitting. Desperately trying to regather her thoughts,

Chloe looked around the more than adequate-sized room.

The other three pieces of sitting furniture—an armchair, a rocker, and a reception chair—all matched the sofa's rich sapphire velour. Her favorite color. She warmed at the thought. Such a small thing, yet Shea had remembered even that.

Green potted plants enlivened the oak-paneled walls and wood floors so shiny they almost reflected her image. Beneath her feet a large Oriental rug graced the center of the room. Chloe eyed the feminine opulence with a curious eye.

Something was wrong with all of this luxury. She did not remember Shea as being one who knew much about such feminine finery. This was not a room decorated by a man. It bespoke a woman's touch.

At that moment, Ushi entered carrying a tray laden with a glass pitcher of lemonade, two tumblers, and a plate of gingersnaps. "I think Meesie like cookie with drink, yes?" She smiled sweetly, her dark eyes pulling to an even tighter slant.

Rising, Chloe clutched the lace collar sticking out above her shirtwaist. She could feel jealousy and self-doubt creeping up within her again. She crossed the parlor to the piano that sat silent in the corner facing her. Why did Shea have to hire such a beautiful housekeeper? She peered around the room again. Was the servant responsible for the luxurious decor? She had to be.

Maybe Chloe had been right. Maybe she was not just a servant after all. Chloe struggled to push the thoughts from her mind. She had to see Shea. Why was he not there? "Where is Shea, Aunt Dudee? Will he be home soon?" Desperate to know of his whereabouts, she turned to her aunt. "And what are *you* doing here?

Both the elderly woman and the servant exchanged questioning glances.

After setting the tray down on a small table to the right of Dudee, Ushi dipped her head, then disappeared from the room in curious haste.

Bewildered, Chloe looked back at her aunt. "What is it? Is something wrong?"

"Why no, child." She waved Chloe back to sit beside her. "I simply assumed Shea had explained everything to you in his answer to your telegram."

"I didn't wait for a reply." Chloe sauntered over to the divan, then sat, albeit as if she were sitting on a cushion of needles. Something was definitely wrong. "I was afraid Shea would tell me he did not want me to come."

Dudee retrieved the pitcher and a glass, then poured. She handed a glass to Chloe. "He did."

Mid-sip Chloe's throat closed as tightly as if she had just sucked pure lemon extract instead of the sweet-tart juice she now fought to swallow. Why had Shea not wanted her? Tears stung her eyes as she lifted them to her matronly aunt. Did she truly want to know? No—not now. She might not be able to bear the reason. "How thoughtful of Shea to ask you here to soften the blow of this dire news."

"Gracious me, child. What on earth are you talking about?"

Unable to trust her trembling hand to hold the tumbler any longer, Chloe returned the glass to the tray. She stiffened her spine to meet the rest of the unpleasant information with dignity. She would not hear it, though. She had already heard the worst. Shea did not want her.

Aunt Dudee had been summoned to ease the truth—a truth Chloe had felt edging destructively closer to her with each mile she had traveled toward Shea. But like a moth flying into a flame, she had to come out to Glenbrook to discover this for herself. She felt the life-light burning within her begin to flicker low. Now, her greatest fear had been said, and was a reality.

A rush of heat consumed her. Her head spun. Somewhere just outside her dizzying thoughts, she heard her aunt call out her name, but she could not bring herself to respond. The room suddenly became unbearably hot. Dudee's concerned face seemed to waver in front of her eyes, but it did not matter. How could it? How could anything matter now that she knew for certain that Shea no longer loved her? He had created their dream with someone else.

THREE

COOL, MOTHERING HANDS ON CHLOE'S FACE COAXED HER to open her eyes. Fluttering her lashes upward, she ventured into consciousness again. She squinted against the late-afternoon sun filtering in through the window at the head of the bed. She blinked once more, then peered at her aunt with a questioning stare. "What happened?"

"You fainted, child." Aunt Dudee smiled. The indistinct lines fanning the corners of her eyes deepened into creases of worry.

Chloe frowned. She tried to rise, but was quickly pressed back down to the massive bed. She glanced around the room. Her hat had been removed and now lay on the table beside her, and her shirtwaist had been completely unbuttoned. She pulled it closed over her blouse. "Where am I?"

"You're in Glenbrook, don't you remember?" Her aunt appeared a little more concerned. "The doctor said the heat must have gotten to you—but if you don't know where you are, well, I'm not so—"

"No, Aunt Dudee . . . I mean, I know I'm in Glenbrook." She took another look around the interior. "But *where* am I?"

Dudee peered up a moment before returning her

attention to Chloe. "Oh. You mean *whose* room are you in?"

Chloe nodded. She had a feeling she knew, but wanted to hear the answer for herself.

"Why, you're in Shea's room, of course."

Ushi shuffled quietly through the door holding a pitcher in one hand and a small bundle of towels in the other. "Meesie feel betta now?" Like a heavy velvet gown on a hot August evening, the Oriental's voice chafed Chloe.

She suddenly remembered the parlor, the elaborate furnishings, and the conclusion she had come to from the woman's presence in Shea's home. It took every ounce of composure she could muster not to leap out of the bed—the bed Shea apparently shared with Ushi. "Yes. I'm fine." She flicked a critical glance across the room. "Thank you for asking, though." She allowed her aloof facade to resurface. She could not let Ushi know of the anguish churning within her.

After setting the towels and pitcher on the bedside table, the small woman smiled timidly and dipped her head. She looked first at Dudee, then back at Chloe. "I will leave you to west, then." She bowed one last time, turned, and hurried from the room.

With dagger-filled eyes, Chloe watched her departure before glancing back at her aunt.

"That was a rather lukewarm response, don't you think?" Dudee lifted one bushy black brow. "Especially since she was only concerned for you. If that's the way that Boston school taught you to behave— well, maybe it wasn't such a . . ."

Dudee's word faded in Chloe's mind as she studied her aunt's countenance more closely. With everything that had happened earlier, she had not noticed how much the woman appeared to have aged in the last eleven years. She reached up and stroked one of the puffy curls arranged in the customary coronet style her aunt had always worn.

"What is it, child?" Dudee's voice edged on curiosity.

"Your hair's almost white," Chloe answered, incredulity filling her tone.

Dudee blinked, and her cheeks flushed. She touched her curls in an unconscious manner, then peered at her reflection in the mirror across the room. "Yes, well, I suppose it just proves that the wind continues to blow through the trees even when no one's in the forest."

"What?"

Still examining her image, Dudee straightened her posture and patted the plumpness under her chin with the back of one hand. "Time marches on, child, even when you're not watching it."

"Oh." Chloe smiled. She had forgotten her aunt's colorful way of explaining things.

"Now," Dudee continued, picking up where she had been before Chloe's interruption. "Why were you rude to Ushi?"

"I was not rude." Glancing down her nose in a disdainful manner, Chloe arched her brows. "As a matter of fact, I believe I was quite tolerant considering the unpropitious circumstances to which I now find myself subjected."

Turning to face Chloe, Dudee frowned. "Unpro—what?"

Chloe rose to a sitting position, then slipped her stockinged feet from the bed to the floor. Her back offered to her aunt, she folded her arms across her chest and gazed past the lacy curtains to the late-afternoon sky. "Is Shea happy?"

Not waiting for the older woman to answer, she stood, then moved to the dresser. Catching sight of a silver toilet set, she picked up the brush and fingered the lovely tiger-lily pattern engraved on the back. It had been Shea's mother's. She remembered him showing it to her once when she was a child.

Keeping her gaze focused on the hairbrush, she prompted with another question. "Have they been married long?"

"Married? Who?" Dudee sounded completely perplexed.

Chloe carefully replaced the item on the dressertop next to its matching comb and hand mirror. Hesitantly, she looked up, her attention trained on her aunt. "Please, Aunt Dudee." She took a breath. "I'm not a child. I assure you I'm quite capable of handling this unpleasant information without succumbing to a tantrum of jealousy."

Chest swelling with her intake of breath, Dudee stood. She clasped her hands in an apparent display of vexation. "Child, if you want me to answer you, you're going to have to stop using all that wasteful stock of words you're tossing out. A body simply can't keep up with what you're saying. Now," she continued without hesitation, "how long has *who* been married?"

Chloe rolled her eyes. "Really, Aunt Dudee, there's no need to play this cordial game with me. I understand how things are between Shea and—" Unable to say the Oriental woman's name with that of the man she loved, Chloe could only indicate her meaning by a sidelong glance out into the hallway.

Dudee followed her gaze, then pinned Chloe with a shocked, yet mirth-filled stare. "Child." With big, round eyes, she peered at the open entryway again, then grinned. "You're not suggesting that Shea and Ushi are—?" She tittered, then hurried toward Chloe with open arms.

Swallowed in the embrace of her aunt, Chloe could do nothing but hold her arms limp at her sides. Why did Dudee find this situation so humorous?

"Shea and Ushi aren't married. Why, Ushi's barely a slip of a girl and only works for Shea." Reaching up, Dudee framed Chloe's face with her warm hands. "He loves *you*, child. This room is to be for you and Shea."

Studying the pale blue of her aunt's eyes, Chloe pulled her bottom lip between her teeth. "Me and—" Could she truly have made such an error in judgment? She wanted to speak, but her voice felt painfully trapped in her throat. A flood of heat rushed through her body. She wavered.

"Oh, no, you don't." Dudee grabbed Chloe's upper arms, then hurried her to the bed and sat her down. She immediately started tugging off the sleeves of Chloe's light wool paletot jacket. After setting it at the foot of the bed, she leaned around and began to unbutton the blouse. "You'll expire in such heavy clothing in all this heat. Living close to the ocean as you did, you're not used to the hot weather we have out here. Of course, it's not always so hot this time of year, at least, so I've been told."

"Thank you, Aunt Dudee," Chloe said after the woman had pulled open the collar. She felt even more uncomfortable from her aunt's insistent attention than from the uncommonly warm weather. "That feels much better."

Dudee grabbed a towel from the side table and dipped it in the pitcher, then wheeled around and sat on the bed next to Chloe. The older woman patted her face with the damp cloth, then handed it to her.

Accepting the towel, Chloe looked down at it a moment, fingering its cool dampness. She felt so foolish. She was always jumping to conclusions when she should not.

"You all right now, child?"

Embarrassed, Chloe looked up and nodded. She swallowed, then took a breath. "Shea and Ushi really aren't married?" she asked in a meek voice.

Dudee laughed again, her amble bosom bouncing with the effort. "Landsakes no, child. Didn't you hear me a minute ago? Shea's in love with *you*. Always has been, I suppose. How on earth did you get such a foolish notion as that anyhow?"

Chloe peered up at the splendor of the huge iron bed and other furnishings. "I—" Her voice caught and she cleared her throat. "I simply assumed that all of this beautiful decor had been picked out by a woman. And with only Ushi here, I—"

"And what, pray tell, do you suppose *I* am?" Leaning back, fingertips against her chest, Dudee appeared offended.

Chloe stared at her aunt for a moment as the sum and substance of the woman's words filtered into her brain. "Do you mean *you* did all of this?" she asked with a sweeping hand.

"I helped. That's why I'm here, child. I've been here for about a month now." Dudee smiled in that understanding way that always put Chloe instantly at ease. "Shea fell in love with this town the minute he saw it. Said it was the kind of setting you two had always talked about. He built this house and sent for me to help him pretty it up. Guess he figured between the two of us, we could fix it like you'd like it."

On the verge of swooning with joy, Chloe jumped up on shaky feet. She grabbed the bedpost to steady herself. "You mean he really did this all for me? He was going to bring me out here to be with him all along?"

Dudee tipped her head to one side and smiled. She exhaled a tolerant sigh. "Well, there *are* some things that haven't changed about you." Reaching out, she took Chloe's hand and patted it. "It's good to have you back, child. I've missed you something awful."

"But what about Daddy?" Though Chloe was delighted with this turn of events, she still was not completely convinced that everything had been done for her. "I can't believe he would just allow you to come at Shea's beckoning without giving you even the slightest bit of an argument." Setting her hand atop her hips, she studied Dudee. "Or has he finally come to his senses about Jerome?"

Dudee shook her head. "No. He still holds Shea responsible for your brother's death."

"Then I don't understand."

"He thinks I'm here visiting some friends," Dudee answered with a mischievous smile. "Besides, Seth Summerhorn doesn't own me. I'm his sister, not his wife, nor his maid. *I* do what I like. Still." She giggled as if she were an unruly child. "No sense inciting trouble for myself. He can't be angry if he doesn't know the truth, can he?"

A knock at the front door below drew Chloe's attention. The stage porters were delivering her trunk.

At once, Chloe bounded for the stairway, buttoning her blouse as she scurried toward the landing. Catching sight of the two men hauling her baggage inside, her excitement grew. "Oh, hurry, Aunt Dudee," she called over her shoulder. "I've got the most exquisite things to show you."

"Where do you want us to put this, ma'am?" one of the porters asked.

"Up here, Zeke." Dudee walked up behind Chloe.

One of the men started grumbling to the other. "Can't fer the life of me figure out how that little lady managed to keep this from being blown up. Monk said they was the same outlaws that's been holdin' up the other stages—"

Dudee turned to Chloe, a look of worry deepening the lines around her eyes. "Why didn't you tell me the stage was robbed?"

Anxious to see how the contents of her trunk had faired, Chloe only shrugged. "It's over. I'm fine, and I did manage to save my things." She hurried back into the room ahead of the two porters. "At least I hope I did."

Once the men had hoisted the trunk upstairs and set it down at Chloe's feet, she immediately sought out the key to her possessions safely pinned to the inside of her reticule.

"But what happened, child?" Dudee appeared determined to hear all of the sordid details.

"Oh, beggin' yer pardon, ma'am." Zeke interrupted. "The boy from the telegraph office was 'bout to deliver this when we got here." He pulled an envelope out of his shirt pocket and handed it to Dudee.

Chloe barely paid the large man any attention, but instead turned her thoughts toward the contents of her trunk.

"Thank you, Zeke," Dudee replied. "I'll get some money for your trouble."

"That's not necessary, Miz Dudee."

Footsteps sounded as the men took their leave.

Chloe inserted the key and turned the lock, then raised the lid and pulled back the cotton cloth she had used to line the large piece of baggage. Carefully, she lifted out several skirts and blouses, then draped them over the footboard of the bed. She had in mind to show her aunt the elaborate wedding gown she had had specially tailored for her marriage to Shea.

"Now, are you going to tell me what happened on the..."

"Who's the telegram from?" Chloe asked, mildly interested now that her aunt's voice had trailed off. When Dudee did not answer, she glanced up.

Slowly a smile grew across the woman's face. It was as if she had a secret to tell, but wanted someone to pry it out of her.

It triggered Chloe's curiosity. She stretched her neck, and tried to steal a peek at the message.

Still looking at her with a playful smirk, Dudee held out the telegram. "Here, child. You read it."

"Why? It can't be for me. Nobody but you knows I'm here." Casting off an interest in the wire, Chloe went back to the rummaging of her trunk.

"Oh, I think there might be at least one other that knows you're here."

Something close to fear lunged at Chloe. She halted in mid-action. Could her father have found out about her departure from school so quickly? She peered up at her aunt. No. Aunt Dudee would not be smiling if that were true. Still, who else could know of her whereabouts?

Accepting the cable, Chloe slowly drew it closer. She scanned the words. Her eyes grew wide with delight. "It's from Shea. He says he'll be home tomorrow evening." Clasping the paper to her chest, she beamed with happiness. "Oh, Aunt Dudee, did you read this? He says we're to be married tomorrow night. Oh Lord, tomorrow night—can you believe it?"

Chloe spent the whole of that night barely able to close her eyes from the pure excitement racing through her body. She beat the dawn, rising even before the first shards of pink and orange could lift the blanket of night.

Searching through the house, she found an old iron and board in the broom closet. She took the board up to her room and unfolded it to a working position suitable for her height. Then, after returning downstairs, she kindled the kitchen stove and placed coffee on to perk. Taking the iron, she put in on some hot coals and set out to press her wedding gown. Everything had to be perfect for Shea's arrival home.

Near mid-morning, her aunt sauntered past her door with an exuberant stretch.

"Good morning, Aunt Dudee," Chloe said in a tone as light as springtime itself. She shifted the weighty wedding gown, repositioning the white lace and satin to press the last of the flounces forming the hem.

Yawning, Dudee halted, her eyes wide. "What on earth are you doing, child?" Wiping away the sleep from her face, she padded inside.

Chloe smiled to herself. The woman still wore the old threadbare robe that had been Chloe's mother's. Both she and her father had given Dudee new robes on different occasions, but her aunt would never wear them, stating that the old one of Etty Summerhorn's still had many years of wear in it. Chloe knew it was just Dudee's way of feeling close to the woman who had been her best friend. "I'm just putting a fresh pressing to my gown," Chloe answered.

Cinching the robe's multicolored cord tighter around her thick waist, Dudee blustered up to stand in front of her. "Why didn't you ask Ushi to do that for you?"

"Because, *I* wanted to do it." Lifting the dress off the board, Chloe held it up to herself. She tucked the collar under her chin, then gripped the sides, and turned from side to side. "What do you think of it now?"

Crowned with a ruffled linen nightcap covering most of her hair, Dudee sucked in an audible breath and clasped her hands to her bosom. Her pale eyes sparkled with a hint of tears. "Oh, Chloe . . . child. If only your mother could've lived to see you this day." Reaching out, she touched the fold of satin edging one of the wide sleeves. "It's beautiful—*you're* beautiful, no—radiant."

Chloe caught up the neckline of the gown with one hand, then spun around to face the mirror. "It is pretty, isn't it?"

Her aunt nodded.

"Do you think Shea will like it?" Her throat closed with the thought of him looking at her.

Moving up beside her, Dudee set an arm around Chloe's shoulders and hugged her lightly. "Of course he will, child. Of course he will."

Chloe spent the rest of the day in her room readying herself for the ceremony. Her aunt had given her strict instructions not to raise a finger to another single chore—no matter what it might be. She was to do nothing but bathe and pamper herself for the remainder of the afternoon.

Still damp from her bath, Chloe stood alone in the room wrapped in a terry-cloth towel. She untied her hair and moved to the wardrobe. Displayed on a hanger hooked over the door was the thin cambric nightdress she was to wear that evening with Shea, fluttering slightly on a whisper of warmth rustling in through the window.

Tentatively she fingered the soft blue ribbon trimming the heart-shaped neckline. The light fabric was so thin, almost sheer. Would Shea think it scandalous? The French dressmaker that had fashioned her wedding gown assured her he would love it. But now, standing here looking at it only hours before she was to wear it, Chloe was not so certain.

What kind of man had Shea grown into? She found herself daydreaming about the coming evening, after the ceremony. Never had she allowed a man to touch her. Shea would be the first. She drew her fingers lightly up her bare arm. What would it feel like to have him caress her skin?

She smoothed her fingertips across her throat, and a tingle of heat skittered low, through her stomach. Her pulse quickened at the thought of his lips lingering on her shoulder, trailing kisses up to her neck, then inching down toward her breasts.

A quiver of anticipation wriggled up her spine. With everything that she had been taught, she knew she should not be thinking of such things. The wedding consummation was merely a formality that had to be passively endured by the woman. But the closer the time drew, the more she found herself fantasizing about the coming night with Shea.

She closed the wardrobe door, then moved to the ornate bed where her undergarments lay. If she did not stop all of this daydreaming the moment would be upon her before she was ready. Looking down at her underthings, she felt a tightness in her stomach. She shivered uncontrollably. Would she be ready?

She shook her head. She could not think about that now. Shea was due home anytime. Taking up her ruffled nainsook drawers, she allowed the towel to fall to the floor in a heap, then stepped into the soft garment.

A knock sounded at her door. "Chloe, it's Aunt Dudee. May I come in?"

Grabbing up her wrapper from the bed, Chloe pulled it on. "Yes, come in." She tugged the length of her golden hair out from the collar.

"Forgive the intrusion, child, but these ladies have come to help you." Without further hesitation, Dudee bustled into the room with an entourage of four other women close at her heels.

Chloe yanked her robe closed. She stared at the strange ladies.

"This is Clarise," Dudee said, introducing a young blond woman carrying a tray with an assortment of hot curling irons. "She's graciously offered to help you dress your hair."

Chloe acknowledged the woman with a forced smile. She pulled her aunt up beside her. "Aunt Dudee, I thought I'd fashion my own hair," she murmured as she watched the other women dither about the room like sputtering flames in a firepot of glowing embers.

"Nonsense, child. I wouldn't hear of such a thing. Besides, these ladies are the wives of some of Shea's associates. They want to help make everything perfect for the two of you." She patted one of Chloe's cheeks.

"But, Aunt—"

"Now, now, child. Don't worry about a thing." That said, she hurried over to where another woman, nearer her own age, hovered over Chloe's trunk pulling out hose, apparently checking them for tears. She glanced back at her niece one last time before taking her departure again. She blew a kiss. "You're in good hands. Now I'm off to see to the rest of the house. The guests will be arriving soon."

"Guests?" Puzzled, Chloe frowned. She had not invited anyone. There had not been any time.

"Why, of course, child. Shea has seen to everything, right down to the minister."

Chloe blinked. But how could he? She remembered the telegram. Now that she thought about, that was really quite odd. According to her aunt, he had figured out that she was coming to Glenbrook all right, but he was not certain of her arrival time. How could he have even known she was here? He was supposed to be out at the logging camp. "Aunt Dudee, I must speak with you," she called out over the din of female voices.

"Not now. I've a million things still left to do." Grasping the doorknob, she pulled it closed behind her. "I'll be back to fetch you when it's time."

"But—" The door closed, sealing Chloe inside the bedroom full of strangers.

The blond woman came up behind Chloe, then ushered her to a chair near the dressing table. She lifted the mass of Chloe's shimmering locks. "You have beautiful hair. I thought I'd pull it up in one of the new styles. Maybe a French twist with coils of curls cascading one ..."

Chloe did not hear any more. Her moment of romance had fled—intruded upon by the bustling and droning chatter of duty-filled women she did not know.

Hours later, alone once more, Chloe ran her hands over one of the wide lace flounces that trimmed her white satin gown. What would Shea think of her wedding dress? She had saved most of her last six months' allowance from her father to pay for the extravagant frock. Of course he would love it. It was so beautiful, how could anyone not?

Breathing in the fresh air whispering through the window, she looked through the curtains and into the yard below. At least twenty-five carriages—sixteen of which she had watched drive up—waited off to the side of the house.

She could hear the myriad voices downstairs and knew the house must be near bursting with guests. It was growing darker outside. She glanced over her shoulder and checked the small cabinet clock atop the fireplace mantel. Six-thirty-seven. Where was Aunt Dudee? She had said she would come back for Chloe at the proper time. But when was that?

She moved across the large room to the mammoth corner window at the head of the bed. She brushed the curtains aside and looked down at all the decorations that had been set up for the reception. Colorful paper pagoda lanterns had been strung across the yard. Tables were heavily laden with food. Even a small stage, obviously for a band, had been set up.

She smiled. Everything was perfect. It could not have been nicer if she had planned everything herself. She would have to thank her aunt later, for she knew it had to have been Dudee who had gotten this together so quickly. Her aunt was like that.

She glanced up at the twinkling evening sky and then her gaze fell onto the lake in the near distance. Large and luminous, a gibbous moon was reflected in the waves rippling to shore. Chloe could not hear their lapping sound over the din below.

Taking in the warmth of the pine-scented air, she sighed dishearteningly. Where was Shea? Had he arrived yet? If not, would he still? Had something happened to cause him to back out? She shuddered. No. She would not allow her restless thoughts to get the better of her again. Shea would not have gone to such trouble if he were not going through with their plans to marry.

A light tap sounded at the door.

Chloe stilled. That was odd. The house seemed to have grown suddenly quiet.

The knock sounded again.

Chloe nearly jumped with excitement. Her heartbeat quickened. Praying with all her might that it was Shea, she swallowed against the dryness in her mouth. She tried to speak, but her voice caught in her throat.

The knob turned.

Hands clasped at her waist, she held her breath in anticipation.

Slowly the door opened.

Clearly outlined by the glow of lamplight on the dresser, her aunt came into view.

Chloe released her pent-up breath in a disappointed sigh.

Handkerchief in hand, Dudee peeked inside. "Are you ready? It's time, child." Upon seeing Chloe, the older woman's eyes filled with tears. She hurried inside the room. "Oh, my. The ladies said you were beautiful, but oh, my ... you're positively breathtaking." Her voice quivered and a tear slipped from her eye.

Chloe moistened her lips. Her blood raced through her veins. Her heart pounded so hard she was certain it would leap from her breast. She could not even think to thank her aunt for the compliment. Her mind was set on a single subject. "Is Shea here?"

Dudee nodded. "He's waiting for you downstairs."

Pure joy, unlike anything she had ever felt before, shot through the entire length of Chloe's body. Shea was finally here—waiting for her. She wheeled toward the bed and picked up her veil. Not wanting to damage the silk tulle, she had waited to put on the fragile train of white until the last possible minute. "Will you help me, Aunt Dudee?"

"Meesie?"

At the sound of Ushi's soft voice, Chloe looked up

at the tiny woman standing in the doorway. "Yes?" Chloe had not seen her since early morning.

"You have no flowas."

Chloe stilled. She peered at her aunt. In all the rushing about to get her ready for the wedding, no one had thought of flowers. She glanced back at the Oriental woman, then shook her head. "No, Ushi." She forced a thin smile. "I guess we all forgot."

Ushi smiled coyly. "May I come in?"

Chloe nodded, smiling at the childlike manner in which the woman spoke.

Gowned in a dazzling red satin shift, Ushi quickly shuffled across the floor. "I have gift fo you, Meesie Chloe."

Remembering her preconceived thoughts about the girl, Chloe lowered her gaze shamefully.

"You like owange blossoms, Meesie?" A light, spicy fragrance followed her inside, filling the room.

Chloe looked up.

From behind her back, Ushi withdrew a small bouquet of orange blossoms in one hand, and a wreath of matching flowers in the other.

Chloe's chest swelled with overwhelming happiness. She could not believe what the woman was extending to her. "You did this for me?"

She replied with only a meek smile and a dip of her head. "You hoowie up and put on. Meesta Shea wait fo you below." With that, she turned and scurried out the door before Chloe could so much as thank her for the beautiful gifts.

Fully crowned with flowers and veil, Chloe peeked over the oak railing marking the stairs. The length of her long train trailed behind her as she slowly descended the steps to the landing below.

She stopped at the foot of the stairs. Cast in the pale glow of two candelabras on the far wall, the parlor seemed to have grown enormous since the previous afternoon. A flurry of murmurs flowed around her. Oh Lord, look at all of those people. The sight of so many overwhelmed her. She had not counted on any of this. Still, she had to get past them if she wanted to be with Shea. And she wanted this more than anything.

Sucking in a breath, she took a step toward the room. Off to one side, a movement—like the swish of an animal's tail—caught her attention. She halted briefly, cutting a quick look to the spot beneath the stairs. For a second she thought she saw the glimmer of a dog's eyes.

Relaxing only slightly, she dismissed the incident and proceeded again. At her approach someone began to play the *Wedding March* on a violin.

The parlor closed in on her, yet the path leading to the opposite side of the room where the minister waited seemed endless. She squinted through the veil.

The man's smile appeared to be painted onto his face.

Chloe hesitated. She felt light-headed. Taking another deep breath to steady herself, she commenced again. Through the heavy tulle she could see an ocean of strange faces looking at her from both sides of the room, but could not make out a clear picture of any of their features.

As she drew nearer, she saw the broad back of a tall man standing at the head of the parlor, facing the preacher. Shea. Her heart thudded against her chest so hard, this time she was certain it would bolt from her body. He *was* here.

Within her moist grasp, the tiny flowers shook. She took another unsteady step. She thought she would never get to the altar. But just when she thought she would surely collapse from the pure excitement of the moment, when she thought she could not force herself to move another inch toward the smiling minister, she took her final step and eased into place beside Shea.

The music ended. The room fell to a hush.

"Dearly beloved, we are gathered here today ..."

Chloe turned her attention toward the man at her side. She cut her gaze in a sidelong glance. In the dimness of the light, it was hard to make out his features. Half-listening to the opening of the ceremony, she squinted through the silk covering her face.

He had shoulder-length hair—brown or dark blond. She could not be sure which. He stood a full head taller than she. She tipped her head for a better view, but he appeared to turn away. Determined to know some part of him before her unveiling, she closed her eyes and inhaled deeply. Desperately she tried to filter out all other scents in the room but his.

There it was.

Ever so faint, she caught the clean balmy aroma of a man's cologne, and something more ... pine? Yes. Opening her eyes, she smiled to herself. Even through the heavy smell of melting candle wax and an assortment of women's perfumes, she could smell the forest scents on him. This *was* her Shea. Nothing could mask the fragrance of the outdoors that had always clung to him.

"Miss Summerhorn?"

Chloe blinked. She looked back at the preacher.

"Do you take Shea Taggert to be your lawfully wedded husband?"

Good Lord. She had almost missed the entire ceremony. "I—" Her voice caught in her throat. She swallowed. "I do."

"And do you, Shea Taggert, take Chloe Summerhorn to be your lawfully wedded wife?"

"I do." Strong and vibrant, Shea's answer echoed through the silent room.

"Then, before I pronounce you husband and wife, let me prevail upon you the blessing of the native people who have lived on the shores of the big Lake Tahoe for hundreds of years." He cleared his throat before continuing. "Where two walk as one, there will be no loneliness. Where one finds shelter, both will find comfort from the storms of life. For where there is one, there is the other. The man takes the woman to his side where from a tiny seed of love life will grow. Turn to your bride, Shea Taggert, so you may seal the promises you have both made one to the other this night."

Chloe held her breath. This was it ... the moment she had been waiting eleven long years for, and now, at twenty years old, it was finally happening.

He turned toward her.

She still could not see him clearly. Impatient now, she nearly ripped the veil off herself.

A flicker of candlelight glinted in his eyes.

As the preacher pronounced them husband and wife, a strange fluttering in her stomach triggered a warning inside her. The instant before the veil lifted, so did the cloud from her memory. The eyes before her glimmered a catlike amber-green. No. It could not be. She shrank back.

Two strong hands held her securely. They clutched her shoulders and drew her nearer that oh-so-familiar face. Slowly, a secret smile grew across the tanned features of the man she had just married. His eyes twinkled.

God in Heaven, no! True fear bolted through Chloe. This could not have happened. But it had. It was not her Shea she had taken as her husband at all. Not her childhood friend. Not the man who had written her such wonderful letters. No, standing before her was the devil's own folly. The man she had just married was the same boorish and vile bandit that had robbed the stage the previous day.

Four

IN THE SHADOWS OF THE CANDLELIT PARLOR, SHEA Taggert looked at the shocked expression of his new bride. He tried to reassure her with a smile, but her countenance remained stunned and confused. Damn. She must have guessed the truth of his deception. But how? He had taken great pains to keep his identity concealed from her during the holdup, and he had remained inaccessible to Chloe throughout the wedding preparations.

He stared into the depths of her questioning blue eyes. Did she know for certain or did she merely suspect? Either way he had to keep her quiet.

He saw the guests stir off to one side. A flurry of curious whispers rustled through the room. They were waiting for the finale to the ceremony.

This would be the test. Did she know? He leaned nearer to Chloe's mouth.

Her eyes grew wide. She stiffened.

His heart hammered. Maybe if he were gentle enough—if he did not frighten her—maybe he could see this through without incident. Softly, he brushed her lips with his.

"No!" She slammed both fists against his chest and shoved.

Shea was forced back a step.

Chloe yanked away from his grasp and spun around. Hiking up her skirts, she dashed down the aisle toward the stairs.

"Damn," he said under his breath.

"Chloe?" Dudee called to her niece from across the room. Her puzzled gaze flew to Shea.

A few of the guests rose to their feet. All eyes shifted from the sobbing woman fleeing the room to Shea. A tumble of questions pitched out at him.

"What happened?"

"Is she all right?"

"Is the girl ill?"

A deep-throated snarl echoed from the hall. A shadow darted after Chloe.

Son of a bitch! Satchel. He had forgotten about the cat.

The minister stepped up behind him. "Shea?"

But he did not wait to be tackled with even one more query before he lurched into action. He bolted into the vestibule and looked up.

They moved as one, the mountain lion and the woman. Like ghosts haunting the rooms of some ancient manor, they rushed toward the upper floor.

Chloe rapidly ascended the steps, her wedding gown flowing behind her.

Yet far from any apparition, powerful and sleek, Satchel tore close to her heels, swiping at the lacy web of her train.

Rounding the curve of the banister, Chloe glanced back and screamed.

The big cat answered with a high-pitched yowl. Claws extended, he struck out at the gauzy fabric, catching Chloe's foot instead.

"Satchel—no!" Shea charged after them.

TENDER OUTLAW 63

Even though the cat was only about eight months old, he was almost full grown. Satchel was only playing. He saw the streaming material as a toy. Shea knew that. But at a little over a hundred pounds the animal could definitely hurt Chloe—at the very least cause her to hurt herself.

Chloe and Satchel hit the landing in a tumble of fur and flounces. Chloe let out a blood-chilling screech.

Again, Satchel shrieked in answer.

Eating up the steps two at a time, Shea had to grab the baluster on the top landing to keep from falling on top of them.

Pulled up in a tight ball, Chloe had herself pressed into a corner at the end of the upper hall. Her face was almost as white as her gown. Wayward curls dangling between her brows, her eyes remained fixed on the big cougar. Her chest heaved so hard it looked as though she might burst out of her dress.

In one quick glance, Shea examined her for any wounds. He could not see any. He looked at Satchel.

Appearing confused, and even more shameless, the cat sat licking his paws in a tangle of torn lace.

Shea tugged the flimsy cobweb off of the animal. "I'm sorry, Chloe. He was just playing—"

"Playing?" she whispered, sounding breathless.

Heavy footsteps pounded up the stairs behind him.

"Landsakes, child," Dudee murmured in a worried tone. "Are you all right?"

Apparently still afraid to move, Chloe only nodded.

"C'mere, you." Shea grabbed Satchel around the head and pulled the beast toward him. Once he had the cat secured at his side, he peered up at Dudee. "You didn't tell her about Satchel?"

Kneeling down to Chloe, Dudee shook her head. "With all the excitement and everything, I forgot."

Slowly Chloe lifted her gaze to her aunt's face. "You mean this animal is a—a pet?" She still sounded winded and shaky.

Hoping to sway Chloe's attention from the incident below, Shea smiled pridefully. "Yup. This is Satchel." He ruffled the top of the big cat's head.

Shifting glances between the animal, Shea, and Dudee, his new bride appeared to relax—but just a little. She clutched at Dudee's arms, then struggled to her feet.

Voices drifted up from the foyer.

"Everything all right?"

"Is anyone hurt?"

Gripping the leather collar around Satchel's neck, Shea stood. He peered over the railing to the crowded entryway. He raised his hand. "Everything's fine. Satchel just got a little excited at meeting his new mistress, that's all."

"She okay?" Doc Jenkins asked from the parlor door.

"Yup, she's fine," Shea answered a bit too quickly.

"Well, what in hell happened?" someone called out. "How come she went flyin' outa here like that?"

Shea looked at Chloe. He still was not sure about her or what she would say. He watched Dudee put a protective arm around his bride.

"It's all the hubbub about the wedding, Shea," Dudee assured him. Without waiting for him to reply, she leaned over and looked through the rungs of the banister. "The child's just fine, folks. The poor thing barely had time to sit herself down before she got word about the wedding plans and had to rush around and ready herself. She's just a bit flustered, that's all." She pulled Chloe closer to her side, obviously showing the guests the truth of her words.

"You sure, Mrs. Taggert?" The doctor looked doubtful. "Maybe I should come up and have a quick look-see just to be safe." He laughed lightly. "I *am* still a doctor first, you know, and a politician second."

Shea opened his mouth to protest.

But this time it was Chloe who interrupted. "Please forgive me, gracious people." Moving on unsteady legs, she looked below, then brushed an errant strand of golden hair from her eyes. "It's uncommonly warm here compared to my Boston home. I'm simply not accustomed to such incremental heat as you have here tonight."

Incremental heat? Shea stared at her. What the hell was that supposed to mean?

"Please, do forgive my unwarranted behavior." She flashed Shea an accusing glare, then offered a smile to the crowd. "Don't let my actions impede on the festivities. I know my . . . Shea must have gone to great pains to see that all was . . . *perfectly* planned for our wedding. I believe you will find refreshments and entertainment out on the back lawn. Do go and enjoy yourselves."

"But what caused you such grief?"

Shea looked down. He knew that rich baritone.

Dressed in his usual impeccable broadcloth suit, William Sharon peered up at Chloe. Even though the man had been known as a wily fox on the Comstock and had made himself a millionaire through some shaky deals, he had still managed to secure a sham respectability within the community of Glenbrook. But he was just a bit too nosy at times to suit Shea.

And Sharon seemed to always make *everything* his business—and why not? Just about every business *was* his—at least, that was the way it was slowly turning out as far as the lumber industry was concerned.

"Come on, now." Dudee stepped past Chloe and Shea to the head of the stairs. She waved her arms as if she were herding cattle. "Don't just stand there chattering. You heard the bride. She wants you to have some fun. There's lots of goodies to be eaten, and music to be heel-toed to. You'll all get your chance to speak to the newlyweds later. But for now, they need a little time to get reacquainted and talk by themselves." She emphasized her meaning with a staunch look at Shea.

Though some still grumbled, most of the guests ambled down the lower hall to the backyard.

Shea exhaled a loud breath. "Thanks, Dudee."

"Don't thank me so quick, Shea Taggert. I'm not entirely happy with the way things turned out tonight." She peered at Chloe before scowling back at him. "I'll take care of your friends. *You* just see that everything's set right up here—and I do mean *right*—you hear me?"

Shea dipped his head respectfully. "Yes, ma'am."

Cutting the couple one last look, she nodded, then patted her hip, motioning for Satchel to join her. "Let's go find something for you, too, boy." Then, without another word, she hoisted her voluminous skirts and descended the steps.

Almost instantly, music rose up above the din of voices.

Shea took the moment to breathe a sigh of relief. He had gotten through the wedding without Chloe divulging who she thought him to be, but now he had to face her again.

Not with the truth, though—he could not risk it—nor risk her knowing it. He turned toward her. Even if it meant facing Dudee's anger later. Dudee was dead against lying to Chloe.

Candlelight from the wall sconces glimmered, showing the anger and hurt shining in her blue eyes.

"Chloe," he began. "Hear me out before—"

She held up her hand. "I don't want to hear anything you've got to say, Shea Taggert." She spun on her heels and stomped toward the room they were to share.

"Hold on now." Not to be put off so easily, he bolted after her. "You think that's fair?"

"Fair!" she all but shrieked from the doorway. In one quick movement, she whirled around to face him again. "What kind of fairness have you permitted me tonight?" She snatched up the hem of her rumpled dress and marched into the room, slamming the door behind her.

Shea stared at the oak barrier that had nearly smashed into his face. Chloe definitely had no plans for making this easy on him. He closed his eyes a second to cool his temper. After all, she was right. He had not been fair to her. He had rushed her through a wedding with little concern for her feelings. But it was something that had to be done—and fast—for both their sakes.

He had to protect her from what she did not know.

But could he deliver the necessary lie so as to gain her sympathy and make her believe it? He did not want to start out their life together with a lie, but he had no choice. He had to go through with it. He gripped the knob and turned it, then pushed open the door.

Standing with her back to him, arms bent up behind her, Chloe was unsuccessfully trying to unbutton her gown. She spun around with a gasp. "What do you think you're doing?"

"I thought I'd help you." He took a step forward.

"Don't!" She lifted her palm to him. She swallowed. "Don't take another step into this room."

He snorted a chuckle. "It is *my* room, too, you know."

As if she had just been presented with an unsolvable problem, she pulled her bottom lip between her teeth, and glanced at the floor. When she looked up, her mouth appeared slightly swollen and a deeper shade of red, yet she still seemed just as bewildered by his statement.

He took advantage of her moment of confusion to study her. It had been so long since he had seen her and he hadn't been able to study her yesterday. Why, they were only kids when her father had had her whisked away to that fancy girls' school back East. And to keep her from Shea, her father had not allowed her a visit home in all the time she was away at school.

His gaze wandered from her large, sky-blue eyes to the golden hue of her mussed hair dangling to her waist here and there where it had escaped the knot of curls. Though lighter now, the freckles he had remembered so vividly from his youth were still scattered across her upturned nose. God, but she was beautiful, tousled and all.

When he had received her telegram, he had not wanted her to come to Glenbrook—it was still too dangerous. There was still too much he had to find out.

But now, standing here looking at her—feeling the longing in himself—he could not help but be overjoyed at her arrival. And though she was slight of figure, and not like the physically endowed females he usually found himself attracted to, he now detected a strain in his body where he had not experienced the uncomfortable tightness in a long time.

No matter how mad she was, no matter what he had to tell her, he *was* pleased to be with her again. He had missed her more than he could ever express in the many letters he had written her.

In a whirlwind of motion, Chloe suddenly snatched up some clothing from the bed, opened the closet door, and yanked out a garment, then whipped back around and charged toward him.

"Hold on." Intercepting her stride, he gripped her shoulders. "What do you think you're doin'?"

"I'm going to find another room." Her voice was pitched high, full of anger. She tried to push past him.

He held her still. "Look, Chloe. Like it or not, we've got some things to talk about." He had to make her see reason.

She glowered down at where he clutched her, then lifted a piercing glare at him. "You don't seem to understand. *I* have no desire to hear whatever lofty and altruistic motives you've conjured up to justify your base actions." Though her voice shook and a glimmer of tears shone in her eyes, her face was a mask of rage. She looked away. "I simply don't care."

Shea stared at her. That was a lie. He knew it—it had to be. She had not come all this way to be turned back so readily—at least not the Chloe Summerhorn he remembered. For a moment he leaned toward telling her the truth—telling her that he was a special agent assigned to the governor of Nevada. And that he was here trying to root out the leader of a band of outlaws stealing payroll money from the logging businesses in the area.

But he could not. If she knew everything, she might slip up to the wrong people—and Shea still did not know just *who* those wrong people were. "Look, Chloe. I don't know how you found out about me—"

"Your mask fell." Her voice was small. A single teardrop overflowed onto her cheek when she peered up at him.

"What?"

"Yesterday." Her lips quivered. "Before you blew up the stage . . . when you were taking down my trunk . . . your mask fell, and I saw your face."

So that was it. He had not known anyone had seen him, least of all Chloe. He had thought he had been quick enough to replace the bandanna.

"I didn't know it was you then, but . . ." Her tone matched the trembling of her mouth. "Why, Shea? Why would you do something like that?"

Hesitating another minute, he began the rehearsed story. "I wanted things. Things for us—for you. Things I couldn't get without money."

She took a step backward and cast him a disbelieving look. "But I've been told your family does quite well. Especially since they've taken a partnership in horse breeding with the Paiute."

Shea nodded. His thoughts turned to his older brother. If it had not been for Lance's solid connections, Shea would not have been able to obtain such good standings with the governor. More than likely, he would still be training with some veteran agent rather than receiving this assignment so early in what he hoped would be a long and fruitful career. "The partnership's Lance's doing." He put a sneer in his tone. "He's the big shot now that Eldon's dead."

Chloe tilted her head to one side and studied him. "I can't believe you said that. You always idolized Lance. More so than Eldon. Now you talk as if you despise Lance."

"Sometimes I do," he grated, then shook his head. "No, not really. It's just that—well—I want something of my own. Something *I* built for myself." Cautiously, he stepped closer. He had to make this good. He reached up and stroked her cheek. "For us, Chloe."

"No," she murmured, disgust straining her voice. "You couldn't have changed so much. You were always so kind, so gentle, so ... loving." Again she backed away.

"But I still am. I didn't mean for all of this to turn out this way. It just sorta happened. I guess I just let myself fall in with the wrong type." At least that part was not a lie. He had allowed many things to happen since this whole charade had begun—unpardonable things of which he normally would never have been a part.

"Shea Taggert never *fell* in with anything. He always did just exactly what he planned. Nobody could convince him of anything if he didn't want to do it."

What could he say? She was right. And he *was* doing precisely as he wanted—it was the only way to smoke out the leader of this gang. "Chloe, I want a good life for us. I love you more than you'll ever know." He motioned toward the door. "Didn't I just prove that downstairs? Doesn't that count for something?"

"Prove what?" Chloe's eyes turned glassy. "That you can trick everybody? That you can rob stages and get away with it? That you can dupe your own fiancée, then marry her before she can discern the truth?" Her face turned a deep red. "And as for counting for something—it does. My father was right about you."

Shea's temper flared. He had known she would be mad—fuming, even—but he never thought she would use her father as a weapon. "You wait just a minute!"

Clothing still draping her arms, she set her hands on her hips. "Maybe Daddy was more accurate about you than any of us knew. Maybe it truly *was* your fault Jerome was killed by those rattlesnakes."

"Chloe!" Jerome's death had always been a sore spot with him. Even though it had been an accident that the younger boy had fallen into the nest of rattlers when they were children, Shea had always felt responsible as he was the oldest.

"Why, you're nothing more than a—a—" Jutting out her chin with a haughty uplift, she looked down her nose. "A—designing prevaricator and a purloiner of a lady's heart."

Shea scowled. He had no idea what she had just

called him, but whatever it was, it made his temper shoot straight up to his brain. "What the hell's that supposed to mean?"

"It means—" Chloe stepped around him, then headed for the door. When she grabbed the knob she stopped and turned back to look at him. "That you've lured me here under false pretenses. That you've lied to me."

"Lied to you?" Until tonight, Shea could not remember ever telling her anything but the truth.

"Yes. When you wrote to me, you professed having obtained some extraordinary job that was going to help us secure our dreams. Robbery, hmph! Some job. You're a thief!"

Shea gritted his teeth to keep from yelling out the truth. "And just what did I steal from you? Seems to me I made sure yer stuff was taken off the stage."

She nodded. "What you stole from me can never be replaced."

Shea tipped his head to one side and stared at her, his arms folded across his chest. "And what might that be?"

Chloe hesitated, a glimmer of tears shining bright in her eyes. "My passion," she said in a small voice. "You stole the passion I felt for you."

Not quite sure how to approach her, Shea lowered his arms. This was something he had not expected. He moved toward her. "We can fix that . . . together . . . if ya just let us."

Taking a step backward, she held up a hand. "No, we can't—not so long as you're unwilling to change your habits." She shook her head. Inhaling, she blinked away the moisture from her eyes, and continued. "I might not be wise to Western lifestyles, *as yet*.

But I'm certainly not some—some dimwitted city doxy ready to catch hold of *your* aspirations, either. I'll not allow you to sweep this all under the door with some soft sweet words of endearment. *I* think more of myself than to let you or anyone else sway me into a life of degradation and falsehoods." That said, she jerked open the door and hurled herself into the hallway.

Dumbfounded by his bride's words, Shea stared after her. He had hoped she would have been easier to bend to his will. Then again, he had not had much of a chance to gain control of the situation. Chloe certainly had changed, at least to some degree.

The woman could talk fancier than any he had ever run across, but what exactly was she saying? He heard a door open at the end of the hall, a shuffling of footsteps, grumbling, then the return of her tread. He looked up.

A jumble of his clothes sailed across the room. His dirt-caked workboots attacked the planked flooring at his feet.

"From the looks of things, the room I've just taken as mine for the night was yours. I'll leave it in better condition than I found it when I depart tomorrow."

Shea narrowed his eyes on his new wife. "What do you mean, depart?"

Bitter laughter gurgled up from deep inside Chloe's throat. "I'm going home tomorrow. I'm sure I can still manage to get a ticket home at such a late date."

"The hell you say." How could she think of leaving him? They loved each other. They had waited to be married for so long. "You're my wife, or have you already forgotten that?"

The pouty curve of her bottom lip trembled. "No, Shea, I haven't. Nor have I forgotten how much I . . . I loved you." Her voice lowered, catching in a whisper. "Nor what we meant to each other at one time." She stood quiet for a long moment staring at him, her eyes filling with tears. She seemed to be waiting for him to say something.

But he could not think of one solitary thing that would not make their predicament even worse. She had believed his lie—and only too well. To her, he was a thief. But he had not expected this reaction from her.

They had not even been married for one hour yet, and already it looked as though they were finished. He had to do something, and fast. "Look, Chloe. You're upset. Let's go down and have something to eat. I've even had some of that champagne you mentioned trying once brought in just for our wedding. We'll have some, you can relax a little, then tonight after everyone leaves we can talk some more." He took a few steps toward her.

She lifted her palm at him again.

Damn it! He was getting tired of that aggravating gesture already.

She shook her head, the bow of her mouth drooping sadly at the corners. "I'm afraid even one sip would choke me." She blinked, spilling the tears down her cheeks. "You go. Enjoy yourself with your friends."

"This isn't a game, Chloe. C'mon, now. Don't be this way." He touched her hand. "I can't go down there without you."

She eased her hand from his. "No, Shea, it's not a game. But you can pretend it is. Once I'm gone, I'm sure it won't be any trouble for you to make up a lie to cover my departure. After all, I'm a Boston woman with no real understanding of how things are done out here. Tell them anything you like. I'm sure nothing you can think of will hurt me as much as . . . as finding out the truth."

The truth? If she only knew the half of it. He cocked his head to one side and studied her.

"They'll believe you, Shea." Sadness filled her eyes, yet she offered him the smallest of smiles. "Just like I did."

"This is ridiculous, Chloe." He suddenly felt as if she really meant what she was saying. "You can't leave me. You love me. You said so yourself."

Reaching up, she stroked his jaw. "Yes," she whispered. "I do love you. And that's exactly why I'm leaving." She turned toward the hall.

He caught her elbow, and pulled her back to him. For the first time since this whole ordeal had begun, he felt frightened. "I don't understand you. You say you love me, but you're leaving me? Why? We can make this work."

She held his stare for a moment, before moving out of his grasp. "No, Shea. We can't."

He swallowed hard. Was he to choose between his job and his wife? But it was more than a job. People were counting on him. He had to put a stop to the cutthroats draining the lifeblood from the loggers.

Chloe swept her hand toward the costly furnishings, then to the noise coming from the wedding guests outside. "All of this is a lie. The house, your friendship with these people, everything. You seem very comfortable with it. But unlike you, I could never live on the appropriations of corruption." She pulled back then, and spun away.

Astounded by his wife's intelligent evaluation of how he had made things appear, Shea stood silent, watching after her.

She made her way to the opposite door.

"Chloe, wait."

Her hand on the latch, she hesitated, but kept her back to him.

He did not know what to say to bring her around to him. She had bought everything he had told her. He could not take it back now. Both of their lives might well depend on the story he had concocted about falling into a life of crime. There was no turning back now. Still, he could not just let her walk out of his life. He searched his heart for the one thing that would hold her to him. "I love you."

She leaned her head back, as if she were seeking help from the heavens. A shudder caught on a sob, but she did not speak. Instead, she opened the door, walked slowly outside, then without so much as a backward gaze, pushed the oak panel closed behind her.

FIVE

FOR THE REST OF THE RECEPTION, SHEA FRETTED OVER Chloe. He did not know what to do. He could not tell her the truth of his business in Glenbrook, yet he could not simply stand by and watch her walk out of his life, either.

Apparently also at a loss for how to handle the situation, Dudee had quietly begged discretion from the female guests. She told them that Chloe had the terrible misfortune of being on her monthlies, and was not feeling well.

Shea had not been quite so quick to come up with an acceptable reason for his wife's failure to make an appearance at her own wedding party.

"I hear your bride is a bit—uh—under the weather," Bill Sharon said after slapping a large mug of beer in Shea's hand.

Ever on the watch, Dudee, standing nearby with some of Glenbrook's more socially notable womenfolk, nodded in his direction. It was only too obvious that she wanted him to go along with what she had told the guests.

Shea did not like Sharon. In fact, he was the one member of the community that Shea was almost positive was behind the stage holdups. But, as yet, he did not have the proof he needed to bring the man to the attention of the law. He needed to know what Sharon's game was and who else was involved with him. "Yup, it must be like she said," Shea said after a moment of deliberation. "The heat's a bit much for her."

"You know I've been to Boston a few times myself."

"That so?" Shea poured some of the foam from his drink onto the lawn.

Sharon dipped his slickly combed head. "Several times."

Shea took a sip of the stout beer. Over the rim of his glass, he studied the dark-haired man with a critical eye. He swallowed. "What's your point?" The man was up to something.

"Oh, nothing." Sharon pulled his mouth into a half-grin. "Nothing at all. It's just that I don't remember Boston as being any cooler than here."

Trying to ignore the irritation mounting within him, Shea took another gulp and looked out over the crowd of contented guests. "Seems to me you're saying a lot." He held his aggravation back. He tried to control his annoyance by keeping time to the lively music with his hand against his thigh.

"Not really." Sharon looked up at one of the windows in the house—Chloe's window—and hesitated. "Yeah," he picked up the conversation again. "I've been back to Boston way a few times—about this time of year, matter of fact."

"That so?" Shea was being polite, but he would have liked nothing more than to shut the man down—permanently. "Nice there, is it?"

Sharon grinned, and he nodded. "Say, did you know Boston was on a river?"

"Really?" Shea did not give a drunkard's snort about Boston, nor hearing about it, either, but he was the host and felt obligated to maintain courtesy. He looked out at the dancers moving to the music.

It was only too apparent that Sharon was not going to let go of the subject, moreover that he had a definite purpose for this little exchange. "Yes, and well, we do have the lake right here, and your bride—"

Shea cut the man a challenging glare. What the hell was he up to? "Speak your mind, Sharon, or keep your mouth shut. That's my wife you're talking about."

"Hey." Bill Sharon held up a hand in a surrendering gesture. "I didn't mean to upset you. I was simply concerned for Mrs. Taggert. I mean, she seems so—so fragile. Maybe it wasn't such a good idea for you two to choose Glenbrook as your home."

"Is that a problem for you, Sharon—my being here, I mean?" Shea continued to glare at Sharon, yet he allowed the tiniest of smirks to mark his point. If Sharon *was* involved with the payroll heists as Shea suspected, maybe it would be beneficial for him to openly stand up to the man.

Sharon raised his brows and his smile faded to a look of uncertainty. He studied Shea for a long moment, then the hesitancy left his features, and the grin returned. "No, not if it's not for you."

There was an insinuation in his tone that unsettled Shea. What exactly was the arrogant bastard suggesting? Or was that a threat of some kind? Was he simply trying to make Shea nervous, maybe even a little careless? Did he know who and what Shea truly was, or was he guessing? Either way, Shea did not like it.

He would have to be extra careful of his actions—especially now that Chloe was here.

Someone stepped up from the side. "The little woman still not feeling so well?" Doc Jenkins asked.

After pinning his glare on Sharon for another warning second, Shea shifted his stare to the doctor. He reached out and accepted the older man's extended hand. Unlike his, the doctor's felt smooth and soft. "It's the weather." He touched the sleeve of his jacket to his forehead. It was not truly all that warm to him, but he felt he should at least defend his wife's absence with some small display of heat. Switching his mug from one hand to the other, he removed his coat, then tossed it over the back porch rail. "She'll be fine."

"I can still go up and check on her if it'll ease your mind." The doctor rocked back and forth on his heels. "I am still a physician, you know. No matter whether or not I'm elected, I'll always be a doctor."

The older man seemed genuinely concerned, but as yet Shea did not want anyone besides himself, Dudee, and his housekeeper too close to his new bride. He shook his head. "Nah, Dudee assures me Chloe's all right."

"Well, if you say so." He turned to Sharon and shook the man's hand. "Bill, how're you?"

"Fine, Congressman, just fine." Sharon always made it a point to use the man's impending political title rather than his medical form of address. He looked back at Shea. "So, the July Fourth celebration will be here before we know it. You ready with your speech? Folks all around the lake will be here to listen to what you got to say, you know."

Shea frowned. He knew the conversation was leading up to a discussion about the movement for free coinage of silver. That was all anyone even remotely interested in mining seemed to be talking about these days. Even the lumber companies were involved. Understandable as it was that the mines were the ones buying timbers for shoring, Shea was growing tired of hearing about it. He did not particularly like politics.

"Sure do. I have it on good authority, too, that all's a go for returning the value of silver to its former merit. I tell you, Bill, we've got a damn good chance of getting the Act of Seventy-Three reversed. Dick Bland's voice carries a long way through the House of Representatives. And if I'm elected in November, mine'll join—" The doctor looked at Shea. He cleared his throat, then rocked back on his heels. "Uh—sorry, Shea, my boy. I didn't mean to turn your reception into a campaign speech."

Shea pursed his lips to keep from grinning. No matter how the old gentleman might try, he always seemed to get going on this subject. He shrugged. "No harm done."

"So, how about a different subject?" Bill Sharon piped in. He glanced at Shea. "How long will you be gone on your honeymoon, Taggert?"

Shea hesitated. Honeymoon? The wedding plans had been so rushed, he had not even considered a honeymoon. He looked at the two of them. Why were they so eager for *this* information?

"You haven't let anyone in on your plans." Bill Sharon leaned nearer, lowering his voice suggestively. "You keeping them a secret for some reason?"

"Yes," the doctor piped in with a smile. "Where are you taking the little woman, son?"

Sharon's interest made Shea wary, but he felt certain the doctor was harmlessly curious. He searched his mind for an answer. "Why, I'm staying right around here."

"Really?" The doctor flashed Sharon a surprised look.

"Yeah, sure." Shea took a sip of beer, then cleared his throat. He had to think fast. He peered out at the glittering waters of the lake. "Summers are short up here, and the Lightning Tree needs to cut all the timber it can before the snows set in. I'll take Chloe up to the camp and let her see what it's like." He cut Sharon a knowing glance. "We don't want to find our company beholden to Mr. Sharon here for too much longer, like so many others are lately."

Sharon sent him a look that could have sliced through the thickest tree trunk, though the man's smile remained fixed.

"Besides," Shea continued, displaying his indifference, "I'd like to take Chloe around the lake and show her some of the local sights like Emerald Bay. Maybe we'll stop in Tahoe City, stay at the Grand Central for a couple of days. Yup." Starting to enjoy the idea, he nodded his head, his thoughts drifting toward more sensual notions. "I think she'd like that. I know I would." The latter, he said more as an acknowledgment to himself than anything else.

Neither of the other two men spoke for a long moment.

Finally, after a few uncomfortable minutes, the doctor took three fat cigars from his pocket and offered one to both Sharon and Shea.

Sharon declined.

The doctor shrugged. "They're Cuban. You sure?"

Sharon held up a hand and nodded.

"Well, then, you take it, Shea." He winked, and smiled a knowing smile. "For later."

"Thanks, Doc." Though Shea did not exactly like the meaning behind the older man's offer, he accepted the tobacco, placing the second cigar into his shirt pocket.

"Now, about that honeymoon," the doctor continued. "I think that's a fine idea, son." Removing a round tin of matches from the inside of his jacket, he struck a match on the bottom of the small container. "What better way to help her get used to the area? She'll love it, I'm sure."

Leaning down to accept the flame to the end of his smoke, Shea was hit with another thought. Chloe had said she was leaving. She was going home. He sucked on the thick roll of tobacco until the opposite end glowed red.

Damn it. He had not wanted Chloe to come to Glenbrook until all was secure, but now that she had and they were married, she would have to stay. Sharon was already suspicious of him. If his new wife left him so soon after the wedding, how would it affect his chances of getting to all the culprits behind the holdups?

He thought of Chloe earlier, lying sprawled at the end of the upper hall, mussed and frightened from Satchel's playful attack. He envisioned her large blue eyes, the slight uptilt of her small nose, and the full pout of her lips. They had waited so long to be together. And although he had allowed himself to be lured by the temptation of other women, he had never wanted to marry any of them. And they had been few. It had always been Chloe's face he had summoned when he had spent time with another. It was Chloe he wanted now.

Looking up at her window, he exhaled a large plume of smoke. And by God, he was not going to let anything stand in the way of sharing his life with her. Not his work, Sharon, nor Chloe herself . . . even if it meant fighting his new wife to keep her.

Once the party had given way, and Shea had seen the last guests to their carriages, he set out for his office in the back of the house—beneath Chloe's room. He knew there was no sense in trying to talk to her tonight. Besides, she needed her rest. But if she tried to leave, he would hear her before she could.

Entering his office, he heard a rustling noise. He stilled, listening. "Who's in here?"

A yawn—like that of an animal—sounded from across the room. Footsteps moved toward him. Then something brushed his leg.

Shea relaxed with a chuckle. "Satchel," he said with a sigh. He bent down and rubbed the cougar's head. "I forgot Dudee put you in here."

The mountain lion purred loudly, then butted his head against Shea's knees.

"C'mon, boy," Shea said, moving through the darkness to the opposite side of the room. "I've got some work to do." After sitting down at his desk, he struck a match to a lamp, then pulled out paper, a pen, and ink.

He had to write a letter to the governor explaining the possible danger surrounding his bride's arrival, but letting him know that he could still handle the situation. It would be necessary, though, for him to take some time away from his duties to gain her confidence.

Apparently seeking more attention, Satchel rubbed against Shea again.

"I can't play now, boy." He gestured toward the braided rug in the corner. "Go back to sleep."

The big cat hesitated.

"Go on." Shea pointed to the corner again.

With a low snarl, Satchel lumbered over to the rug and plopped down. It was only too apparent that he was none too pleased.

Shea smiled. Not once in all the months since he had found the little spotted puma had he ever been sorry for taking the animal in. Except when he was out with the outlaws, the cat was a constant companion, and a good friend to have on Shea's side. And Satchel would be perfect protection for Chloe—if she would be friends with the cat. But after what happened earlier, Shea wondered if that were still a possibility.

He glanced back at the pen and paper. Reluctantly, he opened the inkwell and dipped in the pen point. The governor was not going to like this. Shea had only recently wangled his way in with the outlaws who were actually committing the stage robberies. When Shea had secretly met with him in Strawberry the week before, the governor seemed to be none too pleased at the possibility of Chloe's arrival. He had said she would be a complication.

That was true enough, Shea had to admit. But what was done, was done. Now all he could do was assure the man that he still had everything under control—so far—and that Chloe's presence would in no way hinder his seeing the job completed.

Shea was not certain, but he had a feeling the man had plans for replacing him and he did not want that.

This first assignment was just too damned important. He had to make it work. Looking out the large picture window to his right, he dropped the pen onto the desktop, then blew out the lamp. He leaned back into the comfort of his chair and watched the waning glow of the moon play atop the dark waters of the lake. He had to make everything work—the job, his marriage, everything. He relaxed a bit more, sinking deeper into the tanned-hide bolster against his back. And he would, he just had to.

Dawn came, melting into late morning. Sometime after sealing the governor's letter in an unmarked envelope, Shea had fallen asleep slumped across his desk.

"Meesta Shea?"

A small voice stirred him from his leather chair. He opened his eyes with a start, honing in on the envelope beneath his hand. His heart jumped to a quicker beat. He bolted upright.

"Meesta Shea, you okay?"

Snatching his wits about him, he stared up at the young Oriental woman standing before him. He blinked, looked around his office trying to get his bearings, and then glanced back at her. "Yes, Ushi, I'm fine." He raked his hands through his hair.

"Why you sleep down here again? You say when Meesie Chloe come . . ."

Chloe! His brain seized the name. He squinted out at the brilliance of the morning. "Son of a bitch!" He jumped to his feet.

At that moment, the Rochester clock on the mantel in the parlor struck the hour. Nine o'clock.

"Never mind." He waved a dismissing hand at the

small woman. Normally, he would never speak so harshly to Ushi, but he was anxious to get things settled with Chloe. "Is Chloe up?" he asked as he brushed past the Oriental woman.

"Meesie gone."

Shea halted in the doorway. "Gone?" He frowned. Surely she did not really mean *gone*. Chloe would not leave without at least talking to him again—would she? "Where'd she go?"

Ushi shrugged, her round face filled with sudden anguish. "She not say. She get dwessed and go. Vewy awly."

Shea headed for the front door. "Where's Dudee? Does she know about this?"

"Lord have mercy, what's all the commotion down there?" Knotting the sash of her robe across her middle, Dudee hurried from her room upstairs to the top landing.

Shea gripped the knob and pulled the front door open. "Chloe's gone."

The older woman smoothed back her waist-length white braid. Her posture relaxed. "Landsakes, Shea. That's no call to run around in such a fluster. The child's probably just taking a walk around town." She took a few steps down.

Shea looked at Ushi, then back at Dudee. He shook his head. "No, she's leavin'."

"Leaving for where?" Smiling as she descended the remainder of the stairs, she peered at Ushi, then rubbed her forehead. "Would you fix some tea, dear? I fear I enjoyed that champagne just a little too much last night."

Shea waited until the younger woman had left the

room. "You don't understand, Dudee. Chloe told me last night she was leavin' today."

Dudee's posture stiffened. "Why?" She lowered her voice. "You *did* tell her the truth, didn't you?"

Shea shook his head. "I couldn't."

"Shea." Dudee's tone filled with irritation. "I thought you were going to—"

"I was, but I thought about it again, and—" He paused. "I can't. I think they might be on to me as it is. If Chloe knew all the details, it'd put her life in danger."

"We talked about this before she got here, Shea. I never would've agreed to come and help you fix things up like I did if you hadn't assured me she'd be safe and that you wouldn't allow her to be put in any danger." Dudee peered at him with questioning, stern eyes. "Are you telling me now you can't keep your word?"

"No." Shea swallowed. "Chloe comes first," he said, meaning it. But knowing how important his job was to him, he was uncertain if he could truly maintain a tight hold on that conviction, even with his good intentions.

"Good." Dudee sighed, then just as quickly stiffened again. "So, will you allow yourself to lose her to a lie?"

Frustrated, Shea shook his head. Damn it. This was getting more complicated by the minute. He had to keep that promise to Dudee, the one to the governor, and his vows to Chloe. He loved her.

His mind whirred with another plan. Now, if he could just get Chloe to cooperate . . . Spinning around, he hurried down the porch steps and across the yard. "No, Dudee, I'm not willin' to lose her."

"Shea," Dudee called out behind him. "You can't go off half-cocked like this. You've got to . . ."

Shea did not hear anything more. He had to find Chloe. He had to bring her back. But where would she be? Ushi had said she had left early. She could be halfway to Reno by now. What time was the first stage out of Glenbrook?

"Mornin', Shea."

He looked up just in time so as not to collide with the banker, Ralston. "Will." He nodded acknowledgment, but kept his thoughts trained on finding his wife.

In the distance, he heard the toot of the steam tug *Meteor* signaling its arrival from across the lake. Balloon stacker engines echoed their whistles through the trees as they chugged from Glenbrook to Upper Pray Mountains.

He should be up there working with the men at the logging camp. By now the receiving ponds would be full of cut timber waiting to be hauled down. Except for two short days after his meeting with the governor, he had rarely been away from the company; now he had been gone from the Lightning Tree Logging Camp for nearly a week.

He could not let the wrong people—or *anyone*, for that matter—become suspicious of his absence. It was not that they needed him to complete the sawdowns. The men were competent workers, all of them. But Shea had to keep up his image as foreman.

Galt O'Dell, the owner of the Lightning Tree, was well aware of Shea's assignment. In fact, it had been Galt who had brought the holdups to the governor's attention in the first place. He had even given Shea the position as foreman in his company as cover. He would be understanding, but Shea needed to get back to the job so others did not become suspicious. And he would—right after he finished this business with Chloe.

The sound of his boots scuffing against the wood walkway punctuated the fierceness of his stride. He was angry, frustrated, and even a little hurt that Chloe had left like she did.

He halted at the combination stage station and post office. A huge red-and-blue sash dotted with white stars fluttered overhead. He pushed open the door and searched the small interior. All he saw was the small American flags situated here and there on the counters and tables.

Where was Chloe? Had she managed to take a coach already? He looked in the side office for the ticket master. No one.

"Why, Mr. Taggert." The high-pitched nasally whine of the postmarm assailed his ears. "What are you doing here?"

He veered back to the other side of the room. Apparently, the rail-thin woman had been busy ducked down behind the counter. "Looking for—"

"Your wife?" Miss Henney finished in her usual busybody fashion. She pulled her spectacles a little lower onto her slender nose and peered out over the wirerims at him. She gestured toward the ticket booth with a nod of her head. "Mr. Carmine had to run out on an errand, but he'll be back soon."

"My wife, Miss Henney?" Shea raised a brow. "Chloe Summer—I mean, Taggert. Has she been—"

"Oh, she's gone."

"The devil you say!" He was beginning to hate the word *gone*.

"Mr. Taggert!" She cut her eyes away, as if she thought someone else might be listening in the empty room. "Your language, if you please."

"S'cuse me, Miss Henney, but I—"

"Of course. I understand. You're worried your wife will get lost." Turning a deep shade of red, she smiled. "I understand how it is with newlyweds. They just can't stay away from each other very long."

Lost? What the hell was the old girl talking about? "Miss Henney," he tried to interrupt. "Has my wife been here this mornin'?"

"Yes, she bought a ticket to Reno."

"Damn," he said under his breath. He was too late. No. He could not be. Maybe if he hurried, he could catch up to her. "What time did she leave?"

"Not that I'd know firsthand. I've never been married, you know," Miss Henney continued as if she had not heard a word Shea had asked. "So no one's ever actually been worried about my whereabouts, but—"

"Miss Henney!"

Her huge brown eyes blinked at him with a start.

"What time did my wife leave this mornin'?" Shea asked again, his aggravation growing.

"My goodness, Mr. Taggert." The elderly woman clutched the throat of her blouse and clucked a nervous laugh, her eyes darting around the interior again. "You don't have to shout. There's only the two of us in here. I can hear you just fine."

"Well, then, would you tell me what time—"

"She left right after she bought her ticket—about eight-fifteen, I believe. Now, Mr. Taggert, if there's nothing else I can help you with . . ."

"Did the stage leave on time? Where was their first stop?"

Scooping up a handful of envelopes, the woman squared her shoulders, patted her gray bun atop her head, then turned her back on Shea and began the sorting of the mail. Apparently Shea had unintentionally hurt her feelings, and it was plain to see she meant for him to know it.

Defeated, he wheeled away from the woman. Miss Henney had a reputation for ignoring inquiries in favor of subjects that usually she alone found appealing. Ordinarily, when Shea came to pick up his mail he would follow the old girl's lead, but not today. He did not have the time.

Heading back in the opposite direction from which he had come, he hurried toward the livery. He had to get his horse. The town clock bonged, signaling the half hour. Eight-fifteen, Miss Henney had said. Maybe he *did* have enough time.

"Mornin', Mistah Shea, suh," Bailey called from the corner of the livery where he was mucking out one of the stalls.

"Mornin'," Shea answered as he crossed to his mount's pen. "You done mendin' my tack?" Shea grabbed his palomino's blanket off the gate.

"Sho' am." Bailey carried the saddle over to Shea. "Had ta replace the whole girth. Just weren't enuff braid left worth mendin'. Howja tear it like that, anyhow? Looked like it was ripped on purpose, it did."

A couple of days ago when Shea had brought the damaged saddle in to be fixed, he had thought so, too, but he did not have time to ponder it now. "Sorry, Bailey," Shea answered, taking the seat from the livery hand. "I've got to hurry. I've got to catch the Reno stage."

"You's lookin' fer somebody important, Mistah Shea?"

Shea tossed the saddle atop Topaz. "Yup." He felt no need to disclose Chloe's name to the old man. "I might be gone for the rest of the day, maybe even two."

The man moved to the front of the stall and put the bit into the mare's mouth.

"Would ya mind goin' to my house and tellin' Dudee for me?"

"Sho' thing, Mistah Shea." Bailey raised his brows, almost invisible against the dark hue of his skin. "Would ya like me ta let yer missus know, too?"

Shea halted mid-action. He stared at the man.

"She's right down at the Glen Brook House there." He pointed behind Shea.

"Chloe's at the Glen Brook?" Shea frowned. Surely the man was mistaken.

"Ain't she that woman that came in from someplace up north, the day before yestaday? An' ain't she the one that wears them funny-lookin' hats? An' ain't she the one that everbody's talkin' 'bout cause she's s'pose ta use some kinda big words?" He looked down at the livery floor. "Sorry, Mistah Shea. I didn't mean no disrespect."

Shea peered at the white head of the aged black man. "None taken." He could not be angry. Bailey was right. Chloe did talk like that. So he had to know who she was.

Shea let go of the girth buckle. He spun around. "Never mind about talkin' to Dudee."

"But what 'bout Topaz, here? Aincha gonna be needin' her?"

Shea answered with a shake of his head. All he wanted right now was Chloe. With quick steps, he strode down the walk toward the hotel only a couple of buildings from the stage station. Why had she not left?

When he came to the plate-glass window marked with the words GLEN BROOK HOUSE, he looked inside.

Dressed in a powder-blue traveling suit and a hat with more than an ample amount of matching feathers, Chloe sat at a table in the eatery of the hotel with her back to him.

Glancing away, he took a deep breath. He had to handle this carefully so as not to cause a scene. But how to do it? What was he to say that he had not already? He peered back at her. His stomach knotted and he stiffened.

Bill Sharon stood at her table, smiling that same shit-eating grin he always used whenever he was up to something.

"Damn it to hell!" Shea whispered between clenched teeth. "Now what?" Quietly he stepped inside, halting behind the plant-covered lattice partition separating the entrance from the restaurant. Approaching Chloe in front of Sharon might not be such a smart idea. He would have to wait. Thwarted, he decided to remain in the hotel lobby until Sharon and Chloe parted company.

"Do you mind if I sit with you for a moment, Mrs. Taggert?"

Shea's hearing, not to mention his curiosity, perked to attention. He peeked through the greenery.

"Chloe, isn't it?" Sharon asked after taking a seat before Chloe could invite him.

With an aloof expression, Chloe stared at the man. "*Mrs*. Chloe Taggert, that's correct."

Shea raised his brows with her emphasis on *Mrs*.

"Yes, well, I was wondering how you're feeling today, Mrs. Taggert."

"Quite adequate, thank you." Chloe's voice was noncommittal.

From her tone, Shea guessed that she was not exactly pleased with this intrusion.

She picked up the cup sitting in front of her, her little finger held at a dainty uplift. "Have we met?" She took a sip but kept her stare fastened on the man seated across from her.

"Why, no, ma'am. Not formally." Sharon extended his hand to her. "I was at your wedding last night. William Sharon, Bill to my friends. Perhaps you've heard of me?"

Chloe did not appear too impressed. She leaned back a space as she accepted his handshake. "Well, Mr. Sharon, I don't believe I've heard your name mentioned—at least, not as yet." She took another drink, then set her cup down.

Sharon's posture stiffened.

Folding her hands on the edge of the table, she smiled, though not sweetly, nor demurely as a lady might, but rather coolly and boldly, as if she were a matron experienced with handling men such as Sharon. She appeared to be waiting for something.

Shea listened, straining to hear any tidbit that might otherwise escape him. A shadow caught his eye. He turned with a start.

"Can I get you a table, Shea?" Rupert Thompson,

the hotel desk clerk, leaned into view. He shot a gaze past Shea and into the eatery. "They don't look to be full up. I'm sure Dottie can seat you." He raised his hand, apparently trying to signal for the waitress.

Shea grabbed his arm. "No, Rupe. I'm not hungry."

The skinny man's eyes widened. "You're not?"

"No." Shea snagged the first thought that came to him. "I'm here—uh—waiting for someone."

Rupert frowned, but upon hearing a woman's voice just beyond the partition, he looked up, then smiled. "The missus?"

"Yup. You guessed it," Shea answered a little too fast.

"Well, she's sitting right behind you. Didn't you see her?"

He put a finger to his mouth, signaling the man to silence. "Yup, Rupe, I saw her," he replied in a whisper. He glanced over his shoulder to make sure neither Sharon nor his wife had heard them. When he felt certain they had not he clapped a hand on Rupert's back, then moved toward the hotel counter. "She's busy right now. I don't want to interrupt her. I'll just wait, okay?"

Rupert shrugged. "Sure, Shea, if that's what you want."

Once the desk clerk had taken his place behind the counter again, Shea strode to a settee nearest the partition. He picked up a newspaper, then sat down, smiling at the bewildered Rupert.

"So, I understand you mean to leave our fair little community." Sharon's voice rose.

Shea leaned against the partition, pressing the barrier to its limits. He had to hear what they were saying.

"Do I?" Chloe sounded surprised.

"Yes, well, I understand you bought a ticket to Reno this morning." Sharon's smooth baritone vibrated through the room divider.

"And what if I did?" Chloe asked, her voice even. "What concern is that of yours?"

"Well, I was simply inquiring because I knew you were feeling poorly last night and, well, I just thought since you said you couldn't handle the heat we're having—"

"I never said I couldn't handle it, Mr. Sharon."

"I must beg to differ with you, Mrs. Taggert. I was at the wedding, remember. I heard you."

"You may differ all you wish, Mr. Sharon. But I'm quite confident that if you had truly listened to my ineluctable admission you would know that my precise words were 'I'm not *used* to the heat you're having.' " She paused. "I'm quite durable," Chloe continued. "I simply have to acquaint myself with your unpropitious weather. And as for my buying a ticket to Reno . . ."

Behind his shield of the newspaper, a slow grin began to grow on Shea's mouth. He found himself enjoying her educated speech—especially since it was not directed at him.

The sound of a chair scooting across the wood flooring rose above the other murmurs of conversation in the room. It was followed almost immediately by a duplicate noise.

"I purchased the fare for my aunt Dudee," Chloe stated.

Shea blinked. Had he heard correctly?

"Miss Dudee's leaving?" Sharon asked, his tone shocked.

Chloe hesitated. "As you probably know, my aunt has been here for quite a long time helping Shea with our home." She paused again. "It's a thank-you gift from me to her. I'm certain she must be wanting to return to my father's ranch by now. And, if she's not, then she'll have it when she is ready."

"Do forgive me, Mrs. Taggert. I am sorry for poking my nose in your business. I didn't understand how things were. I should've guessed you were buying the ticket for Miss Dudee. I should've realized you and Shea would want to be *alone*."

The conversation lapsed a moment, making Shea more than a little uncomfortable. What was that good-for-nothing doing?

"After all, you and Shea haven't seen each other for a long time, have you?"

Their footsteps neared.

Shea could well imagine that sly grin Sharon always flashed. He glowered behind the newsprint, wishing Chloe would put the son of a bitch in his place. He peeked around one side of his paper.

Tugging on a pair of white gloves, Chloe stood within a few feet of Shea.

Hat in his hand, Sharon stationed himself on the opposite side of her. His proximity to Shea's new wife was just a little *too* close for Shea's liking.

"That's quite all right, Mr. Sharon," Chloe replied. "And, yes, we have been apart for a long while. Since we were children, if you must know."

Sharon rocked slightly back and forth on his heels.

Damn. She had turned to face Sharon and now Shea could only see her profile. Was that a smile she offered the arrogant bastard? What he would have given to be able to knock that smug expression off the man's face. He watched Chloe's shoulders rise with an intake of breath.

"I do understand how small-town people like to have their fingers in every pie. It *is* so much nicer to encroach on another's life than it is to contain oneself with one's own affairs, isn't it?"

"Why, Mrs. Taggert," Sharon stammered, "I feel I've upset you. Please, let me assure you—"

"Oh, please don't, Mr. Sharon. Let's end this bit of insipid prattle where we are. In the merest of such impressionable moments as we have just whiled away I can tell that you're no friend to my husband and so none to me as well."

She drew herself up and squared her shoulders. "Now, if you'll please excuse me, I must be getting home to Shea. After all ... we're newlyweds, you know, and want to be *alone*." That said, she wheeled away from him and strode out of the hotel toward home.

Still concealing himself behind the upheld newspaper, Shea watched as—for the first time that he could ever recall—Bill Sharon slinked off to whatever rock snakes like him hid under.

Shea had to hold his breath to keep from laughing out loud. Was that *his* Chloe just now? It certainly did not sound like the same woman he had argued with last night—or maybe it did at that. She had definitely taken charge of the situation with Sharon and put him in his place. The same way she had after the wedding with Shea. So why was she staying, and why had she defended him?

Standing, he dropped the paper and strode to the open doorway of the hotel. He stared after her. What had changed her mind? And why had she lied? He knew she had really bought that ticket for herself.

Shea shook his head and grinned, then headed out after her, but not too quickly. He did not want to catch up to her until she got to the house. He wanted her cooled down enough that she would not turn the anger Sharon had stirred up in her on him. That hellish tongue of hers was more than he quite knew how to handle.

His smile broadened as he followed at a leisurely pace behind her. Then again, it might be fun to take up the challenge of her tongue lashings this time. She had said they wanted to be *alone*, had she not?

And right now, he wanted nothing more than to be just that—alone with her. They needed to get to know each other again. They had some things to discuss. Some things like years spent away from each other. Things like why she had chosen *now* to come out from Boston. Or why she had left him this morning without so much as a good-bye.

And, oh, yes . . . lies. They needed to discuss them. His, he was not too sure about. But hers? What about what she had told Sharon? And she had done it so readily, so matter-of-factly, as if it was the most natural thing for her to do. It seemed she was not quite the upstanding *lady* she would have everyone believe.

He picked up his step. His eyes followed the sway of her hips as she pranced toward the house. Boy howdy, had she changed since they were kids. And from where he stood right now, it was all for the better.

He halted a moment, taking the time to appreciate

the womanly curves she had grown into. He rubbed his stubbled chin and arched a pleased brow. Yup, getting to know Chloe Taggert was definitely going to prove to be extremely interesting. Of that he was certain.

Six

CHLOE MARCHED UP TO THE WHITE PICKET GATE IN FRONT of Shea's house—her house, now. She had made *that* weighty decision the moment she had lied to that insufferable Bill Sharon about the ticket she had bought. She stared up at the bedroom window that was to be hers and Shea's. There was nothing to do for the time being but stiffen her spine and make the marriage work.

What else *could* she do? Even as she had made the ticket purchase, in her heart she had known she would never truly be able to go through with leaving Shea—even knowing he was an outlaw. She loved him too much. She had simply needed a push to consciously realize that determination. Well, she had gotten it—now what?

She took a deep breath and pushed open the gate. Now, she would show Shea Taggert what kind of woman he had married. She had come to some practical conclusions as to what Shea would have to do in order to reform. She would simply have to convince him to stop these stage robberies. It was their only hope for survival together.

She would have to make him see reason. Becoming a woman with a mission, she squared her shoulders, crossed the yard, and hurried up the porch, tenacity marking her strides.

Dudee met her at the door. Apparently startled, her aunt sucked in a breath. "You're back."

"Of course I'm back," Chloe responded cordially, yet firmly. Lifting the hem of her traveling suit, she brushed past Dudee. "This is my home."

"But I thought—"

"What?" Once inside, Chloe peeled off her gloves and turned to her aunt.

At that moment, Ushi entered the vestibule. "Meesie Chloe. You back."

Chloe eyed the women. "Why does everyone keep saying that as if they can't believe my presence? I simply took my morning constitutional. I assure you it's quite normal." She tossed her gloves onto the mirrored sideboard against the wall, then unpinned her hat and placed it on top of them. "I'm quite prone to such actions as is my predilection at the time. I apologize if it caused you undue concern."

A door opened behind her.

Dudee's eyes widened, then just as quickly she relaxed.

Chloe followed her aunt's gaze.

Standing at the edge of the lower hallway, shirt half untucked, his shoulder-length hair mussed, Shea squinted at her. He appeared to have just woken up. "What's all the ruckus about?"

"Meesta Shea!" Ushi sounded surprised.

Shea cut her a quick look, then peered back at Chloe. "You been out, Button?"

Chloe's stomach jumped. No one had called her by that name since she had been a child. It had been given to her by Shea's older brother Lance, when she was little more than a toddler. He had said that her small upturned nose looked just like a button, and the name had stuck.

She swallowed.

Shea looked so adorable in his rumpled state—maybe not to others—to her, he was overwhelmingly gorgeous. He appeared as he had when they were children. Rarely had his brown hair ever been combed, and his clothes were always in a condition of disarray, but that had never bothered Chloe. She had loved him no matter how he had looked.

She had seen him spying on her at the restaurant. She knew he had not just awoken, yet seeing him pretending to emerge from sleep ... she felt the irresistible force that had always drawn them together. God help her. It was as if she was that same little girl, so long ago, that had always been spellbound by his boyish charisma. This was going to be hard.

She took a couple of deep breaths to fortify her resistance. "We need to talk, Shea."

His lips spread into an infectious smile. "Sure thing, Button." He gestured behind him with a nod. "How 'bout back here?"

"All right," she answered a bit hesitantly. She had not expected him to comply so readily. She looked back at Dudee. "Will you excuse us?" Then without waiting for a reply, she followed Shea around the staircase. Remembering her ordeal with the cougar after the wedding ceremony, she slowed her step and peeked under the staircase. Her heart picked up its pace. Was the cat still there?

Shea chuckled. "Satchel's outside somewhere." He held out a hand toward her. "You're safe."

Regaining her composure, Chloe lifted her chin,

displaying what she hoped would appear as a regal show of indifference, then continued to the end of the hall. Halting in the doorway, Shea stood to one side, directing her inside a large room ahead of him.

Passing in front of him took great willpower. She could not help but breathe in his heady male scent. He smelled of rich tobacco, morning air, and pine. She fought the urge to pause and enjoy his nearness as she stepped over the threshold.

With hasty strides, she crossed what appeared to be his office to an enormous single-pane window looking out over the lake. She folded her hands at her waist to keep from fidgeting. She could not let him see how strongly he affected her.

The door closed behind her.

A sudden flutter of nervousness caught her by the throat. She whirled around to face him, but was startled to see that he had remained across the room.

Arms folded, he stood leaning against the opposite wall looking at her.

"Shea." Her voice sounded like she had just swallowed a sack full of feathers. She hesitated, fighting back the dryness.

His expression remained blank, but his eyes stared out at her with indulgent interest.

"Shea," she began again.

"You said that," he announced.

She cleared her throat. "It seems I've found myself in a most unusual dilemma. I can neither retreat, nor go forward—at least not in the present state of our relationship."

Shea remained silent. His gaze caused a slow burn as he looked down her body, and back to her face.

Why did he have to ogle her like that? She looked

away for a moment. "I'm not quite certain how to handle this situation, but what I do know is that your unscrupulous business concerning the stage robberies simply must stop."

His expression remained undaunted, yet something in the way he watched her told her she definitely had his complete attention.

She glanced down at her hands. "I'm your wife—" She stumbled over the word. Until now, she had not taken the time to consider the meaning of the term. "And as much as I'm opposed to your unethical choice of preoccupations, I find that I can't report you to the law, or walk away, either. As I understand it, the role of a wife is to remain beside her husband no matter the unsavory circumstances in which she may find him involved."

Shea's expression changed, though just slightly, around his mouth. With the subtle shift, he looked to be almost smiling, yet not quite.

Chloe blinked. How could something so slight be so distracting? "I've spent most of the morning reflecting on this, Shea, and, as I've determined, you simply must abandon your nihilistic ways and conform to the honorable and wholesome lifestyle we both know you were raised to uphold."

Arms still folded across his chest, Shea pushed away from the wall, then crossed the room to a large bookstand. Silently, he opened what looked to be a huge family dictionary. He flipped through the pages, then stopped. After taking a moment to read something, he quirked a brow, then peered up at her. "And all of this?" He swept a glance over the room, apparently indicating the fine furnishings. "What would you have me do about this?"

More than a little taken aback, Chloe held herself to silence. She took in his meaning, then shrugged. What *did* she want him to do about it? She knew how he must have gained the means to purchase these possessions. "Well, I—uh—we'll simply have to find a discreet way of making restitution for the money that was stolen."

"How?" The faint play of amusement on his face grew to a distinct smile. He appeared to be enjoying himself at her expense.

"I—I don't know." It was not the most intellectual response she had ever made but he had caught her off guard. She flexed her fingers, twisting them as if she were wringing out a wet cloth. "We can deliberate that problem later. What I need to know now is . . . are you willing to cease these ill-famed acts of yours?"

He moved to the window, a mere arm's reach away from her, and looked out. "And if I won't?" He kept his gaze trained on the dark waters of the lake. "What then?"

Swallowing, Chloe moved to face him. She had not even considered the possibility that he might oppose her. Surely he realized the robberies had to end? She tried to read the meaning behind his expressionless mask.

Did he not understand how she felt? Did he not care? Could his lust for wealth truly outweigh the love he had professed for her? Was he merely testing her? And what would he do if he did not like her reply? She no longer knew him—not really. She only knew what he had revealed to her through his letters.

He had already proven what a different person he had become over the last eleven years. He had blown up the stage displaying little regard for the passengers. Was he capable of even more unspeakable violence? Would he be so inclined now?

As if he heard the silent questions tumbling through her mind, Shea turned to look at her.

Their eyes met in a tumultuous struggle of wills.

"What then, Chloe?" he repeated. "How will you handle my—" He shot a quick look at the dictionary, then back at her. "What did you call it? My niha—"

"Nihilistic ways," she answered on reflex.

He nodded.

Oh, those green eyes. She had almost forgotten how enchanting they could be with their tiny woodsy flecks. She peered deeper, looking for— what? She did not see even a hint of anger. No savagery, no fury. But there was something.

He lowered his hands, but his gaze never left hers. "What will you do with those nihilistic ways of mine if I don't agree to your terms?"

She blanched. He was calling her bluff.

He touched the fingers of her left hand, then the right. "Will you tell the law? Will you walk away from me then?"

Captivated by the intensity of his stare, her blood heated. Her body warmed, responding to him in ways she had only felt when reading the continuing romances in *Harper's Monthly*.

Moisture covered the palms of her hands. She could not think clearly when he looked at her like that. Did he know what he was doing to her?

She shuddered. It had been so long since she had been this close to him. Of course, as a child she would never have before felt the fire that he now ignited within her. This was something new—

something exciting—and dangerous. She tried to hold her breath to keep from revealing her emotions. Unsure of what to say, she wet her lips instead. It was the wrong move.

His attention slipped to her mouth. Like a panther stalking a wounded fawn, he moved closer. He eased his hands to her waist, and around to her lower spine. "How will you see this finished then?" His voice fell to a whisper. His lips touched hers.

Chloe held herself motionless. A single thought entered her brain. Shea. All concerns for his criminal activity vanished. She had never wanted anything more than she did his kiss at this moment.

She had dreamed about it, fantasized about the texture of his lips against hers, imagined the taste of his mouth. In the privacy of her most romantic notions she had even practiced it against the back of her own hand. But nothing, not even the passionate love stories she had read in school, had prepared her for the torrid sensations that flooded her body and mind this minute.

He drew a wet line across her mouth with his tongue.

Of their own volition, her lips parted. She swayed into him. She inched her hands up to his neck. Her breathing went ragged.

With a rush of breath, he encircled her waist, and pulled her hard against him. He explored the recesses of her mouth.

Timidly, at first, she touched his tongue with her own. Gaining confidence in her actions, she met his intimate advance with newly discovered boldness.

From somewhere deep inside him, he groaned.

She felt the vibration of his urgency ripple through

her entire length. Her body responded in a way she had never known could happen. Her stomach tightened. Her breasts seemed to get fuller, tightening against the ebb and flow of his flexing chest muscles. She felt dizzy.

Gently, he massaged her back, drawing delicious little circles at the base of her spine.

Her head swam with untried longing and the innate thrill of her own uncertainty. Liquid fire melted her insides.

He loosened his hold, moving a hand to her cheek, and down to her throat. His fingers fumbled at the buttons on her jacket. He pushed it open.

Oh yes. She pressed closer, slipping her hands under his hair, beneath his collar. She wanted to touch him, feel the heat of his skin against hers, know the hills and plains of every inch of his body. She wanted to—

Her mind snapped. God in heaven! What was she doing? What was she letting *him* do? She wrenched her mouth from his. "Don't!" She pushed against his strength.

"Why?"

It was a simple question. But for the life of her she could not think of a single justifiable reason for him to stop—none except that she could not think. And she needed to. It took all the inner resistance she could muster, but she held herself apart from him. Her heart hammered against her breast. Blood pounded in her ears. She shook her head. "This isn't right."

"Not right?" He looked hurt, puzzled. "You're my wife. I'm your husband. Of course it's right." He bent nearer her mouth again.

She turned her head. "No, Shea, I mean it." Pressing the heels of her palms a little harder into his chest, she shoved back. "We need to settle things between us. We can't—"

"What?" He pulled her tighter. "We can't do what we've both been aching to do for eleven damn years?"

"Shea!"

"What?" he murmured, though it sounded more like a groan. "Tell me you haven't been thinking about making love with me. Tell me you haven't closed your eyes each night without yearning for my kiss." He stroked her shoulder through her jacket. "That you haven't thought what it'd be like to have me touch you. For you to touch me. To have me lying next to—"

"Don't, Shea!" She grabbed the anger she had felt the previous night. It was her only defense. If she listened to more she might give into the very desires he spoke of. "Please, I just can't do this—not now—not like this. We have to talk."

"Look, Chloe, what do you want to hear from me?" Relinquishing her from his grasp, he threw up his hands and raised his voice. "That I'm sorry for what I've done? That I'll change? That I'll never rob another stage? Is that what you want?"

Chloe winced at the sudden swing of his mood. She glanced at the door, thinking Dudee or Ushi might barge in at any moment, then back at Shea. "They'll hear you."

"It's my house," he stated flatly, though he did lower his tone. Glowering at her, he sucked in a breath; then finally, he abandoned his glare. "Look, I *am* sorry for upsetting you. And I'm sorry about all this business with the stage holdups."

She released a little of the tension with a sigh. "Good."

"But I can't promise I'll never do it again."

"But you just said—"

"I said I was sorry. And I am. But that doesn't change the way things are."

"What does that mean?" He was not making any sense.

"It means, there're problems, reasons that I can't tell you, for what I've done—for what I might do again." He shook his head. "I wish to God I could explain, Chloe, but I just can't."

"Why?" He was confusing her.

He looked down at the floor and rubbed his hand over his mouth.

He appeared just as frustrated as she felt ... but why? She had to know. "Tell me, Shea," she said in a soothing tone. Neither her anger, nor her determination had swayed him over to her way of thinking, maybe her gentleness could. "I'll understand."

He looked up, studying her for a long moment.

She held her breath. It was the test of confidence between man and woman—husband and wife. Would he trust her with his secrets?

A long, drawn-out silence ensued.

"Have you unpacked yet?"

"What?" The question took her by surprise.

"Have you unpacked yet?" he repeated.

"Why ... uh ... yes, I have." What did that have to do with all of this?

"Well, repack—but not too much." He strode past her, toward the door.

Completely astounded by his change of subject, not to mention attitude, she stared openly at him. "I don't understand. Where're you going?"

He spun back to look at her. "*We*, Button. Where're *we* going."

Frowning, she stared at him. What on earth was he talking about?

"We're going on our honeymoon. So hurry up and throw some stuff into a bag for us. I'll go and get the horses." He stopped short. "You *can* still ride, can't you?"

Unable to mask her bewilderment, she could only nod.

"Good." He smiled as if he thought such a statement would set everything right. "I thought I'd take you up to visit the logging camp, and see the sights surrounding the lake."

What was he thinking? She shook her head in disbelief. Did he suppose she was simply going to forget about the robberies and let everything continue as it had before her arrival? She drew herself up. She could not allow this to happen. He was not going to evade her questions. She would not let him. Yet it was quite evident that Shea had no intention of discussing the matter further.

But Chloe did. "I'm not going anywhere until we get things straightened out." She folded her arms across her middle. She had to remain steadfast, for both their sakes. "Not until you promise me you'll stop—"

"Look, Chloe." He hesitated, his gaze darting around the room a moment before finally returning to hers. He took a step toward her.

She backed away. She still was not quite certain of him.

He halted. "The only promises I can make to you right now are the ones I swore to you last night." He indicated his meaning by pointing to the gold band around her finger. "All, that is, but this one. I promise that if you'll just bear with me for a little while. If you'll trust me—"

"Trust—"

He held up a hand. "Hear me out. I listened to what you had to say, now you listen to me . . . okay?"

Was he kidding? After everything he had told her, how could he expect her to put her faith in him—especially when it seemed he could not do the same with her? Still, there was a certain sincerity in his eyes. She bit her bottom lip and nodded.

"Then if you'll trust me," he began again, "I promise it won't be long before you'll know everything you need to. Believe me, I wouldn't be doing all of this if I didn't have to. Okay?"

She narrowed her eyes. He had to give her something more substantial to hold onto than a vague promise. "So you don't really *want* to steal the payrolls?"

Caution marking his movements, he closed the space between them.

This time, she did not shy away. She held herself steady. If he had wanted to hurt her, she felt confident he would have done so before now.

He caressed her upper arms before sliding his hands down to take hers within his grasp. "Trust me, Button. I *am* the same Shea you fell in love with. Trust yourself, and you'll know the answer." He pulled her close then, and placed a light kiss on her forehead. Releasing her, he turned around and made for the door. "I'll be back for you shortly," he said over his shoulder. He left the door open behind him.

Wide-eyed, full of even more unanswered questions than she had had earlier, Chloe stared after him. What had she gotten herself into? He had said he was the same Shea she had fallen in love with—and he was. But he also was not.

He had changed so much. He was so secretive now. Yet in so many ways, he was the same. He was gentle and loving. But something was terribly wrong.

He had asked her to trust him—to trust herself. She could tell he still loved her, so why did he not confide in her? What was it he would not or *could* not tell her? Why did he feel so compelled to continue with these robberies? She felt certain it was not the money as he had at first wanted her to believe. So what was it?

She pulled her mouth to one side and chewed on the flesh inside her cheek. That was a mystery she would have to see solved. Gathering her resolve, she decided she had no other choice but to go with him.

Quietly, so as not to draw attention from either Dudee or Ushi, she hurried upstairs to pack her bag. She did not want to explain their departure to either of them—Shea could do that. She would go on this honeymoon as he wanted, but she would go for one reason—and one reason only. She would not rest until she had discovered the truth behind Shea's charade of robberies—and they were charades . . . of that she felt certain.

In the big bedroom where she had dressed for the wedding, she threw her trunk open. She dug down to where a pair of denim britches lay, then picked out a couple of her less elaborate blouses. She set the pants and one of the shirts aside. She would have to change if she was going to ride astride a horse.

After gathering some underthings, she looked to the closet for a travel bag of some kind. Inside, she discovered a pair of dusty, battered boots next to a travel-worn portmanteau. Perfect. She pulled them out and set them on the floor next to the bed.

After tugging off her jacket, she struggled with the buttons at her throat. She would have to hurry if she was going to be ready by the time Shea got back. She had a new mission. She only prayed she would be able to fulfill this one.

SEVEN

WAITING FOR SHEA TO CHANGE HIS CLOTHING FOR THE trip, Chloe stood out in front of the house with the horses he had brought. After checking the ribbon holding her long hair secure at the nape of her neck, she rubbed the muzzle of the roan mare waiting beside Shea's palomino. "It's been a long time since I've done much riding, girl." She combed her gloved fingers through the lock of blond mane hanging just above the animal's watchful eyes. "Help me out if I get in trouble, okay?"

As if in answer, the horse bobbed its head and nickered.

The front door to the house opened and Shea emerged into the early-afternoon sunlight. "She'll be fine, Dudee, I promise," he said, stepping down from the porch.

Satchel followed closely at his heels.

"She better be, Shea Taggert, or you'll answer to me." Dressed in a simple fawn-colored skirt and white blouse, Dudee marched along behind the animal and Shea. Spreading her arms wide, she hurried to Chloe and hugged her. "You got everything you need, child?"

Smiling, Chloe nodded.

Shea ushered her out of her aunt's embrace and

around to the side of her mount. "We're headin' straight up to the Lightning Tree, Dudee. It's not like I'm whiskin' her out into the wilds of the forest or somethin'. She'll have all the comforts of my cabin up there."

"Hmph." Dudee watched Shea assist Chloe atop the little roan. "That's no more than a shack. I don't see why you have to take her up there. That's not a fit honeymoon. She'll be around all them ruffians you got working for you."

Upon Satchel's approach, the red mare sidestepped nervously.

Shea patted her neck, moved around to his palomino, and swung up onto his own saddle. "They'll be perfect gentlemen." He dipped his head to Dudee. "I'll see to that."

"You'd better." She looked at Chloe. "I found the ticket for Reno and the little note you left me. But I think I'll stay just a bit longer—at least till I see you're back home and settled." She blinked as if she thought she might have overstepped her place. "You don't mind, do you, child?"

Chloe reached down and pecked the woman's plump cheek with a quick kiss. "You'll always be welcome in our home, Aunt Dudee." Straightening, she gripped the reins, then grinned. "And I'd be disappointed if you didn't wait for me." Following Shea's lead, she waved, then maneuvered her mount behind his.

Together they took their departure alongside the edge of the lake. Satchel darted in and out of the trees ahead of them, but always stayed in sight.

Neither Shea nor Chloe spoke for nearly an hour

as they made their way into the depths of the pine-scented forest.

Chloe relaxed, enjoying the tranquility of the woodland. She took in the bright colors of the mountain flowers. Purple heather, yellow columbine, wallflower, white cow parsnip, and, her favorite, the pale purple camas, swayed their regal heads in the gentle wind. Cropping up in little patches among the other blossoms, the tiny pink mustang clovers bobbed like woodland sprites spying on the intruders of their land.

She breathed deeply, reveling in their summer-sweet scent. She listened to the chirp and trill of the mountain bluebird, and the friendly whisper of the warm breeze rustling through the tree boughs. She had almost forgotten how wonderful the mountains and forest could be.

It had been years since she had traveled at such a leisurely pace—since she was a child out on those hunting excursions with her brother, father, and the Taggert family. Shifting in her seat, she wriggled against the tickle of perspiration sliding down her back.

As they were both widowers with children to raise alone, Shea's and Chloe's fathers became good friends. They helped each other out with roundups, branding, and other ranching chores. It was only natural that their children would became friends as well.

Chloe sighed. Oh, how she missed those carefree, serene days in the embrace of her father's love and adoration.

For as far back as she could remember, the two households had been friends. But after her brother, Jerome, had died, it seemed nothing could mend the pain that thrust the two families into a world of conflict and intolerance.

Seth Summerhorn held Shea completely responsible for his only son's death. It got worse when her father realized Chloe would not give up seeing Shea as he had demanded. He had become distant and ill-tempered. And when he had caught Shea sneaking over to see Chloe that awful night eleven years ago—

Chloe shuddered and shook her head, dispelling the turbulent emotions. She had hated her father for a very long time after he had sent Shea running home with buckshot flying after him and her off to the boarding school in Boston. But slowly she came to realize that in his own harsh manner, Seth Summerhorn had only thought to protect her from someone whom he considered dangerous.

"Where are you, Button?" The sound of Shea's caressing voice transported her back to the present.

Looking away a moment, she fluttered her eyelids and shrugged with a smile. "A childhood place, a lifetime ago."

"Mmm." He nodded. "Me, too." Leaning forward, he rested his forearm atop the saddle horn. His gaze swept over the summer-kissed scenery. "No matter how many times I travel this trail, it always takes me back to being a boy when your pa and mine would take all us kids on those trips."

He chuckled. His eyes held a faraway look as he watched Satchel's antics.

Like a kitten at play, the curious beast literally appeared to be poking his nose in every hole and piece of underbrush throughout the forest.

"They always called them *huntin' trips*, but you

know, I don't recall ever huntin' anything to speak of."

A small laugh vibrated up through Chloe.

"We had fun, though, didn't we?" Shea asked.

Enjoying the dance of shadow and light streaking the forest, Chloe nodded. She watched the mountain lion stick his full face beneath a clump of shrubbery.

Satchel sneezed.

Chloe giggled. "Those were happy times."

"Yup, until . . ."

Chloe glanced at Shea.

His expression had suddenly transformed into one of sorrow. His hazel eyes had saddened, taking on a distant look.

She did not even have to question his thoughts. She knew what he was thinking. He was remembering her brother's death. "Don't, Shea."

"You know, I really tried to help him."

"I know," Chloe said, the words catching in her throat.

Straightening in his seat, Shea held his stare to the trees. "If I just hadn't been so wound up in tryin' to catch a damn fish, maybe I woulda heard him laughin' sooner. Maybe I coulda helped him."

"Shea—"

"I'd give anything if it had been me gettin' bit up by all them baby rattlers." Reining his horse to a stop, he turned to look at Chloe.

She pulled up beside him. She could see the ancient pain in his eyes, and knew he was still hurting from it even after all these many years.

"He thought they were worms—dancin' worms." He swallowed hard, his Adam's apple bobbing. "He had tangled his line in mine. He had done it about three or four times that mornin', and I was so mad at him. I told him that we were almost outa bait and to dig us up some more. I just didn't have any patience with him that mornin'. Hell, he was only ten, Chloe, *ten* years old. He mighta been older than me by a few months, but he seemed so much younger. It always seemed like he was such a little kid—" The words caught in a shuddering breath.

Slowly, his watery gaze moved to settle back on the playful cougar. "By the time I went to see what he was up to ... it was too late. The poison hit him almost before I figured out what had happened."

"Shea, please." Chloe was very near tears herself. Over the last eleven years, she had spent many a pain-filled night remembering. And many more before that. Even though she had only been nine when the accident had actually taken place, her father had never let her forget it.

"Jerome was always slow—Shea knew that," her father had said on more than one occasion throughout the years. "I trusted him—loved him like my own son, and this is the way he repays me?"

"Please, what?" Shea snapped.

Tears stung Chloe's eyes. "Don't do this to yourself. Jerome wouldn't want you to. He loved you—he looked up to you. He thought of you as the brother he never had. I know you'd never have let anything happen to him if you could've prevented it."

"But I coulda. If I just hadn't been so damn—" He sucked in a shaky breath and raised his head. He glanced at her, then looked away again. "God, I'd give anything if it'd been me instead o' him."

Chloe took Shea's hand and squeezed. "I wouldn't."

Shea turned a frowning gaze on her.

"Nobody loved Jerome any more than I did, Shea, but if it had to have happened, I'm glad ..." She caught herself, her allegiance torn. "Even though Jerome was—was *retarded*—" There, she had said it out loud. Her father had forbidden anyone to ever speak that word about his only son.

"Jerome knew how we felt about each other. I think deep down inside he knew all along we'd end up together. And I don't think he'd want you to trade places with him, either. You did everything you could. He'd never have held you responsible— especially when you didn't have any control over the situation."

"But your father did. He's never forgiven me."

"He couldn't help it, Shea. He just needed someone to blame instead of himself." It was not that she was all that certain of her father's feelings, but she had to grasp at any small justification for the accusations her father had set upon Shea. "He loved you both. Chances are, he would've felt just as guilty if it had been you instead of Jerome. Surely you know that's true?"

Shea's stare settled hard on her eyes. "Would he?" He took a slow, deep breath, before returning his attention to the woods. "I wonder."

Silently, Chloe slipped her fingers between his, clasping his hand in a display of loving comfort. It had been inevitable that they would broach the subject of Jerome's death. But she had hoped it would wait until she and Shea had reacquainted themselves with each other—until they were more familiar with each others' emotions. But it had not.

She released a slow breath of pent-up anguish. From the beginning, their relationship seemed to be cursed. So much had already transpired between the two of them—Jerome's death, her father's wrath, and now these infuriating robberies. What chance did they have of making their marriage truly work?

Somewhere in the distance, a whistle echoed up the mountainside.

"I didn't know there was a train up here," Chloe said, trying to divert Shea's attention from the pain of those age-old hauntings from the past.

As if he had suddenly become aware of her nearness, he straightened in his seat, then slipped his hand from her grasp. He shifted the reins into the palm she had just been holding, then made a fist and rested it on his thigh. "Sounds like the Number One on its way to Upper Pray Meadow."

Chloe lifted her brows in a thoughtful arch. "Number One? You mean there's more?" She was not truly as interested as she sounded, but she wanted desperately to veer away from their previous conversation.

"Yup." Seemingly just as relieved that Chloe had chosen to escape from the unpleasantry, Shea gestured toward the trees with a nod, then tapped his palomino's flanks with his heels.

Chloe reined her mount up beside his.

The horses snorted loudly in turn, but pressed on up the incline of the pine-needle–littered mountainside.

"We use both, the Number One and the Number Two, to haul the cut timber down to the receiving ponds and on to the mills," Shea told her. Entering upon a hilltop, he guided his horse out of the thick stand of trees and into a clearing. "Each of 'em have five cars that can carry up to—"

TENDER OUTLAW

In the near distance, a terrifying roar rushed at them from somewhere above on an adjoining slope.

Chloe snapped to attention, her eyes wide. "What was that?" She searched the surrounding area.

Tossing its head, her mare lurched forward.

Quick to react, Chloe yanked back on the reins. "Whoa, girl."

"There," Shea said, pointing to the east. "Look at it."

Chloe shot a gaze in the same direction. "Oh my God!"

Hurling down the mountainside at an incredible speed, a rocket trail of white smoke and red fire streaked toward a pond below. The resounding thunder intensified to a deafening rumble, growing continually louder until finally it met the water with an explosive hiss.

"What *is* it?" Chloe said with a gasp.

"A log coming down the chute from the Lightning Tree. That's how O'Dell came to name the camp. It looks like lightning flashing down the mountain when they send timber to the receiving pools. The chutes are angled and greased, but the speeding logs cause enough friction to set up a stream of fire behind them." Shea shook his head, his expression filled with wonder. "Sure strikes a chord of amazement and pure respect, don't it?"

Watching the last of the steam spew upward from the water's surface, Chloe held her gaze fastened to the turbulent scene. "More like stupefaction and apprehension."

Shea looked at Chloe, a frown creasing his brow.

Glancing at him, she could see that he was more than a little confused by her comment. Apparently he had no idea what she meant. She shook her head. "Never mind," she said in a dismissive tone before peering back at the settling mist.

Another groan. A flash of light. A second log, followed by still a third, descended the chute.

For close to half an hour, they sat in silence watching the awe-inspiring sight.

"C'mon," Shea finally said, urging his mount forward in a northerly direction. He lifted his gaze to the brilliant ball of orange hanging low in the sky above the treetops. "I'd like to get to camp before sundown."

But by the time they had followed the trail cut deep into the heart of the Sierras where the Lightning Tree Logging Company had its quarters, dusk was well upon them. Just outside the working community, a wagon clattered toward them at breakneck speed.

Shea held up a hand. "Whoa there," he called out to the driver.

The team of horses skidded to a dusty halt a few yards ahead of them.

"Outa the way," the driver yelled. "I got a hurt man in back."

Shea pressed closer, stopping beside the buckboard.

"Sorry, Mr. Taggert. Didn't notice it was you," the man said in a winded and gruff voice.

"That's okay." Shea narrowed an inquisitive stare on the driver. "Haemen, ain't it?"

The man nodded.

Chloe moved up beside Shea. Beneath the haphazard folds of a threadbare blanket, a man lay bleeding through the dirty bandages wound around his arm.

Chloe gasped. She looked up at Shea. "He's bleeding badly, Shea."

"Yes'm, that's why I was drivin' like I was." Dressed in a soiled blue plaid shirt and dungarees covered in sawdust and blood, the man Shea had called Haemen presented almost as disturbing a sight as the injured man.

"Who's that?" Shea asked, motioning toward the wounded man.

"Tom Bodine. He's hurt awful bad. Got his arm near tore off by one of the adze whilst he was loadin' logs in the chutes."

"How the hell did that happen?" Shea appeared angry. "What were the rest of the pushers doin'?"

"They was there—what there was of them, anyhow."

Shea leaned toward the man. "What do you mean, *what there was of 'em*?"

"Guess you ain't heard that a good number of the men hightailed it out just after you left last week. They said that if'n they couldn't get no wages fer the work they was doin', they wasn't gonna stick around and work fer nothin'." The man swallowed. He appeared to be as upset by the prospect of Shea's temper as by the injuries of his charge. "When Mr. O'Dell told us he couldn't meet payroll cause of another heist—well, sir—it was the last straw fer a lot of the men. Most of us got families to feed."

Shea shook his head and sighed dejectedly. "He gonna be all right?"

"Don't know. Mr. O'Dell told me to take him down to Doc Jenkins."

"Good—but go a little slower, will you? We don't want two men hurt."

"Sure thing, boss." That said, the man slapped the reins against the team's rumps.

"Damn." It was Shea's only reply. He glanced at Chloe. Then, before the wagon had even gotten more than a few yards down the road, he heeled his mount in the direction from which the buckboard had just come.

Chloe urged her mare at an equal pace. Why did Shea seem so distraught? He was the reason his own men had quit their jobs. Maybe now he could see what he was doing to others. Chloe nodded with approval. Good. Maybe this was just what was needed to make him stop.

Entering the camp, they pulled up short in front of a shack marked by a sign that read LIGHTNING TREE LOGGING COMPANY, OFFICE. The grounds appeared deserted. In the distance, a dog yapped outside a huge white canvas tent, but all else was quiet.

Shadowing their every move, Satchel padded up beside them.

Shea looked around with a puzzled expression. "Where is everybody?"

Chloe shrugged. She peered back at the small building. A light burned inside. "Looks like somebody's in there."

The door opened, and a barrel-chested man with a bushy black beard stepped outside. "Shea, boy. 'Tis good to see ya at last." Rushing forward, he reached up and gripped Shea's hand in a hearty shake. He shot a glance Chloe's way. "This be the lassie ye've made yer wife?"

Shea nodded with a smile, albeit a weak one. "Chloe, this is Galt O'Dell, the owner of the Lightning Tree."

"How do, lassie," he said as he released Shea's grasp.

Chloe acknowledged the man with a polite dip of her head.

He peered back to her husband. "It won't be owner again if things don't change soon around here." He shot Shea a meaningful look.

"Yeah. I saw Haemen haulin' Bodine down the mountain. What the hell happened? Haemen said somethin' about Bodine gettin' his arm near sliced off by an adze?" Shea swung down from his saddle. "Ain't that man been around them blades long enough to know to keep clear of 'em?"

Mr. O'Dell cast a cautious glance at Chloe. "This ain't fit talk to be said around womenfolk." He lifted a hand to Shea's shoulder, and another curious look passed between the men. He paused. "Let's talk about it later. You two should get yerselves a bath and some supper, then maybe we can . . ."

Chloe had a feeling there was more to be said between these two than a simple discussion about an injured man. "Shea," she interrupted, "you obviously have been gone a long time and there seems to be an extensive need for the two of you to deliberate a few things."

"What'd she say?" Mr. O'Dell asked in a low voice.

Shea shrugged.

Perturbed by the man's question, Chloe frowned. "Why don't you two take care of your talk? I'm sure it's important." She tried to sound as polite as she could, yet the thought of both a hot meal and a bath did press her good intentions sorely.

She lifted the weighty warmth of her hair off the back of her neck, and sighed. "It'll give me a little time to relax before we eat." She moved to dismount, but stopped mid-action, her foot barely lifting from the stirrup. She groaned. Every muscle in her body—especially those in her lower half—ached with the strain of the day's ride.

Shea rushed to her side and reached up, helping her from her seat.

Stepping to the ground, she moaned painfully and grabbed her bottom. Instantly she realized the error of her unladylike action and snatched her hands to the sides of her skirt. She gripped the fabric.

"You all right?" He studied her, his expression filled with concern.

"I think so," she stated half-heartedly, a forced smile on her lips. It felt as if someone had taken a razor strap and beat her until she could not walk. Stooping, she took an unsteady step, then pressed her hands to her back and arched her spine for relief. "It's been a long time—a *very* long time—since I've done this much riding. I'll be fine. I just need to walk it off, that's all."

Shea appeared skeptical.

She waved a hand, gesturing the men toward the logging office. "Go on," she said with an assurance she did not feel.

Hesitating only a moment, Shea gathered both sets of reins and slapped them around the hitching post outside the shack. "It won't take long, then we can get cleaned up and grab a bite to eat at the cook tent, okay?"

Inwardly Chloe groaned at the thought of what might be served by a logging cook, but outwardly she beamed at Shea. "Sounds extraordinary."

Rolling his eyes, Shea shook his head, then turned

and signaled Satchel to go up to the porch. "You stay with her, boy." He looked back at Chloe. "That all right with you?"

She peered at the big cat warily. It seemed she had little choice but to comply. She was his wife, the cougar was his pet, neither appeared to be going anywhere, so they might as well at least try and become friends—at least friendlier.

She smiled and shrugged. "Of course it's all right. Satchel and I are both here for the duration." With hesitant steps, she walked up to the edge of the porch and leaned against one of the support beams in front of the mountain lion, but at a discreet distance. "By the time you come out, we'll be quite amicable."

"Amicable?" Shea mimicked in a childlike tone. He arched a brow. Then without further delay he turned and motioned for Mr. O'Dell to join him inside.

Chloe stretched forward, extending her hands down over her knees. She flexed her fingers and wiggled her toes inside the large boots she wore. What felt like little pinpricks jabbed her skin, her backside and legs tingling with the effort.

Almost instantly, Satchel jumped down and nudged her hand atop his head.

Chloe flinched. Her breath caught. What did the beast want? Would he attack her? Eyes wide, she held very still, fear holding her as much as a prisoner as did her muscles.

Sniffing, Satchel bumped the palm of her gloved hand with his nose.

Chloe frowned. What was he doing? Somewhere in the back of her mind she remembered her father telling her that animals identified both enemy and friend alike by their smell. Of course. She should have realized.

Moving very carefully, she sat down and slowly removed her gloves. "There now, boy." She offered her hand out for his inspection. "How's that?"

Satchel leaned against her legs. He growled low, though not threateningly, but rather curiously.

Still as yet uncertain of the animal, Chloe swallowed back her anxiety and brushed her fingertips lightly over the top of the cat's head.

Almost immediately he set up a droning purr.

"You like that, do you?" Her nervousness somewhat alleviated, she began to pet the beast in earnest. "You're quite an unusual pet, you know? The girls at school would be quite taken aback if they could see me with you right now." She nodded as if she were speaking to a person.

"Well, well, well. Ain't this a hoot?"

Chloe snapped her head in the direction of the masculine voice.

Instantly, Satchel tensed. His posture stiffened and his ears fell back. He growled deep in his throat.

"What the hell?" The man jumped back. Metal flashed. A gun. A hammer clicked.

Instinctively, Chloe reached out for the cat. She held up a hand. "No—don't! He's a pet." Through the evening's dissipating light, she squinted at the silhouette looming at the edge of the porch. She knew that voice. She looked deeper into the shadows. And that hat. Nothing else could make that ridiculous shape. "Mr. Cameron?"

"Yes, ma'am." He took a step closer, his face coming into view.

Satchel rose up on all fours, his ears still laid back. He snarled, white fangs gleaming.

"That beast gonna attack?" Tyree Cameron held his position, the gun still drawn and cocked.

Chloe slipped her fingers beneath the animal's leather collar as she had seen Shea do, and pulled back a little. "It's all right, Satchel," she murmured in a soothing voice. She kept her focus trained on the cat, but directed a question at the man. "What are *you* doing here? I thought you came out to Glenbrook looking for work."

"I did," Cameron answered.

Only after she heard the sound of the gun's hammer slowly returning to its former position did Chloe shift her gaze from the cougar to the man. "I don't understand. What are you doing *here*?"

Animal and man appeared to relax, though both remained equally watchful of the other.

"I might ask you the same thing, Miss Summerhorn." Mr. Cameron tipped his head to one side. "S'cuse me, I mean, Mrs. Taggert. I heard that you did get married the other evening."

Chloe nodded. "I told you that was my reason for coming out from Boston when we were on the stage."

"Yes, ma'am, you did. And to answer your question as to why I'm here, it's to see your husband."

"My husband?" Chloe frowned. "Whatever for?"

"Work." Mr. Cameron grinned, his teeth flashing in the waning light. "I didn't get a chance to talk to him in town. And when I went to his house, his housekeeper told me he had come up here. I just missed the two of you leavin', I guess, by a half hour or so."

He gestured toward the door to the office with a jab of his hand. "He here?"

Chloe studied the cut of the man's clothing. He looked like he had on the stage—like a rancher, a wrangler, a drifter at the very least—but nothing about his appearance was anything like the lumberjacks she had seen upon her arrival here tonight.

Something about all of this did not seem right. She did not know why, but she had a feeling that Tyree Cameron was not here about a job—at least not as a lumberman—so, what *did* he want with Shea? She had to know.

Stroking Satchel's head, she smiled sweetly. "He's in private conference with Mr. O'Dell, the proprietor of the Lightning Tree Logging Company. But he probably won't mind being disturbed by a prospective employee."

"Great." Mr. Cameron smiled. He moved up onto the porch.

Satchel growled.

"Whoa there, big fella." The man pulled back and held up his hands. "I ain't gonna hurtcha."

Chloe smirked wickedly. "Oh, he's not concerned that you'll hurt *him*, he just doesn't like it when people get too close to *me*." It was a subtle warning, and she was not even certain it was true, yet she could not help but taunt the man. More than a little hesitant herself, Chloe hugged the cat around the neck in an overzealous ruse of confidence.

"Fine animal—good choice of protection," Mr. Cameron stated, his voice hinting of nervousness. With slow movements, he eased up to the door and knocked.

It opened and Shea's face appeared.

"Mr. Taggert?"

Shea nodded.

Chloe could not make out Shea's expression against the lamplight behind him, but she could see by his posture that he was a little apprehensive.

"Do I know you?" he asked Mr. Cameron.

"No, sir, not as yet, but—I understand you're havin' some trouble up here with your men, and I—" The younger man peered at Chloe before returning his attention to Shea. "Well, I'd like to talk to you about some work."

"I guess you haven't heard that we're havin' payroll trouble, too." Shea followed the man's gaze to Chloe, then back again. "This ain't the right time—"

"Here." Mr. Cameron retrieved a folded piece of paper from his pocket, then handed it to Shea. He lowered his voice. "If you'll just hear me out, I think we'll be able to help each other."

After reading it, Shea studied the man for a long moment, then stepped aside, allowing him entrance. Once Mr. Cameron had gone inside, Shea looked out at Chloe. "You all right?"

Chloe touched her head to that of the purring feline. "Indubitably."

"What?" Shea frowned. "Is Satchel causing you upset?"

"No." She giggled. Obviously, he thought the word meant something terrible. "I'm fine, Shea, really. Go on with your meeting."

"You're sure?"

"Quite." She ruffled the cougar's head, for in truth she was getting used to him very rapidly. Having a mountain lion for a friend had already proven beneficial.

Apparently just as content to have a new companion, Satchel began to lick the back of her hand.

"See," Chloe announced, "like I said, by the time you're through in there, we'll be old chums."

"Well, just see that you don't let him lick your skin too long. His tongue's like sandpaper. It'll take the hide right off you if you're not careful." With that, he smiled once more then closed the door behind him.

"What do you think they're up to, Satchel?" She felt the scratch of the animal's tongue and flinched. Slipping her hand up to his head, she absently stroked the soft fur. "I think it's only right that we should find out, don't you?"

Tyree Cameron was up to something—Chloe knew it. She had not liked him from their first meeting. Even then he had seemed the overly curious type— especially after she had mentioned Shea's name. But what *was* the man doing here? He had said that he and Shea could help each other. What had he meant by that? And what had he shown Shea? Did it have to do with the stage holdups? Was he somehow in on them?

No. She shook her head. Shea had not even recognized him. Yet the man had been insistent. Shea told her that there were problems—reasons for his committing these acts of robbery—things he could not as yet control.

She glanced up at the shack. Were these two men a part of these problems? Were they the reason Shea could not end his thievery? If so, why? Could either of them possibly be blackmailing Shea into doing these things?

Turning fully, she shifted her stare to the light in the window. It just did not make any sense—any of it! She strained to clearly hear what the men were talking about, but she could only discern the muffled sounds of their conversation. She had to know what was happening. Maybe if she did, she might be able to help Shea discover a way out of this predicament.

Wetting her lips, she stood. Should she? On occasion, and only out of childish wickedness, she and her friends had eavesdropped on her teachers at school. But this was different. This was on her own husband. She looked around to see if anyone was watching. The camp was quiet, empty. She hesitated. It simply had to be done.

Slinking down to a bent position, she moved toward the window. Shea himself had told her he either could not—or would not—refrain from dealing in these acts of robbery. She had to find out which it was. It was her duty to help him. She was, after all, his wife.

EIGHT

TAKING GREAT CARE TO REMAIN QUIET, CHLOE STEPPED UP onto the office porch, but with the effort the overly large boots she wore clopped against the wood below her feet. She froze. She shot a look to the door, then the window. All remained as it had before.

Phew. The men had not heard her. She relaxed, then took a step backward, and sat down. Bending over, she tugged on the heel of one shoe. "Can't let them know what I'm up to, can I, boy?" she whispered to Satchel.

The cat did not seem to be paying any attention to her. Watchful as ever, his focus appeared to be trained on the forest.

Probably a rabbit. Barely acknowledging the thought she slipped off the other boot, then rose for another try. She had to hear what Shea and the other two men were talking about. With great stealth, she eased up to the building and stopped in between the door and the window.

She tried to peek in through the glass, but the shade was pulled down. She pressed her ear against the rough wood surface nearest the door.

"From where I stand, Taggert, I really can't see as you have much of a choice here." Mr. Cameron's voice filtered through the splintery barrier. "You read the letter. It's an order. You gotta let me in."

"I don't need anyone lookin' over my shoulder—especially somebody as inexperienced as you." Shea sounded angry.

"The way I hear it, you haven't been at this too long yerself there, buddy." Mr. Cameron's tone was smug.

"Look, I told him to trust me. I told him I could do the job." Shea's voice dropped. "Hell, before I joined up with this gang, people were gettin' shot, and one even got killed."

Pulling the length of her hair around to one side, Chloe shifted even closer, trying to hear a little clearer.

"Now nobody gets hurt."

"Yeah, he knows that. And he 'preciates it, too."

"So, what the hell're you doin' here, then?"

Chloe held her breath. They *were* discussing the robberies. And this Cameron person was here to—what? Whatever it was, Shea did not sound happy about it.

"He just thought you might need—"

"What? Watchin' over? Hell, Cameron, I've been doin' my job—and damn good, too."

"Yeah, well, what 'bout that new missus of yers?"

The conversation paused.

"I told him not to worry about her. I told him I could handle things—that she wouldn't get in the way."

"He don't see it that way. He's worried that she'll find out."

Another lull.

"Damn. She knows, don't she?" Aggravation filled Mr. Cameron's voice.

"She recognized me from that last stage we held up."

"Good God, man!" O'Dell broke in. "I heard you used nitroglycerin."

"He did."

"How could you do that, knowing the lassie was aboard?"

A moment of silence.

Mentally, Chloe asked the same question. At least Mr. O'Dell gave the impression that he was a caring person.

"I made sure she was safe—just like I did everybody else. She was never in any danger."

"So how'd she find out? I was there and even knowin' what I know, I wouldn't have recognized ya," Mr. Cameron said in a sarcastic tone. "You were wearin' a bandanna, for Christ's sakes. How the hell did she see yer face? I didn't. Hell, even when you opened the door just now, I wasn't sure you were the same man."

"She wasn't, either—until I lifted her veil after our wedding."

"What's that got to do with it?"

"When I went up on top of the coach to get her trunk down, my kerchief fell. I guess that's when she—"

"Son of a bitch! You should've wired him about this right off. He'd've—"

"What?" Shea's voice lashed out at Mr. Cameron.

Chloe's heart bolted to a faster pace. Now they were talking about her. Why? And who was this other man they were talking about? The leader maybe?

"Wonderful! This's sure a fine piece of trouble."

"She's not your worry, Cameron."

"Not my—"

Footsteps scuffed across the floor toward Chloe.

Oh, no! What was she to do now? She could not let them catch her. Spinning around, she pressed herself hard against the side of the building and held her breath.

The window shade fluttered, and someone looked outside.

Chloe blinked against a wayward strand of hair catching in her lashes, but she did not dare to so much as flinch.

"Where'd she go?" It was Mr. Cameron.

"I told you not to worry about her. She's probably out—"

"That's twice you've said that." The footsteps sounded again, returning to the other side of the room.

Chloe breathed a sigh of relief. He had not spotted her.

"The fact is, Taggert, she *is* my worry. She's all our worry. What if she talks? Then what? She could ruin everything." Someone—most likely, Mr. Cameron—paced across the room. "Don't ya have some family up north?"

"Yeah, so?"

"Well, can't ya send her to them for a while?"

"No."

"C'mon, Taggert. I understand how it must be for ya. She's a gorgeous gal, but can't ya keep yer pants buttoned up for another week or—"

"Shut up!" Shea's voice leapt into the air. "That's my wife—"

"Lads." Mr. O'Dell intervened. "I didn't get involved in all of this to have to put up with nothing but a lot of jaw-jacking. And if anyone finds out, or if I'm openly connected with either of ye—except by the lumber company here—I'll lose more than my ass, in case you two are of a mind to be for noticing."

Chloe's eyes flew wide. She had not heard such language since she was on the ranch back home, listening to the cowhands. Yet something more disturbed her. She had been right. Mr. O'Dell *was* part of the gang of outlaws robbing the stages. In fact, it sounded as if he were the leader.

"We've no time for such things now. If Shea here says he can keep the lassie under control . . . well, then—"

"Hell, he can't keep her under control. I doubt anyone can. That woman purely loves to flap her jaws. O' course, nobody can understand what she's sayin'," Mr. Cameron said with a hoarse chuckle. "On second thought, maybe you *can* keep her under control, Taggert. Just tell everybody she's crazy. That way if she runs off at the mouth about any of this, we're covered."

Anger bolted through Chloe. She flashed a caustic look in Satchel's direction, but he was not anywhere to be seen. Briefly, she wondered where he might have gone. "I should've let you bite the incommodious misbegot—" She mouthed the word to herself, wagging her head like a spiteful child.

Never had she heard anyone speak of her with such rude disdain. She had been correct to feel an immediate intolerance of Tyree Cameron's company.

"I said, I'll take care of her." Shea's voice was low.

"Good enough," Mr. O'Dell piped in before Mr. Cameron could respond. A chair scraped across the floor's wood surface. "Then once ye've finished the jobs ye're supposed to be minding, ye can both go to fisticuffs and beat each other to a bloody pulp if ye've the mind. But for now I'll thank ye to concentrate on working together." He hesitated. "Agreed?"

Neither Shea nor Mr. Cameron spoke.

"Agreed?" Mr. O'Dell was insistent.

Again, nothing from either of the younger men, yet they must have responded silently.

"Good lads. Now," Mr. O'Dell began again, "what say we get down to business, eh? Shea, lad, we're goin' to be havin' to see these robberies put to an end. *Even* if we *can't* flush out the big man standin' behind them, ye know that, o' course."

"Yup." Shea sounded a little more relaxed now. "People're startin' to get suspicious. I'm pretty sure I know who he is, but—"

"And who do ya think they're gonna point at first?" Mr. Cameron's tone had not yet lost its sarcastic edge.

"They?" Shea asked. "Who's they?"

"The outlaws." Mr. Cameron spoke as if he thought Shea were dimwitted.

"I'm not fer seein' yer point, laddie."

"Well, what does anyone around here really know about Taggert?"

"Hmm?" Mr. O'Dell seemed puzzled.

"I mean, all anybody knows is what he's told them, right?"

"Aye."

"He's supposed to've come from some rich California ranchin' family up north, right?"

A second of silence.

"Well, what makes ya think everybody believes him? Nobody ever heard of him till he moved here. So how does any of them know it's true?"

"It's easy enough to prove, Cameron. Quit dancin' and just spit out whatever it is you're tryin' to say." Obviously Shea had about as much tolerance for the younger man as did Chloe.

"Well . . . if anything goes wrong, yer gonna be the first one they point a finger at."

"Yeah, so?"

"So." Mr. Cameron sounded frustrated. "The way I heard it, everybody in the gang of outlaws is men from Glenbrook and the surroundin' area, right?"

"Mmmhmm?"

"So . . . the way I heard it from him, just before you came here, you were supposed to've robbed the Wells Fargo office in Carson City. They had to've heard it, too, *and* that there's a reward out on ya."

"Nobody saw the thief's face. They don't know if it really was me or somebody else. I just convinced 'em it was."

"So, was it?"

No verbal reply.

Chloe blinked. She could only pray it was not true.

"Still, *they* think it was. And when push comes to shove, those men're gonna throw you to the law—just like some kinda fresh bone to a starvin' dog."

"That's been evident since day one, Cameron. Why the hell *do* you think they let me—a stranger—in on their little setup in the first place? Hell, it was my idea. I had to cozy up to 'em somehow," Shea said matter-of-factly. "Things were gettin' too hot for 'em. They needed somebody for a pigeon, and I gave 'em just what they wanted—a rich rancher's son with a price on his head."

Cameron did not speak for a minute or two. "Ya mean, *you* set *them* up?"

Both Mr. O'Dell and Shea laughed.

"It seems you don't have everything figured out as good as you thought, doesn't it, Cameron?" Even a fool could tell that Shea was pleased with himself.

But Chloe was not. This was the first she had heard of the Wells Fargo holdup. How had he gotten so mixed up with all this stealing? He had spoken the truth. His family *was* well-off—maybe not as wealthy as her father, but well-off nonetheless. She had never known Shea to be so prideful before that he could not accept help from his family, so why was he doing this to get money now?

"Look, Cameron, Mr. O'Dell's right, here. Things're definitely heatin' to a boil. I got a feelin' if the holdups ain't put to a halt, and quick, things're goin' to turn out bad—for everybody."

"So what're we gonna do 'bout it?"

Chloe took a chance and leaned over to peek inside past the shade.

In the yellow glow of a single lantern, Shea's features appeared distorted, like a child's mask on Hallowe'en. He leaned across a desk, staring at who she could only assume to be the Irishman. "Mr. O'Dell, I want you to leak word out that you're sendin' for another payroll shipment—double what it should be—to make up for the wages lost on the last robbery."

"But most of the men around here know I don't

have that kind of capital, lad. They'll know there's devilment afoot, 'tis certain o' that, I am."

Shea shook his head. "Not if you tell 'em you got a loan from some bank in—oh, say—Sacramento?"

"Aye, that'll work."

"Good. You leak that out and it won't be no time before the boys'll get in touch with me. They'll want that money and, with such a large sum, I think we'll even be able to nab the real leader behind all of this."

"And me? What do ya want me to do?" Cameron seemed overly eager to get involved in whatever underhanded scheme Shea was up to.

"Since it's like you say, Cameron, I don't seem to have any choice in acceptin' your help. So I want you to sit on top of things with the outlaws."

"And just how am I gonna do that?"

Chloe pressed her nose against the glass, trying to see more clearly through the tiny space between the window and the drawn shade. Shea was still in view, but neither Mr. Cameron nor Mr. O'Dell was in sight.

"Don't worry, I'll tell you where they meet—later. I just need to know that you'll be there when I need you."

"Count on it." He hesitated. "But what 'bout yer—uh—Mrs. Taggert? How ya gonna fix things with her so's she stays outa the way?"

Shea rose to his full height. He seemed to be contemplating his next decision with great care.

Chloe held her breath, straining against the distressing silence. What *would* Shea do with her? Surely he did not think he could just tell her he was going out on another holdup—like he was going off to work or something—and simply expect her to understand. Could he? No, surely not. He knew how she felt. So how was he going to explain things?

"Chloe and I are on our honeymoon. I was goin' to take her on a tour around the lake and on to Tahoe City for a stay at the Grand Central Hotel tomorrow anyhow." He paused as if formulating his plan with more precision. "So right after we leave, Cameron, you go back to Glenbrook and wire me that there's been more trouble here at the Lightnin' Tree."

"Sounds good, but whatcha gonna do with her?" Mr. Cameron asked. "You said you two're on yer honeymoon. She ain't gonna like it if ya just up and leave her stranded."

"She'll be fine once I show her around town and she gets a gander at all them shops with their pretty female frills. I'll leave her with some money for shoppin'. Yup, she'll be just fine with that."

Like hot coals sizzling through snow, Chloe's eyes burned with rage. *Just fine with that.* With the backs of her hands against her spine, she leaned against the rough-hewn siding of the building.

Of all the nerve! He thought he could *buy* her into submission. Well, if he thought she was going to stand idly by and watch him ride off to perpetrate another calculated and unpardonable stage robbery, Shea Taggert had another think coming. Something else he had said—something confusing enough to thwart her anger—rolled through her mind.

I think we'll even be able to nab the real leader behind all of this.

What had Shea meant by that? Was not Mr. O'Dell the *real* leader? When they had first started talking, she had thought so, but now she was not certain.

More than a little perplexed, Chloe frowned. What did it all mean?

"It's gettin' late. Chloe's tired. So'm I."

The sudden nearness of Shea's voice snatched Chloe from her suspicions and speculations. Her heart leapt to her throat. She could not let him catch her spying on them. She shot a glance to the woods. Grabbing her wits about her, she shoved herself away from the shack and bolted for the trees. But she had only managed a couple of steps before she remembered her boots.

She veered to the edge of the porch, seized the tops of the shoes, and lunged for the shadowy cover of the forest. She barely cleared the side of the building before the door opened. Half-running, half-skipping, she tugged on the sloppy boots. She did not stop to catch her breath until she hit the treeline.

"Satchel—here, boy," she called out, hoping to appear as if she had been searching for the animal all along. "Come here, Satchel." Staying just inside the stand of pines, she followed the edge of the encampment around to the front of the shack.

"Chloe, you all right?" Shea shouted into the night air. Moving to stand at the rear of the horses, he peered into the darkness.

Pretending not to hear him, she whistled for the big cat to come to her. "Come on, Satchel."

"Chloe?" Shea sounded concerned.

Taking advantage of the moment, she stepped out from the shadows and into the moonlight. "I'm here, Shea. Satchel ran off. I was looking for him."

"He's a mountain lion. He was born in those woods. He can look out for himself."

"Oh," she answered, hoping to sound suitably embarrassed. "I hadn't thought of that."

Shea smiled and held out his hand to her. "C'mon, let's go get somethin' to eat. That's more than likely what Satchel's doin'. He'll be back soon. He comes up here with me all the time."

Dutifully, Chloe hurried to his side and accepted his grasp.

He pulled a small sprig of pine from her hair, then guided her toward the white canvas tent. He shrugged. "When he's had his fill he'll come to the cabin."

The mention of Shea's lodge sent a slight tremor through her body. Absently, she brushed a few wayward strands of hair behind her ear. Tonight would be their first night spent together as husband and wife. She swallowed. Until now, she had not given that any consideration. Head bent, she shot him a nervous glance.

"I've got a surprise for you," he suddenly announced.

Chloe blanched. Her step faltered.

Shea grabbed her around the shoulders. "You all right?"

"Mmmhmm." She tried to conceal the tumultuous undercurrent rolling through her emotions. She was not yet certain she was ready to be alone with Shea in the customary manner expected of a wife—especially with the misgivings that shadowed their present relationship.

How could she be expected to fully give herself to him when she could not as yet trust him? She could not. A marriage was supposed to be built on trust as well as commitment and love. The love and commitment were there—of that there was no denying. Otherwise, she would never have decided to stay with him. But trust? Of that, it seemed, they both were sorely lacking.

Maybe once she helped him see these robberies put to an end, they would be able to add that missing element. But, for now, she would have to set her goal on a more urgent objective. No matter what the risks, she would see Shea saved from his own corrupt self.

"Are ya sure ye're okay, Button?"

"I'm sure."

"Ye're awfully quiet all of a sudden."

Remembering the tender regard he had shown earlier when he had seen the effect the day's ride had had on her, she leaned into him, feigning more weariness than she actually felt. "I guess I'm more fatigued than I realized." She faked a yawn, then sighed soulfully. "I'm sure I'll love whatever it is you have for me, but would you mind holding your surprise until tomorrow?"

He chuckled deep in his throat. "Don't fret, Button. The surprise *is* for tomorrow." He hugged her a little tighter against him. "Soon as we get some food in ya, I'll take ya to the cabin and ya can go right to sleep. Good enough?"

A rush of relief flowed through Chloe's limbs, but in its wake a little piece of her earlier anger returned. Apparently, he had been thinking of the covert plan he had disguised as a honeymoon.

So he though to woo her into looking the other way while he plundered the stage lines, did he? And tempt her with *shopping* and *female frills*, hmm? She smiled up at him sweetly. "A good night's sleep sounds positively wonderful. Thank you, Shea, darling."

Yet behind that mask of unsuspecting innocence, her thoughts were not quite so honeyed. *But once we get to Tahoe City, Shea Taggert—I have a surprise for you, too.*

NINE

EARLY-MORNING LIGHT FILTERED INTO THE SMALL CABIN that Shea called his Lightning Tree home. Quietly, so as not to awaken Chloe, he took up the end of the leather strop attached to the edge of the washstand and sharpened his razor. He held his jaws tight against an insistent yawn. He had not slept well—in fact, he had hardly slept at all.

The bed had not been big enough for the two of them to lie comfortably together. At first, he had enjoyed their closeness. For tired as he had been the previous evening, he had wanted Chloe—wanted her with a fiery passion he had not even known existed within him. Yet he had felt uneasiness in her whenever and wherever his body had touched hers.

After an agonizing hour or so, he had made a pallet on the floor next to her. He could not stand lying so close and not being able to hold her. It had caused him more tension than he could handle. Rather than making them both suffer, removing himself from temptation had seemed the better plan.

He glanced up and looked at her reflection in the mirror. Like the play of a sunrise across water, the fullness of her golden hair spilled across the pillow. Asleep, she appeared so naïve and fragile. Hell, she *was* naïve and fragile.

He would never tell her so, though. She seemed to be under the unmistakable delusion that just because she had been to school back East, she was worldly and ... He looked down at the blade and the strop. Tough as old leather. Yup. Arching a brow, he nodded.

He returned his attention to his shaving. Tough was just what she thought of herself, all right—tough and sure of herself. But he knew deep down, she was not tough at all. She had proven it last night when he had moved to kiss her. She had not exactly pulled away. No—it was worse. She had flinched, turning rigid within his embrace.

Chloe was not yet ready to give up the flower of her body. And he would not take it. He loved her. He had waited this long, he could wait a little longer. She needed time. He knew her fears about the stage robberies were putting more pressure on what would have been, at the very least, an uncomfortable situation. Especially for two people who had not seen each other in eleven years.

Setting the razor down, he picked up his mug of soap and brush, then dabbed a thick layer of foam onto the heavy stubble covering his jaws. He turned the left side of his face to the mirror. First one stroke with the sharp tool, then another.

He was going to have to finish this secret undertaking for the governor, and quick. He had a strong feeling that Bill Sharon already suspected that Shea might know of the part the man played in the holdups. It would not be beneath the bastard to get to Chloe somehow—to put her life in danger so as to keep Shea under his control.

Hell, he had as much as admitted that this was his

intention with his veiled threat about Chloe on the night of the reception, and then again when he had taken it upon himself to approach her at the Glen Brook House.

Chloe moaned. In one swift movement, she turned, plumped the pillow with a fist, then plunged back down, one side of her face exposed to his view beneath a finespun web of hair.

Smiling, Shea shook his head. She was still asleep. He watched the slow rise and fall of her shoulder within the folds of the shirt he had given her. Chloe appeared to be extremely organized at all times. He had been surprised that she had forgotten her own nightdress. He followed the stretch of her limb atop the bedsheet to where her slender fingers barely peeked out beneath the cuff of the garment.

At that moment, he prayed for an unusually long life with her. A hundred years would not even be lengthy enough to tire of waking to such a glorious sight.

He sucked in a slow breath. What could a ten-year-old boy have ever done to make one beautiful little girl of nine fall so deeply in love with him? Shea stood in awe of his own good fortune.

With no more than words of endearment passing between them over the miles, their love had endured the test of time. He exhaled. But would it endure all that was about to take place? The lies—the dishonesty?

Chloe would never understand his deception. Yet he had no choice. He had to leave her in Tahoe City where she would be safe. He had to execute this one last robbery. He had committed himself to this job.

He lifted his gaze from his task of shaving to his

own eyes. In the mirror, he stared hard at the overly ambitious man he had become. *But what of your commitment to her?*

Once the dispute had been settled between his family and the Paiute back home, Shea had not been able to wait to get hooked up with the agency. He had been in a hurry to get through his training and on to his first real undercover job. He had wanted to find the exciting adventures he was certain his older brother had lived.

Shea had worked hard. He had been tops in his class. And once he had acquired the knowledge and experience necessary, he had finally landed the opportunity he had been waiting for.

But his brother, Lance, had been right when he had told him about working as a special agent for the governor: "Sometimes even the most experienced don't see things coming." He had told Shea not to be in such a rush. It was not always so glorious as Shea had believed.

Until now, he had not known what his brother had meant by that. Damn. If only he had seen this one coming. He could have stopped Chloe from traveling out to him until he was through. He had tried, but it had not been soon enough. Now here she was.

He swept her form with another glance. He would be damned lucky if he was able to pull this one off. If he could just see it finished ... If he could just keep her out of the way and unharmed ... If he could just manage to keep the love they had for each other from being damaged ... Damn. There were an awful lot of *ifs* involved.

He wiped the foam on his razor onto the towel draped over his shoulder. A movement caught his eye. Head tilted downward, he slowly lifted his gaze to the mirror again.

Chloe remained as before. She appeared not to have stirred.

Hmm. He must have imagined it. He lifted his chin to scrape away the beard from his throat.

There it was again—another movement. Barely noticeable, the flutter of an eyelash against a wisp of hair.

He stilled, squinted, cut her a look. Chloe was watching him. He smiled to himself. His stomach constricted. He had never had a woman do this before. It excited him to think that she was watching but did not want him to know it.

Two can enjoy this. With slower strokes than was necessary, he began the task anew. Then he struck a pose that showed off his well-built body. With lingering deliberation, he stroked first one side of his face with the razor, then the other, removing the soapy stubble with more enjoyment than he had ever felt.

After drawing the task out as long as he could, he dipped his hands into the basin and wiped the remaining foam from his face. He glanced at Chloe.

Was she still watching?

This was too much fun. He could not let it end here. Pouring some water from the commode pitcher, he filled the bowl. He leaned down and splashed up the cool liquid onto his face and into his hair.

When he had doused himself completely, he rose, smoothing both water and hair down over his head. Rivulets trickled down his torso like tantalizing fingers teasing his senses. Relishing the feeling, he shivered.

She stirred ever so slightly again. This time a finger twitched, parting a tendril of hair away from her view.

He held back a satisfied smirk. He picked up a bar of soap and pumped it slowly back and forth in his palms until he had a thick lather, then washed his upper body. Giving her something to watch, he took great pains to flex his muscles in the process. He kept a discreet eye trained on the looking glass, trying to appear as if he were deeply absorbed with his morning ritual, but was secretly watching *her* watch *him*.

Unmistakable. He caught the sight of her soft blue eyes glimmering between slitted lids.

Was that desire shining in her eyes?

He groaned inwardly. His groin tightened. The excitement was almost unbearable. It was like some erotic love ritual—the more attentive she became, the more he wanted her to look.

His gaze followed the seductive sight of her legs being drawn up beneath the coverlet.

Softer than a whisper, she sighed.

Oh God, this was good. He had never noticed this from any other women. Chloe was aroused. At least, it appeared that way. He knew *he* certainly was. Would she respond so easily if he were actually touching her?

He took a towel and plunged it into the basin, then wrung out most of the liquid. Straightening his spine, he wiped off the soap from under his arms and off his chest with slow and deliberate movements. He could feel the play of his muscles across his shoulder blades and knew she was studying their rippling movement. Never had a bath been so stimulating.

He dunked the cloth back in the water and, for a

moment, allowed himself to think of her being in a huge tub of warm suds ... then of him being in it with her. He squeezed the rag. His manhood twitched. Damn. This was becoming almost painful. He had to end this—now!

Without thought of his actions, he grabbed the bowl of cool liquid and flipped its contents over his head. He groaned again—this time from shocked relief.

Chloe bolted straight up. "Are you all right?"

After returning the basin to its spot, he peered up at her startled reflection. He grinned. "So you *were* watching."

Like a cornered child caught with a stolen handful of licorice, her eyes flew wide. "I—I wasn't watching you bathe. You—you frightened me awake."

He wheeled around to face her. "If you weren't watching, how'd ya know I was bathin'?"

Her face flamed red. She flicked a glance around the room before looking back at him. Apparently bent on another denial she opened her mouth, but quickly clamped it shut. She hesitated another second, then all at once her eyes turned a sassy shade of gray-blue, twinkling mischievously. "Oh, you!" She snatched up the pillow and hurled it at him. "You knew all along, didn't you?"

In one quick movement, he lunged forward, leaping onto the bed. He shook his shoulder-length mane like some wild beast of the forest. Beaming with pride, he grabbed her upper arms. "Admit it. Ya were watchin' me."

"Never," she shouted with laughter.

He showered her with another spray of water from his hair. "No?"

"Don't!" She tried to shield herself with her hands.

He moved up to straddle her thighs with his knees. "C'mon, Button. Tell me the truth." He grabbed her hands. Thrusting his fingers in between hers, he rubbed his freshly shaven jaw against her cheek, across her lightly freckled nose, and over to the opposite side of her face. "Tell me. I want to hear ya say it."

"No—why?" She giggled, squirming beneath him like a basketful of wriggling puppies. "If you think you know so much, why do you want to hear it?"

"Tell me!"

"Let me go, you—you—brandish bogtrotter!"

Stunned, Shea pulled back with a stare. "What? I'm a what?"

Chloe laughed. "A bogtrotter."

Making a mental note to look that one up in the little dictionary he had brought along, he scowled down at her. "Ya think so, eh?"

With a childish titter, she nodded, a daring taunt twinkling in her eyes.

"We'll see." He bent near her ear and nibbled her lobe. "Admit it, Button. Tell me ya were watchin'." With intent to torment her further, he nipped at her neck. He released her hands, then snaked his fingers around to her ribs and began to tickle her mercilessly. "Tell me."

"All right! I admit it!" she shrieked, laughter bubbling up from deep within her. Leaning her head back, she screeched at the ceiling, "I was watching you—I was watching you!" She shoved her palms against his chest and pushed, kicking her feet all the while. "There! Are you happy? I said it. Now let me go." Like a battering ram, she lunged her body against his.

A button on her shirt popped off. The fabric fell open.

In that movement, he caught sight of the soft mound of pale flesh rising just above her camisole. The luscious view threw him off guard. He stilled. He could feel the warm surge of her rapid breathing. His gaze slipped lower to where his hand rested beneath the underswell of that same breast.

She gasped.

His eyes found hers.

But she did not shrink away from him this time. She did not stiffen. Could this be the moment—the signal that she was ready and willing to give herself to him?

Neither moved. Time and silence circled around them in a dizzying spin, holding them suspended.

She wet her lips with her tongue—that same fateful action she had taken in his office when he had held her like this. It was his unbridling.

Slowly, so as not to frighten her, he bent toward her, his stare shifting between her eyes and her tempting mouth.

Even before he touched her lips, she slipped her arms up around his neck.

Shea felt as though he were in one of the boiling hot springs back home—only this one was a lot more dangerous. If he moved too quickly—if he made the wrong advance—Chloe might dart away from him and he would lose this chance. His chest tightened, threatening the air in his lungs. He had to take the risk.

Hesitantly, she closed her eyes.

He flicked his tongue across her lips, softly at first, tasting their sweetness.

Her lower lip quivered, yet she did not so much as flinch.

Seizing her surrender, he captured her lips fully. With a deep-pitted moan, he pulled her hard against him.

She shuddered within his embrace, and clutched a shock of his hair at the base of his skull. Her tongue parried with his. Her breathing sped to rapid pants, filled with impassioned whimpers.

She smelled of sleep, sweet and warm, tasted of early morning and virginal innocence, felt like fire and ice, melting beneath his touch. It was more than he could resist. Desire flamed through his body. A stab of raw savagery shot through his limbs as his baser needs gripped him.

He secured one arm tighter around her, then eased the other palm up to the fullness of her small but heaving breast. He squeezed her gently. It was not enough. He wanted to feel the softness of her form against the hardness of his.

Smoothing her shirt aside, he eased his hand beneath the fabric. He tugged the ribbon holding her camisole closed free.

She shuddered, stiffened. Her breath caught in a throaty gasp.

No. He would not let her retreat now. Coaxing her back to the mattress, he shifted his weight to lie beside her. He brushed the tip of her nipple with his fingers.

She trembled against him. She was afraid.

He knew that. No one had ever touched her so intimately. He was certain. He had to calm her fears, but how? For as unseasoned as she was with men, so was he with an untried woman. Freeing her mouth, he worked a path of light kisses to her ear. "Shh, trust me, Button."

He cupped her breast and thrummed his thumb back and forth across the hardening peak, taunting it to a tight bud. "Relax, Chloe. Let yourself go," he murmured in her ear.

She closed her eyes and stilled. Her arms fell away from him. Her muscles went taut. She balled her fists against the bed, gripping the sheets.

He had reached her, whether with his touch or his words, he did not know, and cared even less. He could feel the pounding of her heart within his hand. His own called to hers in a deafening drumbeat. Rising up on one elbow, he began unbuttoning the rest of her shirt.

Eyes still clenched, she squeezed them tighter. Her chest rose and fell in a feverish staccato.

It urged him on. He brushed the thin garment to one side, exposing her breast to his view.

Rose-brown, her nipple stood erect from his caressing.

A dark, groin-gripping sensation, like that of some ancient cave dweller claiming possession of his woman, clutched his insides. Damn it to hell! If he did not watch himself, he was going to ruin everything.

He held himself in check. He would have liked nothing more than to stretch out on top of her and take her with all the fierce urgency rocketing through his being—make her his—become that cave dweller. But he could not. He would not do that to her. He had to take it slowly. Let her learn to enjoy, want, and even seek the pleasure his touch could bring her.

He could feel the heat radiating from her body. It

fed the volcanic flames that lapped at his. Sliding his hand down to the curve of her hip, he lowered his head to her breast.

In that instant, someone pounded at the door. "Mr. Taggert."

"Damn it to hell!" Shea complained with a groan. It was Cameron.

Chloe gasped. Still passion-flushed, her expression registered fear—or was it embarrassment? Her gaze flew from Shea to the door.

He reacted instantly, snatching Chloe's shirt together, concealing her from any prying eyes that might be lurking around. "What the hell do ya want?" he yelled at the man.

"I brought yer horses—saddled and ready—just like ya ordered."

Eyes still wide, Chloe looked back at Shea. Sitting up, she quickly gathered the sheet up to her neck.

"Sorry, Button," he whispered. "I forgot about Cameron. I'll get rid of him."

Rolling off the bed, he stood and crossed to the door. He opened it with an angry jerk.

"Oh, hey," Cameron said. He looked almost as startled as Chloe had. "I—uh—got the horses—"

"Yeah, I can see that." Shea did not intend to sound so angry.

Cameron took in Shea's barefoot, shirtless appearance, and grinned. "You—uh—" He leaned ever so slightly to the side as if he were trying to see into the cabin.

Shea yanked the door up behind him.

Cameron snapped his attention back to Shea. "I'm sorry for the intrusion, Tag—Mr. Taggert," he announced in an overly loud tone. "Butcha did say to have yer horses brought to ya by dawn."

Shea stiffened against the brisk chill of the morning air. He folded his arms across his chest and nodded.

"Well," Cameron stammered. He pointed toward Topaz and the roan. "Here they are."

"Thanks." Shea had no intention of carrying on casual conversation with this man when he had Chloe warm and waiting for him inside. "Just leave 'em there." He turned back to the door.

"Um—"

He shot a hostile glare over his shoulder at Cameron. "Ya forget somethin'?"

"Nah, I was just wonderin'—"

"What?" Shea did not have the temperament to deal with this man.

"Well—I—uh." The man's intolerable smile grew wider. "Should I tell Mr. Mapes over at the cook tent to drop somethin' off to ya and the missus, or will ya be comin' to eat with the rest of us?"

The door suddenly flew wide behind Shea.

"Shea, darling, whatever are— Oh, Mr. Cameron, it's you." Chloe emerged from behind Shea, completely dressed. Her voice held an overly gracious quality. She sounded as if she had not a care in the world, as if she had known the man was there. Clad in blue jeans, Shea's old boots, and the same shirt he had just taken great care to unbutton only minutes earlier, Chloe stroked a hairbrush through the length of her hair.

He shot a quick glance down her front, assuring himself that the studs were now fastened. They were.

Relieved, yet at the same time a little disappointed, he turned back to face Cameron.

"Morning', ma'am." Cameron, too, looked a little discontented. What had he expected?

Chloe stepped up beside Shea and slipped an arm around his waist. "Was there something you wanted?" She beamed Cameron a stout-hearted smile.

Shea felt reasonably certain it was forced. Nobody could recover that quickly, yet Chloe appeared the picture of confidence and poise. "It seems Cameron here was concerned about our eatin' breakfast."

"Really?" Her eyes went wide with a suitable display of amazed appreciation. "How thoughtful."

Hiding a smirk behind a cough, Shea could not help but find her amusing. He looked down at the tops of his bare feet. In no way was this woman going to give Cameron the satisfaction of thinking the man had interrupted his and Chloe's moment together. He had to admire her spunk. Most females would have shrunk into the shadows with embarrassment. He shot her an applauding look. But not his Button, no sirree.

"You may tell your chef that Mr. and Mrs. Taggert will be joining the others for breakfast momentarily."

"Chef? Oh, yeah. Of course, ma'am." Cameron tipped his hat. "My pleasure." He cut Shea a queer, somewhat apologetic frown, then stumbled off toward the cook tent.

Together, Chloe and Shea watched after him until he disappeared with several lumbermen into the white tent at the opposite end of the path running through camp.

"*You* were great," Shea told her with a pride-filled smile. He kissed her temple.

Easing out of his arms, she whirled around and returned inside. "Are we going somewhere today?" A little of her earlier nervousness echoed in the vibration of her voice. Moving to the bed, she slipped off her shoes. Her feet were bare. Apparently, she had snatched them on without thought of stockings.

Thrown for a loop, Shea followed her into the cabin. He closed the door behind him. He knew she had been playacting, but he had not realized she was as ruffled as she now seemed. "That's the surprise I told ya 'bout," he said, trying to sound cheerful. "I'm taking ya to Tahoe City for a stay at the Grand Central Hotel." The latter he said with dramatic flair, hoping to lighten her mood with a little humor. He plopped down on the edge of the bed beside her.

She did not appear to be impressed, neither by his spirit nor his wit. She peered around the room. "Where's Satchel? Isn't he going with us?"

"Nah. O'Dell's goin' to keep him till we git back. Tahoe City ain't exactly the place for a cougar."

"Hmm." Head held at a slight tilt, she held her concentration on a pair of socks she had retrieved from her traveling bag. "Sounds like this *Grand Central* of yours is quite an estimable establishment. I didn't bring anything to wear befitting such a place."

Lounging back on his side, Shea propped himself up on an elbow, then slid a hesitant hand around her hips. "That's no problem. We'll go shoppin'."

She stopped mid-action, her expression turning mildly tolerant. With as much warmth as a freak snowstorm, Chloe leveled her gaze on him. She smiled. "We will?"

He had to fight the shiver that threatened to race up his spine. What had he said? "Well, sure—why not?" He did not like the sudden coolness in her attitude. "I brought some money just for the occasion."

Appearing as if he were about to hand her a stolen bone from a starving dog, she narrowed her eyes, then turned her face away from him.

He suddenly realized why. "Hey," he said, grabbing her arm. She thought the money he had mentioned was stolen. Gently, he pulled her back to look at him. "I *earned* this money. Working here. It's honest cash. You don't have to worry."

She studied him long and hard for a lengthy moment. Then, without further convincing, her stoic features slowly softened. "You wouldn't lie to me, would you, Shea, darling?"

He was not sure he liked the way she said *darling*. If memory served him, she had only used it with his name when she had been trying to impress someone, or when being sarcastic. Which was her intention now? She made him feel as though she could read his mind.

"No," he answered simply, yet it had taken every ounce of strength he could muster. God, he hated lying to her, but it had to be done. In truth, the money he had on him was honest. But he had earned it for his undercover work with the agency, not from the lumber company as he had told her.

She deepened her stare, piercing him with a can-I-really-trust-you look. She must have decided the answer was yes. She smiled. "Good," she finally said, her voice dripping with pure sweetness and unexpected liveliness. Jumping to her feet, she clutched his hands in hers, and tugged. "Then let's go have breakfast. The quicker we get going, the quicker we arrive in Tahoe City for that shopping."

TENDER OUTLAW

Rising to a sitting position, Shea watched Chloe flutter about the room like an energetic butterfly darting from flower to flower. Something was not quite right. Her attitude had shifted too quickly. Why?

Confused, he stood, gathered his shirt and boots, then finished dressing—all the while keeping a well-trained eye on his wife. When Shea had told Cameron that he planned to keep Chloe out of harm's way with shopping in Tahoe City, he had not actually thought she would be so easily persuaded.

True, she had an eye for quality—that was evident in the garments she had brought with her from Boston. But had she become so frivolous that the simple prospect of buying clothes could sway her to his bidding? Disappointment flooded his senses. He observed her more closely.

"Hurry along, Shea, darling," she said when she had finally ceased her unnecessary business long enough to notice him. "As Daddy always says, 'Make hay while the sun shines.' The shops will be all closed by the time we get to Tahoe City." She looked at his half-dressed appearance and rolled her eyes with a huff. Smiling like an impatient mother over her child, she hurried to stand in front of him, then began buttoning his shirt. "Here, let me help you or we'll be here all day."

Shea eyed her skeptically. This was a side of Chloe he had not seen before. Never as a child had she seemed so—passionate—yeah, that was the word. So passionate about shopping—for anything. Briefly, he wondered if her father knew of this trait. Hell, he must. He had been supporting her, had he not?

"Oh, I can't wait to see if they have any new fashions from Europe. Oh, and the hats. How quickly do they get the latest styles out here?" She all but skipped to the bedside, fluffed the pillow, and pulled the blankets straight. "Oh, but you wouldn't know ..."

Shea frowned. Chloe was acting like some high-strung, ravenous monster. He had never seen her so excited about anything.

"Coming?" she asked from the doorway, her traveling bag already in hand. But before Shea could so much as nod, she rushed outside. The woman sure was fired up all of a sudden.

Shea shook his head. What had he started? Reaching in his pocket, he pulled out the clip holding the wad of money he had brought with him. He vaulted a brow, a sorely rankled sigh escaping him. "Sure hope it's enough to keep her busy for a week."

TEN

ABOUT AN HOUR OUTSIDE TAHOE CITY, CHLOE'S MARE pulled up lame.

Shea climbed down from his own mount and inspected the roan for the reason behind her limp. He retrieved his knife from his belt. "She's got a rock wedged inside her shoe," he told Chloe.

"Can you get it out?"

"Yup," he answered, as he scraped away the stone. "But it cut into her hoof. Ya won't be able to ride her."

Chloe sighed heavily. "She'll be all right, though, won't she?" She patted the mare's neck.

"Sure. She'll just have to stay off it till it heals." He replaced his knife and moved to assist Chloe from her saddle. "When we get into town, we'll leave her at the livery. They'll see she's fixed up fine. But yer goin' to have to ride the rest of the way in with me."

Turning back the edges of her leather gloves, Chloe dabbed at her forehead with the back of one wrist, then nodded. She handed him the reins. "How long before we're there?"

Shea retrieved his watch from his vest pocket and checked the time. Four-twenty. After a little over ten hours of riding, Chloe still appeared to be in a hurry to get to Tahoe City, though her earlier display of enthusiasm had diminished a bit.

"Shouldn't take no more than an hour." He looked southward over the treetops edging the lake in the distance. He squinted, the brilliance of the late-afternoon sun blinding his right eye. He could barely make out the *Governor Stanford* steaming across the water toward their destination. "It's only about a couple miles farther."

She exhaled again, but said nothing.

He glanced at her. Not once had she complained about the strenuous ride. Even though they had stopped for a picnic at noon, and several times later to stretch their legs and give the horses a breather, he could see by her worn-out expression that she was exhausted—bone weary, more than likely. "Ya tired?"

"A little." She smiled. "I'm fine, though, really." She pressed her palms to her spine and reared back, a soft groan escaping her lips. A sudden frown knitted her brows and she shielded her eyes with her hand, peering out at the lake. "That's not the same steamer from Glenbrook, is it?"

"Sure is," Shea answered before he thought of the consequences.

"You mean, we rode all the way around the top of this huge lake, when we could've just as easily taken that ferry?" She sounded more than a little perturbed.

Shea had to think fast. They had had a pretty relaxed day together and he did not want to incite trouble now. "I wanted ya to see this beautiful countryside," he stammered. "Ya can't see nothin' but water on that boat."

If the truth be known, he had actually brought her

around on horseback so she would be ready to fall into bed, sound asleep, as soon as they got to the hotel. He had vowed to keep his thoughts trained on his job until after it was finished. And if Sharon and his gang of outlaws were involved as Shea believed, he had to see them put behind bars.

But if Shea had to spend even one more night in the same room with Chloe, he was not certain he could hold back his desire for her. Hell, after the previous evening's torment and the impassioned incident this morning, he was *certain* he could not. Chloe was too much of a distraction. He could only pray that Cameron had carried out the order Shea had given him and sent the telegram.

"How many trips a day does that steamer make across?"

Shea shrugged. "Depends if it's goin' directly across or tourin' around the lake."

"So we could've already been to this Tahoe City by now if we'd taken it?"

Suddenly anxious to be on his way, Shea checked Topaz's cinch. He had been victim to Chloe's anger the night of their wedding and had no desire to repeat such a scene now. He gestured for Chloe to join him. "We better git goin'." He swung up atop his mount, then reached down for her. "Like ya said, those shops won't be open all night."

After they had been riding double for about half an hour or so, Chloe rested her head on his back. "Shea?"

"Hmm?"

"It really has been kind of a nice day today." She slid her hands up from his thighs to encircle his waist, then squeezed. "Thank you for bringing me this way. It really *is* beautiful country."

He looked down to where she held onto him and smiled. It felt good to have her clinging to him. "Yup, it's been real nice." He listened to the sound of her breathing mingling with the clip-clop of the horses' hooves against the hard-packed earth.

While they had spent all those years apart, Shea had imagined, on many an occasion, how wonderful it would be to hold her against him. But nothing in his musings had even come close to the pure heaven he experienced now.

Somewhere in the distant tree boughs, a woodpecker rapped against a pine trunk looking for insects to feed its squawking young. Chirps of mountain blue jays, thrushes, and wrens blended with the songs of the robin and mockingbird in a soothing chorus.

He relaxed and listened. Everything seemed to be so much more alive for him today. He smiled at two chipmunks lost in a game of tag atop a fallen log and wondered why he had never taken such notice of the simpler forms of life at play. Or how the forest shades of muted green could suddenly give way to the stabbing of the afternoon sun's fiery rays of gold and orange.

Chloe sighed softly, wriggling ever so slightly against him.

Gradually, he became aware of the intense heat growing steadily between them. Noting something moving along the outer length of his legs, he glanced down.

Chloe had returned her hands to their former position, and now she smoothed her fingertips back and forth along the outside seams of his pants.

Whether or not she was conscious of her actions, Shea did not know, but *he* most certainly was. Within the easy gait of the horse beneath them, he felt the steady friction of the very female stomach riding flat upon his back, up and down against him. Of the graceful curve of her body clinging to him. The movement stirred him.

He returned his gaze to the path ahead of them. But the sensitive touch of her inner thighs rubbing his legs set off a charge of rhythmic undercurrents flowing through his lower limbs. It grew like a wave traveling upward through the length of his entire body until it finally reached his brain in a thunderbolt of intense excitement. He could not get away from it, nor could he simply turn off his mind to it.

His groin tightened. Instinctively he looked down at her hands.

Her palms were still on his legs, her fingers still toying with the seam of his Levi's.

Damn it. Did she know what she was doing to him? The breeze picked up and he caught the warm, clean scent of her hair, the soft, heated fragrance of her skin. It teased his senses.

Moisture sheened his upper lip. He wiped it away, then switched Topaz's reins, with the lead from the roan, into his other hand for diversion.

The path took a sudden decline and the horses trotted faster against the downward slope.

Chloe's breasts bounced, taunting the muscles in his back. Son of a bitch! This was too much. How much provocation could he be expected to take? He had never felt so much excitement from a woman pressed up tight on the wrong side of his body. Hell, he had never before *had* a woman on the back side of him.

Shea ground his teeth together. He had to fight the demons clawing at his insides. He throbbed with the pure want of her. He wanted to stop the horses, snatch her off, and take her right there on the grass for all of nature to watch, but he knew he could not—would not allow that to happen. God, it was hell being this close to an innocent woman—glorious hell!

Little by little, the distant drone of civilization penetrated the forest noises, coaxing his mind back to more acceptable thoughts. Thank God, he groaned inwardly, when the main stem of the city finally came into view. Another minute and he would have undeniably broken his own vow of self-control with Chloe.

Never before had Chloe been so delighted to enter a town as she was at that moment. Without thought, while riding behind Shea, she had been tracing the seams in his pants with her fingers. She had not even realized she was doing it until a few minutes ago.

She loved the feel of his leg muscles flexing against her palms beneath the fabric of his jeans. It had seemed so comfortable and natural to be close to him that until now she had not even considered how unladylike her actions might have appeared. She felt as if God had put her and Shea on this earth just to be together. Like that morning ... oh, how wonderful they had felt together.

She had been so excited, so thrilled, and so filled with passion by his kisses, and by the way he had kissed and fondled her. Even if she had wanted to, she could not have resisted his advances. It was as if he had ignited some sweet, soul-scorching fire that, until now, had been sleeping within her, waiting for his touch—and his alone.

She had not wanted it to end. And when it had, and so abruptly, it had left her empty and unfulfilled. Embarrassed as she had been, she was even angrier than Shea that Mr. Cameron had intruded on them. Their lovemaking—when it happened—promised to be beautiful.

"What'd ya think?" Shea asked, pulling her from her musings.

Leaning around him, she looked down the wide thoroughfare cutting through the center of Tahoe City. Her breath caught. She had not seen such a grand setting since she had left the East. Maybe these streets were not paved, or lighted with ornate gaslamps like Boston, but the town appeared quite distinguished just the same.

Buildings of every size, some as tall as three stories, lined the lane. Cardwell's Bowling Alley and Billiard Rooms, the Grand Central Meat Market, an interesting place that looked like a mercantile marked J. A. TODMAN'S. She would have to take a peek in there later.

"Oh my good Lord," she murmured, clutching the open throat of her shirt. She could not believe the large green area of grass near what was posted as being *Commons*. "Croquet grounds, Shea? And swimming baths? You didn't tell me this place had anything so—so—"

"Civilized?" he interrupted.

Her mouth hanging agape in a quite unladylike

manner, she nodded, though the words *refined* and *splendid* were what she would have chosen if she had not been too stupefied to speak. She swung her head from side to side, looking everywhere and at everything. Still, she could not seem to take in all of the indescribable pleasures offered by what until now she had only envisioned as a crude little urban sprawl—a dusty speck in the wilds of the West.

Several saloons loomed up, flaunting themselves quite flamboyantly between the other more respectable businesses throughout the town—the Tahoe House, Kincaid's, and another that appeared to have been built out over the water called the Custom House, to name a few. But the most impressive, by far, was a bar posted as "BIG MOSE" STAPLES'S BIG BONANZA. Phew! What a mouthful.

Chloe giggled at her own wit. Why else would a body go into such an establishment but to find themselves a *mouthful* of spirits and to get primed to the sticking point?

Throughout the town, Tahoe City's citizens met her with general jollification and sparkles of laughter in their eyes. She had never before encountered so many smiling, seemingly carefree and happy people.

Shea reined to a stop in front of a fine enterprising-looking building, so opulent that no sign was needed to tell Chloe that *this* was the Grand Central Hotel he had told her about earlier. She lifted her gaze to the three-and-a-half story edifice. Never would she have expected anything so splendid.

Elaborate balconies ringed the white L-shaped hostelry. And off to the side of the porticoed entranceway, white fir trees had been planted, giving the hotel a deft touch of sweet-scented High Sierra atmosphere, as she had overheard another patron of the hotel describe it.

Even before they had retrieved their bags from the horses, two Oriental men hurried up to them and gathered the reins. Shea explained about Chloe's mare, then gave the men instructions to take the animals to the livery for a good feeding.

"Shall we, Mrs. Taggert?" He offered her his arm.

Automatically, Chloe reached up to straighten her tousled hair, then brush at the dust on her clothing. She shook her head. "Oh, Shea. I can't go in there looking like this."

"Oh, yes, ya can." He clutched her elbow before she could muster resistance, then entered through the huge glass doors, pulling her along with him. "Dirty or clean, my wife's every bit as good as anyone else in here."

No finer quality could be found anywhere, Chloe decided as they crossed the expensive Brussels carpet covering the floor.

Shea released her and walked up to the front desk.

"Why, Mr. Taggert. We haven't had the pleasure of accommodating you since your arrival in the Tahoe area," the clerk said in an almost bleating voice. "Your reservation wire said you've married."

"Yup." Shea grinned back at Chloe and winked.

She smiled at the pleasure in his expression.

"Wonderful." Dressed in a gray pinstripe suit, the man peered up at her over the tops of his wire-rimmed glasses. He did not seem to be impressed with what he saw. "How long will you be . . ."

Chloe winced. She did not like the way he had snaked his gaze over her. Moving away from the desk, she explored the lobby, though not with her usual self-confidence. Dressed as she was, the moment called for subtlety. She had no wish to arouse attention to herself, although it seemed that few had even noticed her.

In truth, there were a number of people arriving outfitted no differently than she. Briefly, she wondered how many times *she* had ignored others under such circumstances, due to their outward impressions.

Peeking into the huge parlor, she discovered ladies and gentlemen resplendent in their evening wear milling around a magnificent cherrywood piano. She shot another glance down the front of the overly large man's shirt, soiled jeans, and filthy boots she wore, then cringed. The matrons of Miss Hauser's Young Ladies' School of Social Prominence would most certainly have swooned at her distressing appearance.

Why had she not brought at least one dress with her on this trip? *Because you're a snob, and you didn't think the West had anything so spectacular.* Chloe blanched at the truth of her own conscience. She *was* a snob. *Serves me right for being so arrogant and condescending.*

"Chloe?" Shea called out as he approached.

Startled, she spun around to face him.

"You ready?"

She nodded.

He slipped an arm around her waist, then ushered her toward a wide staircase and a porter waiting with their things. Shea remained silent, keeping a prominent smile on his face while the servant inserted the key and opened the door to their room.

Upon entering, Chloe marveled at the luxurious

black walnut furniture. She hurried toward a huge bouquet of wild cow parsnip and yellow monkey flowers. "Oh, look, Shea." She leaned down and sniffed their sweet fragrance. "There's even some of those beautiful purple camas, like the ones in the woods." She had seen some rich accommodations in the more elite homes of Boston, but none were any more regal than the bounty spread within this room. She spun around. "Everything's so lovely."

"Thank you, ma'am. We're glad you like it." Dressed in a smart red jacket and black trousers with gold braid, the diminutive servant deposited their saddlebags and Chloe's satchel onto the huge four-poster with all the skill of a well-trained steward. "Now, if there's nothing else—"

Shea shook his head, acknowledged the porter's departure with a cordial thank you, then flipped the man a gold half-eagle.

"That was rather indulgent, don't you think?" she asked once they were alone.

Shea shrugged. "It's only money." He moved to the bed, then lounged back, his hands behind his head. "Isn't that what it's for?" he asked, crossing his ankles, yet keeping his boots over the edge.

Halting mid-stride across the room, she stared at him. Every time she thought she had money as the explanation for his stealing scratched off the list, he would make another confusing statement like that one.

"You look tired."

She rubbed the back of her neck and nodded. "I feel tired."

"Tell ya what. I've ordered up a bath. Why don't ye

take a soak, and I'll see if I can't scare up somethin' more—uh—suitable for us to wear out to supper."

"Oh, Shea, can't we just stay in tonight?"

"Not a chance, Button." He grinned, his gaze flitting suggestively up her form. "I wanna show off my beautiful new wife."

A knock sounded at the door.

Shea jumped to his feet. "That'll be the hot water I had asked for, now."

He crossed the room and pulled the ornate bronze doorknob.

"Mr. Taggert, there was a slight oversight at the front desk." It was the porter who had brought up their bags. "It seems the clerk forgot to give you a message that came earlier this afternoon."

"What is it, Shea?" Chloe asked, though she suspected she already knew.

After closing the door, Shea tore open the envelope he had received. He frowned as he read.

Chloe waited expectantly, praying all the while that he would not go through with the arrangements she had overheard him planning with Mr. Cameron and Mr. O'Dell.

"Trouble." Shea hurried to his saddlebags. He appeared properly concerned.

"Where?" Dread coursed through her. She knew what he was doing.

"Back at the Lightning Tree." He tossed the telegram onto the bed, then picked up his bags, checked inside, then flipped them over one of his shoulders. He turned back to face her. "There's been some unexplained explosions and a couple more men were hurt."

"Oh, no."

Shea came to stand in front of her. He clutched her upper arms. "I've got to go back. O'Dell needs me." He glanced in the direction of the window, then back at her. "If I hurry, I can catch the *Governor Stanford* and get to Glenbrook by midnight."

"Of course." she nodded, frowning suitably. She studied his features, looking for any small clue that would surely prove this to be the lie she knew it to be. Nothing. So, he was a proficient liar as well as a thief.

He reached into his pants pocket and pulled out a clip of money folded in half. After removing two bills, he took her hand and set the rest in her palm. "You stay here."

"But I—"

"No buts," he said, placing a finger to her lips. "I don't know how long all this'll take, but I'll try not to be gone long."

"Let me come with you." She knew he would say no, but she felt it was only right that she should play out her role in this scheme of his.

He shook his head. "I don't know what's goin' on at the camp. It could be dangerous. And I'm not about to let anythin' happen to my wife."

"But maybe I could help—"

"No buts." He cocked his head to one side. "Remember?"

She masked her indignation with a sullen look. Of course not, Shea, darling. *No buts.* "So you want me to just stay here? Without you?"

"I think that's best. I'll send word for Dudee to come and stay with you."

"But I don't know anyone," she whined in a sulky tone. "What'll I do till she gets here?"

He squeezed the hand holding the money. "Go shoppin'. Find somethin' pretty to wear for when I get back, okay?"

With a pouty scowl, she looked away.

"Okay?" He leaned into her view.

"You'll hurry back?"

"Fast as I can," he said, rubbing her arms. He raised his brows, obviously waiting for the appropriate reply.

She sighed, a heavy note of resignation in the sound. "All right, Shea. If that's what you want me to do."

Grinning with more than adequate little-boy-charm, he kissed her nose. "That's my Button."

His overly satisfied tone caused her instant irritation. He seemed quite pleased with the way he had thwarted her argument. Oh, how she would make him pay for treating her like such a child and discarding her so readily so that he could get back to his thievery.

Why, if she was not so positive that he *did* love her, she would— She blinked. What? Leave him? No. She could never do that. She loved him too much. No, she would just have to be happy with seeing these robberies put to an end. Then she would make him so happy with his life he would never want anything but her.

Once Shea had left the room, Chloe crossed to the window.

He waved to her from the street.

Forcing a smile, she blew him a kiss. "We'll just see about those *buts*, Shea Taggert," she said scornfully, though her lips still curved in a sweet crescent. She looked at the money she still grasped in her hand, then watched as he made his way across the street and down the boardwalk where the steamer was docked. "If you can't stop yourself from performing these crimes, I have no other choice but to do it for you."

A moment later, the *Governor Stanford*'s whistle blew. People crowded on deck for the return trip across the big lake to Glenbrook.

Wheeling around, Chloe made for the door. She would have to hurry if she was going to sneak on board the boat before it left, and without Shea seeing her. She was not quite certain, yet, just how she was going to accomplish it, but she had to confront Shea—head-on—face-to-face, and put an end to these robberies, once and for all.

ELEVEN

CHLOE HAD NO DIFFICULTY BOARDING THE *GOVERNOR Stanford* without Shea spotting her. She purchased her ticket at the dock office, then slipped on with a large group of last-minute travelers bound for Glenbrook. That part had been easy enough. But now that she was on the vessel, she would have to stay out of sight. *This* might not be such an easy feat.

Filled to its capacity, the boat could hold well over a hundred people, but there were only about half that many milling around the large open deck this night. She could only stick to the shadows and pray that the cover of darkness would be enough to keep her presence concealed for the next hours.

Mindful to watch for any familiar faces, she sought out Shea. She had to know where he was in order to keep her proximity to him stretched to the limit. It seemed the smartest thing to do, considering the dilemma she had thrust upon herself. After about fifteen minutes of careful searching, she found him standing in the stern house chatting with the captain.

She decided that a stack of cargo crates a few yards away from the pilot would be the best place to set up her vigil. Crouching down, she huddled close to the planked boxes, shielding herself from the rush of cool air coming off the water.

"Mrs. Taggert?" A man's commanding voice sounded behind her.

Her heart bolted. Wheeling around, she jumped to her feet, certain Shea had somehow found her out. Eyes wide, she peered at the unfamiliar silhouette looming before her. Within the shadow of the masculine form, she caught sight of a glowing ember. "Do I know you?"

"Why no, ma'am, not exactly." The advancing figure moved into the dim but silvery light. The white-haired man leaned on the cane he was carrying, took a long draw on his thick cigar, then exhaled a plume of smoke. "I've not as yet had the pleasure of an introduction, but I attended your wedding."

Chloe swallowed. She cut a nervous glance over her shoulder, checking on Shea.

He was still with the captain.

"Really?" She smiled obligingly, though she did not feel it.

"Yes. As I recall, neither did anyone else that particular evening."

"Oh, well, I—uh—didn't feel very well."

"So I understand," he said in a smooth, affluent tone. He flicked off the ashes from the end of the burning tobacco. "Damn poor timing for such female trouble as monthlies."

Chloe blanched. Her face heated red. What was this man talking about? And how uncouth and presumptuous for a stranger to even mention such a thing.

Without encouragement, the man took her hand, then swept off his hat and bowed his head. "I *do* apologize, Mrs. Taggert. How rude of me to speak of such delicate matters when you have no idea of who or what I am."

Shocked at his forward behavior, Chloe looked down at where he touched her. His fingers felt warm against her cold skin. "I assure you, sir, I have no idea what it is you're talking about. Nor do I wish to." She pulled her grasp from his. "Now if you'll excuse me, I must locate my husband."

"You know very well where he is, Mrs. Taggert." The man gestured toward the stern house with a dip of his head. "You've been covertly watching him since we first boarded."

Instant fear gripped Chloe by the throat. She took a step backward and bumped into the crates. Instinctively, she grabbed for them, keeping them balanced. Who was this man? And how had he known she was spying on— Her lungs constricted. She gasped. He could only know this if *he* had been watching *her*. "Who *are* you?" she finally asked. "And what do you want with me?"

"Again, forgive me for not coming right out with the introduction. I'm Donovan Jenkins, M.D., presently from Glenbrook." He dipped his head again and smiled. "Soon to be Congressman Jenkins, if all goes well at the next election."

Chloe blinked. "Doctor? You're a doctor?"

"Yes, ma'am. That's how I knew about your—uh—problem the night of the wedding. Your aunt confided in me." He replaced his hat, then gestured toward the railing. "I was concerned for your well-being. I offered to look in on you, but your husband assured me it wasn't necessary."

So *that* was the excuse Shea and Aunt Dudee had given. Remaining in the shadows, she shuddered at the thought. How embarrassing. "What a lovely way to be introduced into your quaint little community."

"Please," he said, motioning again toward the side of the boat.

"No ... thank you, Doctor, but I'd rather not." Shivering from the damp chill coming off the lake, she shot another look toward the stern house.

"Ah, yes, I see." He moved back to his former position. He glanced around. "How about inside, where it's a bit warmer, then?"

Clutching her upper arms over her chest, she peered back at the lantern-lit dining room. It looked inviting, but she could not risk the chance that Shea would come down and see her. She shook her head. "I rather like the briskness of the evening," she lied.

"Mmm-hmm." He paused, then pointed to a corner with his cane. "There's an empty bench over there. Would that be more acceptable? I really would like to talk to you."

Chloe swung her gaze from the seat to Shea and back again. From that vantage point, she would still be able to keep a watchful eye on her husband. She nodded at the doctor, then without waiting headed for the long seat and sat down.

The man quickly joined her, filling the space beside her. "So, why aren't you with Shea?" Doctor Jenkins asked, his tone personable. "Aren't you two supposed to be on your honeymoon?"

Chloe sighed. "We're supposed to be."

"But?"

She peered up at the older gentleman, noting the expensive design of his cutaway suit. She had not seen anything so extravagant since she had left Boston. Doctors must certainly be paid well out here.

"My dear, is there something wrong?" he interrupted her perusal. "You seem to be unhappily preoccupied. Are you and Shea having trouble already? Is that why you're out here?"

Chloe stared at the man. She stiffened. She did not care how genuine he appeared. He was intruding into her personal business and she did not even know him. "It seems I've erred in accepting your company, sir. If you'll—"

"I am sorry for prying, my dear, but I do so admire Shea. I have since his first arrival in Glenbrook. He's always appeared to be a very honest and forthright young man. Please talk to me. Let me be your friend, too. Let me help."

Chloe rubbed the cold from her fingers. She did not know what to say to such an appeal.

"If it's what I think it is," he continued, his gaze wandering from her to the pilot room then back again, "if you believe him to be seeing another woman—let me assure you I've know Shea for almost a year and I've never seen him with anyone else. You're all he's ever spoken about." He shook his head. "No, my dear, it's simply not the case."

Chloe had to swallow to keep from chuckling. Another woman? If that were only the problem . . . she might be better equipped to see that put to an end. She might even be able to understand the reason behind it. "No," she said with a gracious smile. "It's not that."

He studied her for a brief moment. "I see," he said, his voice filling with disappointment. He stood. "Then if you'll forgive my intrusiveness, I'll—"

"No—please, Doctor." On impulse, she reached out

and caught his hand, then just as quickly released it. "I didn't mean to offend—" She hesitated.

He retook his seat.

Chloe looked back at her husband's dark figure. She took a deep breath. If only she could trust someone. If only she could tell the good doctor here what was truly happening—maybe he could help her figure a way out of this for Shea. The thought prompted a question. Could she trust him?

"I *am* a physician. People do tend to confide in their doctors from time to time with things of a more ... personal nature." He waited, but when she did not respond, he moved to leave again. "Well, if you change your mind, I'll be here for you."

Chloe watched him disappear around the outer corner of the dining room. She glanced at the reflection of the moon rippling across the water. She had to talk to someone. Aunt Dudee would certainly never understand. She did not know anyone else in town. The doctor had said he and Shea had been friends for nearly a year. And he *did* seem sincere with regard to Shea's happiness and well-being.

Chloe chewed on the inside of her cheek. Should she? Standing, she moved across the deck and peeked around the edge of the structure.

At a leisurely pace, the older man strolled toward the rear of the steamer, a thin wisp of smoke trailing from the thick cheroot clamped between his teeth.

She cut Shea another glance. She loved him more than words could ever convey. She had already decided she had to help him. But how to go about it? She did not know the countryside. Once they left Glenbrook, if he veered from her sight she would never be able to follow. She needed someone to guide her. She looked back at the doctor. She really had no choice.

The decision made, she crept out from the cover of the shadows. "Doctor Jenkins?" she called softly. "Could you wait a minute?"

Stopping mid-ship, he turned toward her and smiled.

Upon her approach, she hesitated again, doubt pricking her conscience. "Do you know what you're doing, Chloe?" she asked softly. Maybe she should not do this. *No.* She gave herself a mental shake. *I have to.* Swallowing, she began anew. "There *is* something—something important that I'd like to talk to you about."'

When Chloe had finished explaining to the doctor the unfortunate and sordid details behind her dilemma, she peered up at him through teary eyes.

"Shea's a good man, my dear," he said, brushing away the moisture from her cheeks. "I'm sure he's just fallen in with a sorry lot of bad characters and can't figure a safe way out, that's all."

"So you'll help us?" she asked, her voice trembling.

"Of course I will. As I told you, Shea's my friend. I admire him deeply. As a matter of fact—" He rubbed his smoothly shaven chin. "I know just the person to help us."

"Oh, no!" She shook her head. "We mustn't tell anyone else. It's too dangerous for Shea."

"He's quite trustworthy, my dear," he assured her, the pale cast of his eyes shimmering with what she could only hope was honesty.

"But what if this person doesn't share your respect for my husband? What if, after you tell him, he doesn't want to help? What if he reports Shea's actions to the law?"

"He won't, I promise you that." He leaned closer, his tone deepening. He gathered her hands together in his, then patted the back of the top one. "Trust me, Chloe, my dear." He shrugged, then grinned playfully, apparently trying to coax her into relaxing. "I'm a doctor, and a soon-to-be congressman, for pity's sake. If you can't trust someone like me, then I ask you, who can you trust?"

More than an hour after Chloe had finished explaining the situation to Doctor Jenkins, the steamer docked in Glenbrook. Chloe waited until all but the crew had departed from the decks, then she, too, took her leave.

It had all seemed so simple the way Doctor Jenkins had explained how they should proceed with helping Shea put an end to these inexplicable crimes of his. She would secretly go back to the house, change into some warmer clothing, then meet the older gentleman at sunrise.

He would in turn speak to his influential friend and, together, the three of them would confront Shea with the knowledge of his contemptible deeds. Then, if all went well, they would convince him of the error of his ways and see that he delivered himself up to the law.

In all probability, Shea would have to spend some time in jail. But the good doctor had assured her that if her husband did so, it would most likely be a short sentence. It was Shea's first offense. More than likely the judge would show leniency. Especially if Shea gave evidence against the other men involved—most importantly, the ringleader of the gang.

TENDER OUTLAW

Chloe had to remain outside of the house until Shea had left town. She did not want to run the risk of having him return home and catch her. Once she felt confident that he was gone, she quietly entered.

She was so cold from her boat trip across the lake, she halted in front of the kitchen stove, warming herself a few minutes before she would tiptoe up to her room. And to think she had complained of the heat when she had first arrived. Rubbing her hands together above the iron oven, she tightened her jaws to keep her teeth from chattering. How could anyplace so hot in the daytime be so cold at night?

Quickly, quietly, she ascended the stairs. In a fleeting thought, she remembered her wedding night and Satchel. She sent a tiny prayer heavenward, thanking the Almighty for Shea having left the cougar at the logging camp. Still, he would have been a fabulous source of protection.

Don't be silly, she silently berated herself as she turned the knob to her bedroom door and entered. The doctor would be with her.

A floorboard creaked beneath her weight. She froze, waiting, listening. Nothing stirred.

A sigh of relief slipped out from between her lips. A sudden notion overwhelmed her. She had an unmistakable niggling feeling that something was just not right about all of this. What did she really know about the doctor? She only had his word that he and Shea were friends or, for that matter, even acquainted.

After tossing off her dampened, soiled shirt, she replaced the garment with a fresh one, her favorite sloppy blouse—a light turquoise cotton. She pondered the thought more thoroughly. Still, the doctor *had* been invited to the wedding. She had not remembered seeing him herself, but he had known about her incident with Satchel and about her taking to her bedroom after the ceremony.

On the other hand, he could have simply heard about it from someone else.

She slipped off her pants, pulled out a clean pair of faded jeans from her bag, and stepped into them. Gathering the hand-tooled leather belt her father had sent her last Christmas, she threaded it through the loops on her pants.

Maybe she *should* confide in Aunt Dudee. She would be able to tell Chloe whether or not Donovan Jenkins was a friend of Shea's. She tugged on a pair of thick wool socks, straightening the red seam across her toes. *No, Chloe. You'll only upset Aunt Dudee. Trust your own judgment.* "That's the trouble," she mumbled to herself as she pulled on her boots. "I don't know *who* to trust anymore—not even myself."

She crossed the room to the front window, pulled aside the lace curtains, and peered out. Except for the light tinkling of chimes on some unseen porch and the ruffling of ribbons decorating the streets for the impending Fourth of July celebration and debate, nothing stirred but the breeze. The town remained quiet.

The clock downstairs chimed twice. She still had about three hours until she was supposed to meet the doctor. She looked at the bed. It beckoned to her. She was too tired to think anymore. If she could just close her eyes for a while, she would be better able to reason out the situation.

Taking care to be as silent as possible, she moved back to the huge mattress and lay down across it. She seized a pillow, plumped it, then popped it under her head. Briefly, she thought about removing her shoes. No, she could not afford to get too comfortable. She could only allot herself a couple of hours of rest. That was all she needed. She yawned, her eyes drooping heavily. Just a couple of hours ...

Somewhere in her fatigued mind, Chloe was roused by the husky sound of a man's voice.

"The old girl's sawin' logs in the next room."

Was she dreaming? Chloe fluttered her drowsy eyes open.

"Hey. She's wakin' up."

"Grab her—quick—before she starts screamin'."

Screaming? Far-reaching fear charged through Chloe's body. This was not a dream! Someone was in her room. Sleep still fogging her brain, she sat upright.

The bed pitched downward. An arm snaked around her shoulders.

Instinct bolted her into action. Her heart pounded. She tried to yell.

A hand clamped over her mouth. The stench of sweaty skin, grime, and unwashed maleness assailed her nostrils.

She fought against the grip.

"Damn it! Hold her."

Chloe struck out. Flesh caught in her nails.

"'Son of a bitch!" A man's beer-soured breath hit her ear. "Get her hands tied."

"Hold her still, I said."

"No! No!" Chloe shrieked into the brawny palm. She thrashed from side to side. What was happening? Who were these men?

"Who's there?" Dudee's voice rose above the commotion.

The man pinning Chloe down pulled her tighter against him. "Make another sound and the old lady's dead," he threatened in a whisper.

Someone got off the bed and the mattress eased up a little.

Chloe froze. Terror unlike any she had ever felt held her immobile. *No—no*, her mind screamed. *Don't come in here, Aunt Dudee.*

But it was too late. The bedroom door squeaked open. Lantern light pressed into the darkness.

A thud. A groan.

The flame sputtered. Glass shattered against the floor.

The oil ignited, and in its wake, Chloe saw her aunt's slumped form lying in the doorway.

"Damn it, boy. Get a blanket and put out that fire. Ya want the whole town swarmin' around us?"

Chloe shot a glance at the man hovering over her aunt. It was not a man, but a youth. Her eyes flew wide. One of the porters from the stage depot!

"Look there!" He pointed at her. "She's seen me."

"Damn it to hell!" The man holding Chloe spun her around to face him. "We shoulda done this to begin with." He raised his fist.

Chloe screamed. Pain sliced through her jaw. All went black.

Shea took in the band of men huddled around the fire inside the chasm in Shakespeare Rock. Cameron was with them. "Who's he?" Shea asked, sauntering inside the cave.

"This new gun we took in," One-Eyed John, a Paiute renegade from Truckee Meadows, announced. John had always considered himself the leader of the gang. And if it were not for the strong evidence pointing to Bill Sharon being the mastermind behind the robberies, Shea might well have believed it to be true.

One-Eyed John was well-known for his ruthlessness. He and Shea had come to blows on more than one occasion since Shea had been involved with this mission. If the rest of the members had not broken up the fights when they had, Shea had often wondered who would have been the victor. Though John stood taller than Shea, both seemed equal in strength, as well as will and temper.

Shea strode over to the fire, removed his gloves, and warmed his hands. He glanced around, making a mental note of the faces he saw. "Where's Hank and Jimmy Lee?"

"They come," John told him. "They busy with more things—important things. You no worry about them."

A couple of the others snorted a chuckle.

Shea shot a questioning look Cameron's way.

Over a tin cup of coffee, the younger man pulled a face as if to say, *How the hell should I know what he means?*

The Indian jabbed a finger at Shea. "You make blasting water ready for stage. We leave early."

Shea bristled at the renegade's sharp command. It was going to give him great pleasure to see the hulking man brought down to a mewling beggar when this was all over. But not before Shea settled a long-awaited score with the Indian.

Just before dawn, Shea stepped outside the cave for a smoke.

Cameron joined him after a few minutes. "Got another'n?"

After taking one last drag off the thick roll of tobacco, Shea handed it to the younger man. He shook his head. "This one was given to me. You finish it."

"Ya sure?"

Shea nodded. He glanced back at the firelit cave, then moved off a distance. "You sure got in with the boys quick."

"Hey," Cameron said with a grin. He followed Shea. "All ya got to do is drop a few choice words about needin' money and not carin' how ya git it." He sucked on the cigar, then blew out a puff of smoke. He chuckled.

"Better watch yerself, Cameron." Shea turned toward the lake, his gaze gliding over the glassy water. "Ya start enjoyin' this too much and you could get in over yer head."

"Enjoy it? Hell, Taggert, I love it." Cameron grinned, his teeth flashing in the growing morning light. "I ain't never felt so alive in all my life."

"This yer first assignment?" Shea asked.

"Yeah. Finished my training two months ago."

Shea turned his attention to Cameron.

The overconfident man made a familiar picture as he leaned against the cliff face.

It had not been more than three years ago, that he, himself, had probably appeared to be that same type of cocky, adventure-seeking man to his older brother Lance.

"They told me I'd have to work at least a couple times with somebody else before they'd turn me out on my own with an assignment." Cigar clenched tightly between his teeth, he crossed his arms over his chest. "Hell, that might be necessary for some but—"

"Relax, Cameron," Shea ordered a little too sternly.

The younger man tensed, his expression turning defiant.

Shea took a cleansing breath. Try as he might not to, he found himself liking Cameron. The younger man reminded him too much of himself. "Let's just get through this mess before we get too excited. Ya keep yer edge or ya might find yerself dead." Training an ear out for any stray listeners, he shifted his weight, settling his foot atop a crag in the rocks. "And, friend, there ain't no excitement in dyin'."

"Yeah, well, you relax if ya need to." Cameron tossed the cigar down near Shea. "Me, I keep my edge better with a little well-honed frenzy worked up in my blood." He turned to leave, but stopped short before moving back into the cave with the others. "Ya know, if ya ain't high-strung enough to handle the excitement, maybe ya oughta think about gettin' out. After all, ya got that purty little wife o' yers to take care of now."

Shea watched the man return to the fire. He held his jaw tight, his body rigid. The whole time he had been growing up, *this* was the life he had always wanted to lead. But now . . . he was not so sure anymore.

Cameron was right. Now there was Chloe to consider. How could he continue this line of work and never place her life in jeopardy? His gaze veered toward Tahoe City. He could not—not if they were to live together. Damn. This was more complicated than he had ever imagined it could be.

"Taggert," One-Eyed John called out, "get over here. We go now."

Keeping his gaze riveted on the tiny buildings becoming more visible in the distance, Shea gritted his teeth, and nodded. He breathed in a long, deep breath. At least Chloe was safe *this* time. He had seen to that. But what about the next assignment, and the one after that?

He exhaled with an audible sigh. Once this was over, he had some hard decisions to make. Hesitating another moment, he watched the slow, stretching fingers of sunlight reach toward the town of Tahoe City.

The crispness of the air reminded him of the previous morning, and Chloe's softness beside him. He envisioned her large blue eyes, and her upturned little nose sprinkled with freckles. He would give up everything to enjoy the next lifetime of mornings like that with her.

Hard decisions? Maybe. But finding a way to spend the rest of his life with her was worth every one he knew he was eventually going to have to make.

TWELVE

CHLOE OPENED HER EYES WITH A START. SOMETHING DUG into her stomach. An up-and-down motion flooded her with nausea. The heavy scent of sweaty animal flesh penetrated her nostrils. She stared down at the sage- and thistle-covered ground passing below her. Where was she? She tried to push herself upright for a look, but her hands and feet were tied beneath the girth of a horse.

Shocked, she glanced around, but she could only see the legs of a big bay. She looked up. A man's broad back pressed close against her side. Panic filled her being. Who was he? What did he want with her? And what on earth was she doing trussed up like so much meat on a pack animal? She struggled against her bonds, but to no avail.

"Hank, she's wakin' up," a youthful voice announced.

Chloe raised her head and peered behind her. Vaguely familiar, a boy came into focus. She blinked, sudden realization gripping her senses. Now she remembered. She had been attacked in her room. Oh Lord! Her eyes went wide with fear. Aunt Dudee. What had happened to her?

She deepened her study of the young man. It was the boy from the stage. Kicking and squirming, she yanked against the ropes. "What did you do to my aunt?" she railed, tears threatening to betray her forced show of courage.

"Quit wigglin' back there!" the man riding with her commanded in a harsh voice.

"Let me go!" she screamed.

The horse came to an immediate halt.

"Stop that!" He smacked her bottom.

She yelled, though the blow had not hurt, only shocked her. "Don't you touch me!" she spat. "Where's my Aunt Dudee? What did you do to her?"

The man swung his leg over the horse's head, then jumped to the ground. He jerked her head up by the hair to face him. "You should be askin' what we're gonna be doin' ta *you*."

She inhaled sharply. It was the same porter that had delivered her trunk to the house when she had first arrived in Glenbrook.

"Look, now." He poked a finger in her face. "I don't wanna have ta hurt ya, but if ya don't stop, I'm gonna—"

"Sharon didn't say nothin' 'bout hurtin' her, Hank."

"Shut up, Jimmy Lee." The grizzly faced man shot the youth a piercing stare, then glowered back at Chloe.

An uncontrollable shiver bolted through her entire length. Her stomach rolled. "Please," she whimpered, ashamed that her fear had gotten the best of her. "I'm going to be sick."

"Let 'er up, Hank. She's a city woman. She ain't used to bein' handled rough."

"I don't give a shit what she is." Narrowing his eyes, he shifted the huge wad he had in his mouth from one cheek to the other. He seemed to be contemplating his next move.

"Please?" Chloe asked again. She had to sit up. "I can't ride like this any longer. I'm going to be—" Another wave of nausea rolled up from her stomach. She blanched. She swallowed it back, her throat burning against the effort.

"Son of a bitch!" The one called Hank appeared disgusted.

"Look at her. She really *is* sick." The boy sounded worried.

"I kin see that."

Chloe squeezed her eyes tight against another onslaught of bile threatening her system.

"Hey, girl." The older man smacked her face with light pats.

Startled, she peered up at him.

"You all right?"

"Just let me down, please." If she could only get her feet on the ground and stand up straight, Chloe felt certain the sickness would pass.

He hesitated. "I dunno—"

"Aw, cut 'er loose, Hank. Ya can see she ain't fakin' it. Leave 'er hands tied. I'll watch 'er." The younger man swung down from his saddle. "We're already at the cliff anyway. What'll it hurt to give her a breather first?"

"Yeah, yer right. Prob'ly ain't gonna matter none whether she's sick or not, though," Hank said as he pulled out a knife from his pocket, then severed her bonds from around the animal. He grabbed Chloe unceremoniously under her arms, then jerked her off the horse. "Like Sharon said, she'll prob'ly fall by herself anyway—"

Fall? Chloe shot them a startled look of inquiry. What did he mean by that?

"Hank!" Jimmy Lee cut in. He gestured off to the side with a nod.

Chloe leaned against the bay. Dizziness buzzed through her head. She grabbed her stomach, waiting for the rush of blood to ease from her brain, and back into her limbs. The somersaulting slowly began to subside.

"She don't need to hear all this stuff 'bout Sharon and what we gotta do," the boy murmured to his companion. "It'll jist scare her, and make her harder to handle's all."

"What the hell's wrong with ya, Jimmy Lee?" The older man chuckled gruffly. He did not make any effort to lower his voice. "Ya goin' soft or somethin'? I thought ya liked danger and excitement."

Oh God, they meant to kill her. But why? Except for their brief confrontation over her luggage, she did not know either of them. Surely that incident had not angered them enough to cause them to want to kill her.

They had mentioned someone named Sharon. She paused on the thought. Who was that? Were they working for a woman? She did not know anyone named— No. Not a woman—a man. The man who had introduced himself at the hotel restaurant a couple of days before. He had said *his* name was Sharon. She glanced at the men, hoping that looking at them would trigger a memory. Wayne? Wilton? No, none of those sounded right.

"I don't give a damn who Bill Sharon thinks he—" The youth cut her a sidelong glance.

That was it! William—Bill Sharon—that's what the

man at the Glen Brook House had called himself. She strained to hear anything more from the two men.

The young blonde turned his back to her, continuing his argument in a more subdued tone.

She was glad she had trusted her initial instincts that day and gotten away from the pompous man. But why did this Bill Sharon want to have her killed? He had even told her that he was a friend of Shea's. Was this how he treated a friend's wife? It appeared her suspicions were correct. Bill Sharon was definitely no friend of Shea's.

Good Lord in Heaven. Did everyone in Glenbrook lie? No one was proving to be who, or what, they professed. She swallowed back the awful taste in her mouth. But if that were true— Her eyes flew wide. *Oh, Chloe, you little fool!*

The doctor—what about Doctor Jenkins? He had said he was a friend of Shea's, also. Did that mean that he, too, was Shea's enemy? Oh God, no! You told him everything. About the stage holdup when you saw Shea, his and Cameron's plan for the next robbery, everything!

Her jaw throbbed where Hank had hit her. She rubbed her cheek. What if the doctor and this Bill Sharon knew each other? Chances were, they did. Maybe the doctor had something to do with her abduction. But why? It was all so confusing.

And if, indeed, no one was who they appeared to be, then what of Shea? Could it be that he, too, was the opposite of what she believed him to be? Maybe he was not a criminal? Could he actually be some kind of lawman?

Her mind flitted back through the many letters she had received from Shea. Had he not written her a few years earlier about Lance having been a special agent of some kind? She could not have been more stunned by the realization of this new conclusion than if someone had slapped her.

That was it—it had to be. She should have known Shea could never have been swayed to become a true outlaw, no matter what the reason. How could she have thought such a thing? Lost within the realm of her own deliberations, she did not hear the men's approach.

"Woman, ya ain't doin' nothin' stupid like tryin' ta figure a way ta escape, are ya?"

The older man's rough voice startled her. She stared at him a moment before his question penetrated her brain. She shook her head. A truthful answer. She had not as yet had time. But now that he had brought the idea to her attention, it was clearly the most logical thing to do.

She peered at the boy called Jimmy Lee. He seemed like her best chance. "Please don't hurt me," she whimpered. "Please—" She clutched at the first thought whispering through her mind. "I—I'm with child."

Jimmy Lee's dark brown eyes rounded. He shot a startled glance at his partner.

Even as the words left her mouth, Chloe flinched. What had prompted that? It was the farthest thing from the truth. Yet it had been so easy to say. Still, why not? Everybody else was lying. Why should she not do the same—especially if it saved her life?

"Nobody said nothin' 'bout killin' no woman carryin' a baby." Jimmy Lee held up his hands and took a step back.

Hank studied Chloe for a minute. "Ah, hell, boy.

Ya really are one dumb, snivel-nosed pup, aincha? She's lyin'. Look at her."

Jimmy Lee's expression was skeptical.

Good. It just might work.

"She ain't gonna have no kid. Leastways if she is, *she* don't even know it yet."

"How da ya know that?" The boy leaned forward a little, inspecting her features more closely.

Chloe held her breath. She was as curious as Jimmy Lee. She had seen a few pregnant women before their babies had begun to grow large within them and *she* had not been able to tell. Surely the man was bluffing.

"Hell, boy," Hank said with laughter deep in his throat. "She jist got married three days ago, fer Christ's sake. She ain't had no time ta know nothin' yet."

Chloe's hopes plummeted. She held back an agonizing groan. She had been so quick to speak, she had not taken that one little detail into consideration.

"That true, lady?" The boy sounded angry. "Are ya tryin' to play me fer a fool?"

Chloe cut her gaze askance. What was she to say? Should she try to continue with the lie?

Suddenly, Hank began to laugh in earnest. "Why you little tramp. You *are* carryin' a kid in yer belly, aincha?"

Startled, Chloe peered up.

"What're ya talkin' 'bout, Hank? Ya jist said she weren't. Ya said, even if she was—"

"I know what I said. But think about it." He squinted, his tobacco-stained lips curving upward in a smirk. "She got married the very next day after she got here. And, don't ya remember everybody talkin' about her bein' sick the night o' her weddin'?"

"Yeah, so?" Jimmy Lee cocked his head to one side and frowned. "Folks said she couldn't tolerate the heat."

Hank's bushy brows shot upward. He grinned, his eyes raking lecherously over her form. "We're in the mountains, boy. It ain't never *that* hot up here."

Chloe blinked. What was he insinuating? She held his stare, curiosity mingling with more than an ample amount of fear.

"You sayin' what I think yer sayin'?" Brushing a thick shock of white-blond hair from his eyes, the youth scowled at Chloe.

Hank nodded with a shrewd chuckle. "Most likely *Taggert* don't even know she whored 'round behind his back. Poor bastard." Sneering, he leaned into Chloe's face and clutched her abdomen. "Savin' that special surprise fer a little later, were ya?"

Repulsed, Chloe clutched his wrist and shoved his hand away. "Don't touch me!" she shrieked with all the venom she could muster. She could not believe what he had said. She wheeled around and took a step backward. She bumped into the boy.

He grabbed her upper arms and whipped her around to face his partner, slamming her back against him. "Whored around on yer intended, did ya?" he seethed in her ear. He shook his head. "And I liked Shea, too."

Hank grabbed her out of the youth's hold. He jerked her up hard against him. "Yeah, well, good thing he ain't never gonna know then, huh?" His piercing gaze roved over her face. He clutched her hair and yanked her head back. "Ya know, that kinda thing don't bother me none, though. 'Specially seein's how ya ain't gonna be 'round much longer."

Chloe pushed against his chest, holding herself as far away from him as possible. God, help me, she silently prayed. What had she gotten herself into?

"Yeah, matter o' fact, it makes me kinda hot thinkin' 'bout it," he said. He unbuckled his gunbelt and tossed it to the ground.

The stale stench of his beer-ladened breath rocked her senses, adding to her growing terror. Her lungs nearly exploded with the force of her rapid breathing. She had never before been so afraid for her life.

"What, Hank?" The younger man's excited voice slithered up behind her. "What're ya thinkin'?"

"I'm thinkin' . . . she's already spoiled." He cut a savage glance around, then spit out the mushy hunk of tobacco. "We could have a little fun a'fore we toss her over the side. Hell, who's ta know?"

Chloe's heart leapt to her throat. Rape? She choked back the word. "No!"

Hank held her fast. He licked his lips and grinned. "I ain't had me a taste of female flesh in a long time." He shot a look past her to the boy. "Ya game, kid? Ya want some of her?"

Apparently hesitant, Jimmy Lee did not answer.

"Ah, hell!" The older man yanked her a short distance away from the horses. "Who the hell's gonna stop us? Ain't nobody but you, me, and the woman here." He shoved her to the ground.

Chloe screamed.

In one move, he grabbed the front of her shirt and knelt down. He tore open the outer fabric along with her camisole, ripping off the buttons to her waist.

Hands still bound, she tried to cover herself. She

thrashed against him. Shea! God, where was he? Screaming for all her worth, she scratched her attacker's face.

"Git over here, boy," Hank hollered.

The kid dashed forward. He fell to his knees.

"Hold her, damn it!"

Chloe fought with all her might. She could not let them do this. She had to save herself. There was no one else to do it for her.

Jimmy Lee grabbed her wrists, slamming them to the ground above her head, exposing her breasts to his view. "Do her!" His voice pitched high with enthusiasm.

She dug her nails into his flesh.

He yowled.

Hank backhanded her.

Pinpricks of light exploded in her head. "No—no!" She squeezed her eyes closed, kicked and squirmed. They would not take her without a fight. The buttons on her pants suddenly gave way.

Hank ripped the tight-fitting garment down over her hips. He fell on top of her. Hunching against her, he held her fast. "Ooo-yeah," he rasped against her mouth. "That's nice."

She gagged. The bulk of his huge frame nearly crushed her. Her earlier nausea returned. Darkness threatened. No. She whipped her head from side to side. She could not black out.

"Don't even twitch an eyelash." A man's angry, throaty voice intruded.

Hank stilled.

An audible click echoed sharp in her hearing.

The boy gasped.

Slowly, she opened her eyes. She saw the small

barrel of a derringer first. Then, as she lifted her gaze, a familiar face came into focus.

Scowling with more fury than she could have ever imagined, Bill Sharon leaned down, the tip of his gun pressing against the temple of the heaving man on top of her.

Hank scowled into her face, his gray eyes bright with rage. Then, suddenly, they dimmed a bit. His body relaxed. "Ooowee." Pushing himself off of her, he laughed out loud. "Almost lost it, didn't I, boss?"

Bill Sharon held the position of the gun steady, its new location becoming even more formidable as the older man regained his height. "More than you realize," he told Hank, the threat, inches from the older man's crotch, only too apparent.

Jimmy Lee released Chloe.

Uncertain what to do, she remained on the ground in a defensive curl. Shielding her bosom with her forearms, she held her hands to her quivering chin. Scared beyond control, she could not stop shaking.

Bill Sharon gestured the men away from her with a wave of his gun. "Get over there with the horses," he told them.

"Sure thing, Mr. Sharon." Jimmy Lee did not hesitate.

Still smirking, Hank did not appear as worried. As if he did not have a care in the world, he sauntered over to stand beside the boy, tugging up his britches with the same nonchalance that he showed in his gait. He moved to retrieve his holster.

"I don't think you need that right now." His gaze tethered to the men, Bill Sharon reached down and clasped Chloe's hand. "Let me help you up, Mrs. Taggert."

Caution warning her to remain still, she stared at him. Why was he attempting to be so nice to her? Did he not realize she knew who, and what, he was, or that she guessed that he was the person behind all of this?

"Come now, Mrs. Taggert." His hand still extended, he motioned for her to rise. "I won't hurt you."

Wary, she reluctantly accepted his aid.

He pulled her up to stand beside him. "Are you all right? They didn't harm you, did they?"

Struck speechless, Chloe could only shake her head. She stared at the man as if he were crazy. Was that concern in his voice? She could not believe his gentleness. What did he hope to gain by it?

"Good." He cut the rope that secured her hands together, then stepped in front of her, gallantly shielding her from the other men. "I should've known I wouldn't be able to trust you two alone with Mrs. Taggert."

Free at last, Chloe looked for an escape. No. There were three of them. They would only catch her again.

"Why the hell did ya send us ta git her, then?" Apparently, Hank found Bill Sharon's conclusion humorous.

Chloe took advantage of the moment and pulled up her pants. Once she had done up the buttons, she tried as best she could to fasten her shirt closed, but it was useless. Most of the buttons had been torn away. Tugging out the hem, she opted instead to tie it together at her waist. The alteration offered only the meagerest degree of modesty.

"I couldn't afford to lose any of the other men. I

need them," Mr. Sharon answered matter-of-factly, his tone smooth.

"But ya *can* afford to lose us, is that what yer tellin' me?"

Peeking around Bill Sharon's fastidiously clad shoulders, Chloe watched Hank stiffen, his expression sharp as a blade.

"It seems I've underestimated you, Hank. You're smarter than I thought."

The older man flicked a gaze down to his gun, only a few feet away.

"I wouldn't if I were you."

Hank chuckled. "C'mon, Sharon. What the hell do ya think yer gonna be able to hit with that little pea—" He dove for his weapon.

Mr. Sharon fired.

Chloe flinched.

Bristled jowls fixed in a grin, Hank peered down at the blotch of red oozing through the thick cloth covering his belly. He touched it, smearing crimson on his fingers. He dropped to his knees and looked up.

Fear held Chloe stock-still.

The man opened his mouth, but said nothing. His eyes clouded over and he fell facedown on the hard-packed dirt.

Both Chloe and Sharon glanced at the boy.

Trembling, Jimmy Lee lifted his hands. "Don't shoot me, Mr. Sharon. I ain't gonna give ya any trouble."

Sharon lifted the smoking barrel, then smiled. "Good boy." He shoved the derringer into his coat pocket. "Now. You dressed, Mrs. Taggert?" he asked over his shoulder.

Chloe could not speak. She had never seen anyone killed before.

"Mrs. Taggert?" Mr. Sharon turned to face her. "Ah, I see that you are dressed. Good. Now ..." He took her arm. "If you'll be so kind as to step over here with me."

Chloe pulled her gaze from the lifeless form lying in front of her, then shifted it to the man at her side.

Smiling, he gestured toward a cliffside she had not noticed until now.

She swallowed. So, he did not intend to be *nice* after all. He still planned to kill her. Her legs felt like lead weights. She had to consciously lift each foot, one at a time, then set it down, step by step.

"Do hurry along, Mrs. Taggert." He pulled against her resistance. "I must be getting back to town before someone misses me. There's still lots to do before the Fourth of July festivities tomorrow."

"Why did you stop him if you were just going to—" She fixed her terror-filled gaze on the open terrain below. She could not bring herself to say what she knew was about to happen. "Why're you doing this to me?"

"Jimmy, bring me your rope," he called to the boy, then returned his attention to Chloe. "I didn't want you marred. And, please, don't fret yourself over this. I assure you, it's nothing personal, Mrs. Taggert." He took the coil from the youth; then, after shaking it loose, he returned one end to the younger man. "Secure that around that tree over there." He pointed to a nearby yellow pine.

Jimmy scurried off to do Sharon's bidding.

"I don't understand." Chloe shot another glance

over the edge of the slope. "Why do you want to kill me?"

Bill Sharon stopped short, his hawklike brown eyes piercing her. "I'm not going to kill you." He motioned for the boy to move up behind her, then looped the rope over both of their heads, and cinched it tight around their waists. "I'm just going to put you on that ledge down there for safekeeping."

"Ya want me ta go down with her?"

"She's not going to lead herself down there, boy. Somebody's got to do it for her."

Looking over the edge, Chloe nearly swooned. The so-called ledge he had mentioned was at least twenty or thirty feet below, and only about two feet wide. Beyond that, she could not even begin to estimate how far it was to the bottom of the face.

"Signal when you get her down there, Jimmy, and I'll pull you back up."

"Sure thing, Mr. Sharon." Though he appeared to still be quite nervous, the younger man seemed overly eager to please his boss. With that, Jimmy clutched her around the middle and moved to the edge.

"Wait!" Chloe dug her heels into the earth "Can't you at least tell me why you're really doing this to me?"

Sharon picked up the slack on the rope, then leaned back, bracing himself against their weight. "I told you . . . for safekeeping. You're my insurance policy."

Her heart racing like a wildfire, Chloe pulled on the hemp. "Insurance against what?" she all but shrieked. She had to know.

"Calm yourself, Mrs. Taggert. You don't want to fall, do you?" He signaled to Jimmy with a nod.

Chloe felt the rope cut into her sides. Fear attacked her senses. She looked down. The ground fell away beneath her. A whimper shuddered through her body and she gripped the coil. "Please don't do this," she begged Jimmy.

"Shut up and just do what you're told, and you won't git hurt."

"But why're you doing this?"

"Mr. Sharon's told ya all he wants ya to know."

They slipped down a few more feet. The rope jerked.

Chloe screamed.

The ledge seemed to move nearer and nearer toward them. Finally they reached it.

Chloe almost collapsed with relief when she felt solid rock beneath her feet. But her respite was short-lived.

After easing her over to a wider crook in the stone wall, the boy removed the rope from around her, then shoved her down in the corner.

She flattened herself against the sheer surface, spreading her arms out wide from her sides. "Oh, no, please!" she shrieked. "Don't leave me—don't leave me." Her blood raced through her veins.

Jimmy moved off a space, then cinched up the rope tight around himself again. "Just stay still, and you'll be okay." He tugged on the hemp. Almost immediately, he began to ascend the stone face of the cliff. "Mr. Sharon'll come back fer you later. He promised."

Chloe could not move. She heard the boy speak,

TENDER OUTLAW

but she was so frightened, she could not completely understand all that he said.

Suddenly, Jimmy screamed.

Chloe looked up just in time to see his flailing body plummet downward.

She gasped, her gaze riveted on the still, broken form lying mangled below on the rocks.

"Mrs. Taggert? You all right?" Bill Sharon called down to her.

Squinting against the late-morning sun, she peered up. She could barely make out his silhouette against the brilliant glare.

"I said, are you all right, Mrs. Taggert?"

She tried to answer but could not. She swallowed against the dryness in her mouth. She leaned out a little for a better glimpse of him. The world tilted around her. She slammed herself back against the stone. "Y—yes."

"Good. You sit tight now, all right? I'll be back for you once my business in Glenbrook is finished tomorrow." He started to move off, then stopped. "Now, if you get too impatient and want to strike out on your own, that ledge down there'll eventually take you to a gorge below and off the cliffside."

She peeked over the edge and shivered.

"You need to be careful, though," he instructed as if he were speaking to a small child. "There's a seventy-five-foot cavern just under you. So do watch out. Like poor Jimmy there, I doubt you'd survive the fall." He left her then—left her to the screaming silence of her own fear.

THIRTEEN

IT HAD TAKEN SHEA AND THE OTHER MEMBERS OF THE gang of outlaws about four hours to make it from their camp at Shakespeare Rock to the strategic point they had chosen for the holdup below Spooner Summit. Tired from their ride, the men sat or squatted in close proximity, checking their weapons and gear.

Shea stood with one foot braced against the bottom of a tall fir trunk. He picked absently at its purplish-red bark. Squinting, he shot a critical glance from the horses, still belly-heaving from their morning climb, to One-Eyed John. The damned Indian was crazy.

In the months since Shea had taken on this assignment, he had managed to successfully arrange and artfully accomplish the many heists he had been involved in without so much as a single bruise on any of the passengers. Now, here was this son-of-a-bitchin' renegade ordering him to set up a bottle of nitroglycerin right in the path of the stage trail.

Shea looked back at Cameron.

Crouched on his haunches, the younger agent shot a quick glance up at Shea, but he did not display any sign of emotion. He was playing his part well.

"You do not like my plan?" One-Eyed John asked in his clipped nasally dialect.

Shea tossed a piece of broken bark to the ground. "As a matter-of-fact, John, I don't."

"Good." The Indian dipped his head. "That make me like it better."

"Why?"

"I have not seen the blood of a white man spilled in a long time past." Though he did not smile, his one good eye crinkled at the corner. "Good thing you do not take ride on coach today, hmm?"

Shea stiffened. The hair on the back of his neck bristled. This damn Indian was nothing like the agreeable Paiute back home, that was for sure. "What the hell's that supposed to mean?"

The big red man shrugged.

Shea knew there was no love lost between himself and One-Eyed John, that had been apparent from the first. But until now they had at least managed not to kill each other. Once this job was finished, Shea was not certain he would be able to hold on to that practice.

One-Eyed John was notorious for disliking anyone with pale skin. It was said that he could use that huge blade strapped to his hip with the skill of a surgeon. He had no tolerance for whites and was not afraid to let them know it. Hell, around the Tahoe area, the mere mention of his name made people shiver in their tracks. And for some reason he had taken on a special hostility toward Shea.

"You go." The renegade pointed to a spot a short distance down the road. "Set blasting water in path of stage."

Shea hesitated.

"Go." One-Eyed John straightened to his full height. His hand resting on the hilt of his bowie knife, he glared at Shea, defying him to disobey. A threat of death glimmered in his dark stare.

Shea met his glower second for dangerous second. He knew he should not tempt the man's temper, but he could not back down, either. If he were to show any glimpse of cowardice, the Indian would not hesitate to kill him—any way he could. At least this way, when the time came—and it would, of that there was no doubt—it would be face-to-face.

"C'mon, Taggert." Cameron stood up. As casual as if he were out on a Sunday stroll, he walked up to Shea. He slapped him on the back. "We don't know how soon that stage's gonna git here. Let's jist git the job done, okay?"

Shea held the Indian's stare a second longer, then slowly he shifted his gaze to Cameron.

"C'mon." The younger man lifted his brows. "I'll help ya. Jist tell me what to do, okay?" He smiled.

Behind that nonchalant expression, Shea could see that Cameron was more than a little nervous. And why not? This was the man's first assignment in the field since his training. At least Shea had been on at least a dozen or so missions with veteran agents before this one. Now, *he* was supposed to be the senior member. He sighed heavily. He sure as hell felt like a *senior*. He nodded, then moved off toward the box he had set down a few yards away.

Once he had a small hole dug out for the nitro, he reached inside the wooden case and retrieved the tiny bottle of liquid explosive.

"What'll this do to the stage?" Cameron asked, sweat glistening through his black mustache.

Shea waited to answer him until he had knelt, unwrapped the cotton from the glass vial, then set the container down. He took a minute to relax before covering it with dirt. "You were on the same coach that Chloe came in on." He peered up at the younger agent.

"Yeah."

Shea dipped his head, his eyes trained on the little flask. "There's twice as much in this bottle as I used on that holdup."

"You shittin' me?"

"Nope." Sitting back on his heels, Shea rested his hands on his thighs and took a few deep breaths. Handling dangerous explosives always made his nerves jitter. It was one of very few things in his training that he had immediately learned to have a deep and abiding respect for.

"There'll be passengers on that stage, Taggert," Cameron said in a choked whisper.

"Don't ya think I know that?" Shea did not try to hide his annoyance, though he kept his voice low. He glanced up at the outlaws in the distance.

"We gotta do somethin', then." Cameron followed Shea's line of vision. "We gotta bring down the odds."

"Yup." Not counting himself and Cameron, there were four other men.

"Well?" The younger agent shifted his gaze back to Shea. "You got a plan?"

Shea started to gently push up the dirt around the bottle. Cameron was right. They *did* have to do something. They could not allow anyone to get hurt, least of all killed, if they could help it. But at this moment, Shea had no idea what he was going to do to stop it.

"Taggert? Ya hear me?"

"Mmm-hmm." Shea continued to press the dry earth up into a mound around the glass container.

Cameron stared at him.

From the corner of his eye, Shea could see the frustration on the younger man's face. He knew the agent was nervous. So was he.

"Damn it, Taggert!" Cameron whispered. "What the hell're we gonna to do?" He looked back at One-Eyed John and his boys. Slowly, he unfastened the leather loop on his Colt.

Shea stopped mid-sweep. "Don't try anythin' stupid, Cameron."

The younger man shot an angry glance back at Shea. Perspiration soaked the dark hair cropping out beneath his large hat.

"Look, we're outnumbered two to one. If we try gunplay with 'em, they'll more than likely win." Shea brushed the dust from his hands. "Even if we were to manage to best 'em, odds are that one of us'll be killed—wounded at the very least."

"Not without takin' one 'r two of them," the younger man sneered.

"Ya figure that's good odds then, do ya?"

"Well, what the hell else 're we gonna do? Ya got another idea?"

Pursing his mouth, Shea took a minute to think. He looked down at the man's gun. "How good a shot are ya?"

Cameron shrugged. "I ain't no sharpshooter, but pretty fair, I suppose. Why?"

"Pretty fair ain't good enough." Head at a downward tilt, Shea looked up at the Indian from beneath his brows. "Guess it's gotta be me, then."

"What does?" Cameron darted the gang a sidelong glance. "What're ya aimin' to do?"

"The stage's goin' to be comin' down around that bend there." Shea nodded toward the curve in the road half-hidden from view by a stand of sugar pine. "We won't be able to see it till it's almost on us. But when I do, I'm goin' to shoot the nitro."

Cameron shifted his gaze between the turn, the explosive, and the nearest possible cover of boulders only a few yards away. "You'll have to be over there to hit it."

"Uh-huh." Shea knew what the man was thinking. It would be a dangerously close distance to hit his target and not get hurt in the process.

"That's cuttin' it too close. Ya wanna blow yerself up?"

"Nope." Shea raised his brows. He could only pray luck would be with him. They had to stop the stage somehow before it got to the nitroglycerin. This seemed like the only hope they had for coming out of this alive. "We just ain't got no other choice, now, do we?"

Cameron hesitated. "So what do ya want me to do?"

"Ya see ol' One-Eyed over there?" He glanced back at the man with the black patch.

"Yeah."

"Ya keep yer sights on him and don't let him shoot me in the back. I got a queer feelin' he's gonna try his damnedest to see me leave this spot in a pine box."

Cameron nodded. "Yeah, I noticed you two don't get on too good."

Shea snorted a chuckle. "That's puttin' it gently."

Once the men had taken up their places to await the coach, Shea, like the others, took a practice bead on the curve in the road. But unlike them, his weapon was a Winchester 44.40. It was the best rifle known to the West for accuracy. Now, if only *his* aim was as good as the firearm's boast.

He sucked in slow, even, and deep breaths. This was the excitement—the thrill of danger—he had always wanted to experience. But now that it was here, he was not too sure he liked it.

He checked the sun. He guessed it to be about ten o'clock. If the stage was on its normal schedule, he would not have much longer to wait. He strained his hearing, listening for the first telltale sound of the coach and horses. Only the soft hum of the wind blowing through the needles of the pines murmured around him.

At that moment, he and the outlaws appeared to be the only intruders upon the enormous extension of road. But all too soon he knew a Wells Fargo stage filled with unsuspecting passengers would come barreling down off the summit toward them at breakneck speed. Those people had to be protected at all costs—even his own life.

He looked down the long barrel of his rifle again. From his vantage point, he could easily shift his sights from the point at which he was supposed to be preparing to shoot to the mound of earth concealing the nitro, without any of the others noticing. He ran his gaze over the positions of the gang members.

As he had expected, One-Eyed John had taken a spot to the rear and slightly off to the side of Shea. And, as he had asked the agent to do, Cameron had situated himself nearest the renegade.

The clatter and rattle of horses and coach suddenly echoed down the mountain road toward them.

Shea wiped away the sweat beading up under his eyes. This was it. He crouched as low as he could into the mound of boulders while still being able to clearly see the little hill of dirt in the road through his sights. He had not remembered praying in a very long time. He cut one last look between the Indian and his fellow agent. He prayed now—prayed in earnest that Tyree Cameron's "pretty fair" shooting would be good enough to cover his back.

Seconds later, the first horses came into view. The driver cracked his whip over the team's heads. The wheels on the stage kicked up a cloud of dust.

Shea tipped the rifle barrel down. The morning sun glimmered off the glass bottle imprisoned in his sights. He fought the urge to check the aim of the Indian. No. Cameron was there. He had to trust him.

The coach closed in on his mark.

He had to do it now. He took a breath. Held it. Gently, he squeezed the trigger.

A flash of light erupted from the ground. Thunder deafened the quiet. Rocks and dirt pitched into the air in a blinding mushroom of dense smoke. Horses squealed. The stage skidded to a shuddering halt.

Gravel blasted into Shea's face. Flying earth and stone pelted him from above. He ducked down behind the boulders. It was not enough. Something hot shot across the upper portion of his left arm. It felt like a bullet.

Gunfire blazed all around him. He raised up, trying to see through the curtain of debris. Barely visible, he focused on Cameron.

The agent fell. He had been hit.

Shea dashed toward the man. Bullets pinged into the rocks nearest him. He jumped down beside Cameron. With a quick perusal, he saw that the younger man was bleeding badly from the chest. "Damn it, Cameron," he said, lifting the agent's head.

Lead whizzed past them.

Using a huge ponderosa pine to their advantage, Shea pulled the man up beside him for protection.

"Guess ya figured out by now that I lied."

After firing off a couple of shots, Shea stared down at Cameron with a frown. "Lied?"

The younger man nodded, then coughed. Blood erupted from his mouth. "I'm a lousy shot."

All around them, men were yelling and guns were blasting.

He looked up through the spray of bullets for the Indian. "What the hell're ya talkin' about? Ya kept that damn renegade from killin' me." He showed the agent his arm. "See, he only creased my shoulder."

Cameron shook his head, then laughed. Another bout of choking caused him to gasp for air. He grinned through the blood staining his teeth. "That was me. I missed the red son of a bitch." He swallowed. "Hit you instead."

A slug pinged into his rifle. It stung Shea's hand. The weapon flew from his grasp. He glanced at the gun. It lay off to the side, splintered almost in half. "Shit!"

The gunshots subsided.

Shea looked up.

"Pinkerton agents!" a gravelly voice called out from behind the stage. The unmistakable sight of a Colt barrel wavered into view. "Throw down your guns and come out with your hands up." Hesitantly, a silver-haired man came out into view, followed by three others.

Shea cut a glance around for any remaining outlaws.

One lay facedown over a fallen tree trunk. Another crawled out from behind some shrub-infested rocks. The third tossed out his pistol, then moved from the shadows of the forest and into sunlight, his hands over his head.

Still crouched behind the huge pine, Shea squinted at the spot where he had last seen the Indian. "Where the hell's One-Eyed John?"

"He run off," Cameron said, the words leaving his body in sputters. He cut a gaze in the direction they had left the horses.

"Damn it!" Shea watched the stage driver crawl out from beneath the coach. "We'll never get Sharon without that red devil."

"You there," the Pinkerton agent called. "Come out from behind that tree."

"Shit!" Now what was he going to do? He did not have the time to explain things to these men if he was going to catch One-Eyed John.

Cameron clutched Shea's sleeve. "Go after him." He swallowed hard, his breaths coming in heavy pants. "I'll cover for ya here." He lifted the pistol he still held and eased the cocked hammer back down to the firing pin.

Shea stared at him. "I gotta see you get help first."

Cameron looked at the flow of crimson blotching his shirt, then back at Shea. He shook his head, a forced smile on his lips. "I'm coming out," he half-yelled, half-gasped, then tossed the Colt into the dirt a few yards away from them.

Shea scowled. What the hell was he up to? "You can't go out there without proof that you're a special agent." He felt around the man's shirt pockets. "Where's your badge?"

Cameron glanced away. He looked like a scolded child. "I was afraid they might be suspicious of me." He swallowed. "I left it in my hotel room."

Shea closed his eyes and shook his head. He should have thought to tell the younger man to keep it on him at all times. He knew it had to have been part of Cameron's instruction when he had joined the force. Why had he not listened?

Gripping the material covering Shea's arm tighter, Cameron pulled himself up. "Get the hell outa here and git that damned Indian."

Shea hesitated. He reached down inside his boot and removed the silver special agent shield. "Here, hang on to this."

Cameron glanced down at the badge, then nodded. "I'll get it back to ya as soon as I can." He grinned. "Now go, will ya?" With a groan, he rolled away from Shea onto his belly, then scooted a few inches out into the clearing. He looked back one last time. The full spread of an appreciative smile stretched beneath his bloody mustache. "Tell the governor I did good, okay?"

Shea swallowed the lump in his throat. Now he knew how childlike he must have appeared to his older brother a couple of years back, when he had been so carried away with becoming an agent. The man was dying, and all he cared about was the spine-tingling embrace of the moment.

But was it enough to warrant this man losing his life? And what about Shea's? It was a question he had never asked himself. He could not now. "Yeah," he choked out. He held the agent's meaningful stare for close to a full minute. The implication of Cameron's request hit a nerve. Shea knew that if the younger man lived an hour, it would be a miracle. "I'll do just that."

"And Taggert . . ."

"Yeah?"

"Give that purty wife o' yers a kiss fer me." He winked. Then, without another word, Cameron shifted his attention back to the Pinkertons.

Shea did not hesitate to take advantage of the younger man's ploy. He had to catch One-Eyed John. He did not have any evidence on Sharon and he would need the renegade's confession if he was going to see the real leader behind these robberies brought to justice. Wheeling around, he silently put as much distance between himself and the Pinkertons as Cameron's maneuver would allow.

Shea followed One-Eyed John's trail for more than a mile before he ever got sight of him. At the edge of a stand of depleted timber where the ground turned to rock, he watched the Indian snake his pinto through the boulders. If Shea had not been so quick to follow the renegade, he might very well have lost him over the stony terrain.

He shifted his attention to a spot above the Indian. If he hurried, he could beat the man to that point and have him caught. He reached down for his Colt. His hand touched leather, but no metal. He glanced down. His holster was empty. "Damn it to hell!" he rasped between clenched teeth. He must have lost it somehow during all the commotion back at the stage.

Now what in all the blazes of Hades was he going to do? Serenade the savage into submission? He looked down for the skinning knife he kept strapped on the opposite side of his gun belt. Good. At least he still had that.

After quickly maneuvering the sorrel he used for the holdups ahead of the Indian, he dismounted, then wedged himself into the cleft of a huge, split boulder. He did not have long to wait.

Moments later, One-Eyed John approached.

Shea lunged from above him, slamming his full weight into the unsuspecting renegade. He knocked him to the ground.

Leaping to his feet with a growl, One-Eyed John cocked his head to one side and shot a look at his rifle, lying a few feet away.

Shea was closer to the weapon than the renegade, though the gun was still too far to reach. He snatched out his blade and crouched low.

Seeing Shea's intention, the Indian sneered. He withdrew his own steel.

Sunlight glinted off the metal.

Shea looked back at his. The entire length of it was only about eight or nine inches long, and it did not seem much of a threat compared to that of the Indian's murderous-looking bowie. Still, it was better than going up against a rifle.

They circled each other for a minute.

"Why you follow?" One-Eyed John asked. "You know I kill you."

"I'm not dead yet."

The Indian curled his upper lip. "That yet not long. Soon you be with your woman." He lunged forward.

Shea ducked just in time to miss getting his shoulder stabbed. He swung up his blade, sliced air. He wheeled around.

One-Eyed John slashed out. He caught Shea across the chest.

Jumping backward, Shea groaned. Pain cut into his flesh. A thin line of crimson stained his shirt. Fury charged through his veins. He swiped at the Indian's belly.

One-Eyed John veered to the side. He whipped back toward Shea and thrust.

Too quick, Shea crashed his empty fist down atop the renegade's wrist. He knocked the bowie to the ground.

Enraged, the Indian flew at him.

They locked in combat, each holding the other prisoner.

Shea clutched his small knife tighter, but the Indian held Shea's wrist secured.

Shea glowered into the renegade's black-patched face. His muscles strained. Sweat stung his eyes.

One-Eyed John was taller than Shea by nearly a full head. The Indian nearly overpowered him with strength.

Shea ground his teeth together. He forced his brawn to stretch to the limit. His arms shook. He could not hold out against the renegade much longer. He smashed his forehead into John's broad nose.

The bone cracked.

The Indian groaned. Blood gushed from his nostrils. His eye flew wide. A predatory snarl ripped from his throat. He clasped his hands together and swung, catching Shea under the chin, and pitching him to the ground.

Shea landed spread-eagle upside a tumble of boulders. His head struck the stone. Dizziness threatened. He shook it off and started to push himself up.

"Now you die, white dog!" One-Eyed John shrieked.

Shea looked for his knife. He had lost it. Something shiny flashed in the sunlight. It was a blade. He glanced up.

One-Eyed John flew at him.

Shea dove for the weapon. Clutching it, he flipped over to face his attacker.

The Indian crashed on top of him.

Shea stiffened.

The renegade went rigid. A groan slid from his lips. Slowly, his shock-filled gaze moved to Shea's.

What had happened?

One-Eyed John pushed himself up to his knees. He looked down.

Shea followed his line of vision.

Protruding from the man's belly was the handle of the Indian's own bowie knife. The man scowled, disbelief marking his features.

"No!" Shea yelled. He caught One-Eyed John by the collar just as the Indian collapsed. "Ya can't die, yet, ya son of a bitch! I need ya to—"

One-Eyed John grinned. "I wrong. Now, *I* join your woman."

Shea grabbed the renegade and shook him. Fear stabbed through his heart—a more deadly pain than any the knife could have inflicted. "What do ya mean, *join* my woman? Did you do somethin' to Chloe? Did ya hurt her?"

The man's stare turned glassy.

Shea yanked the renegade up closer to his face. "Damn you, don't you die! Tell me—where's my wife? What'd you do to her?"

The Paiute shook his head. "I not . . ." He closed his eye. "Sharon . . ." One side of his mouth twitched in a mocking smile, his breath rushed out in a hiss, then, nothing.

Crumpled down on his knees, chest heaving, Shea stared at the man for a drawn-out moment. Time spun around him in the deafening silence. He trembled, sudden realization seizing his unguarded soul.

Bill Sharon had Chloe.

Mad-dog angry, Shea thrust the dead man away from him. He lunged up to his knees with a throaty growl. He had to find Chloe—and fast. Bill Sharon was a murderous bastard. What if he tried to kill her? What if he already had? No! He could not even think like that.

He ran to the sorrel and leapt atop the animal's back. He had to get back to Glenbrook to find Sharon. He did not care what the cost, he had to save Chloe. He had been foolishly reckless to leave her alone and unprotected.

Now, even if he had not committed himself to this job and the demise of Bill Sharon, he would see the bastard brought to his knees. He heeled the horse's flanks, wheeling the beast southward. He only prayed his blind commitment to his work had not cost him the only love he had ever wanted—the pure and passionate devotion Chloe had so trustingly committed to his protection.

FOURTEEN

SHEA TOOK GREAT PAINS TO KEEP HIS PRESENCE UNknown as he entered Glenbrook. At the edge of town where the livery was situated, he dismounted, then led his mount around to the back of the building. If luck were with him, Bailey would be the only one inside. The old black man liked Shea. He knew he could count on him to help Shea get another horse ready and get out of town again before anyone else could discover his whereabouts.

Coming to the back entrance, Shea tied up the animal, then checked the nearby street.

Everywhere, people were bustling around, putting up the last touches of patriotic decorations around the community, but no one appeared to have noticed his approach.

Carefully, he peeked inside the huge livery.

Except for the usual animal sounds, all was quiet. Then, from out front, the lively hum of Bailey's voice filtered into the barn.

Shea fell back behind the door, but peeked inside through the cracked opening.

The old man sauntered into the straw-littered area, a mucking rake in his hands.

Shea took one last look around. Everything remained as before. Good. He pulled the huge doors open a little wider, then slipped inside. He scanned the interior. Nothing appeared out of place. He approached Bailey from behind.

Apparently sensing Shea's advance, he wheeled around. His eyes shot open wide. He gasped, clutching his chest. "Ya nearly scared ol' Bailey half ta death."

"Sorry, Bailey, I had to make sure ya were alone."

The man's gaze flittered upward, then back to Shea. "Why's that?"

"No time to explain, now." Shea shot a look toward the front doors. "Can ya get me another horse ready right away?"

"Where's Topaz?"

"I had to leave him in Tahoe City."

"Tahoe City?" Bailey's large brown eyes grew wider still, his gaze darting around the interior. "So's ya been in Tahoe City, ya says?" he asked, his voice pitched high.

"Keep it down, will ya?" Shea frowned. Why had the man almost yelled?

Bailey looked up at the hay loft again. "How's come ya had to leave Topaz?" He moved back to his chores.

"I really need that horse, Bailey." He crossed the floor to the large empty stall where Bill Sharon always kept his horse penned.

"Mistah Shea, suh, I ain't so sure I kin help ya none today."

Shea caught the note of nervousness in the man's tone. He watched the him cut another look upward. He followed the man's line of vision to the hayloft. What was he looking at? Shea froze. Was someone up there? He glanced at Bailey.

The black man's brows raised. He backed up a step or two, but kept the rake moving back and forth through the soiled hay.

There *was* someone up there. Damn it! Shea looked around for anything that he might be able to use as a weapon. Hay hooks. He moved to the wall where the tools here hanging—the wall closest to the ladder leading to the upper floor.

Bailey stilled, his mouth agape.

Quitely, Shea removed one hook. He peered over at Bailey.

Swallowing, Bailey held his attention riveted on the loft.

Shea gripped the implement tighter. Who was up there? He clutched the side of the ladder. Whoever it was, it did not look like he was going to come down and introduce himself—he would have to climb up and find out for himself. He eased his foot up the first rung.

A reverberating click sounded behind him.

He stopped dead in his tracks.

"You looking for somebody, Mister?" Deep and gravelly, a man's voice attacked his hearing.

Shea started to turn around.

"Slow and easy."

Setting his foot back on the ground, Shea moved to confront the intruder. Stark blue eyes set in a face lined like parched earth, framed by a thick shock of silver hair, met his gaze. It was the same Pinkerton agent from the stage. How the hell had he gotten here so fast?

"Drop the hook, son," the man ordered. He waved his gun, punctuating his meaning.

Raising his hands, Shea let the tool fall to the ground. He looked at Bailey.

The black man appeared as surprised as Shea.

"Kick it over to the side there."

Shea obliged. "Look, ya don't understand what's happenin' here."

The older man chuckled. "I understand a sight more than you think. The name's Angus Gentry, Pinkerton Agent, Illinois Division. I understand only too well. I was at the—"

"Yup, I know you were."

"Then ya know why I'm here. So, if you don't mind, I'll thank ya to be more cooperative this time, son." He glanced at Bailey. "You mind going for the sheriff?"

"Me, suh?" Bailey darted a look between the two men.

"Uh-huh. Would you do that, please?" Gentry motioned for Shea to take a seat on a bale of hay. "I don't want to have to shoot you, but if you try to cut out on me again like you did back—"

Shea took note that Bailey had not as yet left the barn. Maybe he could convince the man to help him escape. "Look, didn't ya talk to Cameron?" After doing as the older man had wanted, Shea shifted his attention to the gun barrel staring him down. "Didn't he tell ya who I am?" The younger agent was Shea's only hope.

The Pinkerton tipped his head to one side. "If you mean that young fella you sent crawling out—yeah, I talked to him."

Shea let out a relieved breath. He started to lower his hands.

"Talked to him about two minutes before he died."

The Pinkerton man shook his head. "I knew I had that boy pegged for a nice fella. Rode into town with him on the stage the other morning. You know, the last time you robbed a coach?" He shook his head. "Didn't know the boy was a—"

"Cameron's dead?" It was a foolish question. He had guessed the outcome even before he had left the man. Shea's hopes dashed by the wayside. His stomach tightened.

"Yeah, poor fella." He glared at Shea. "Bet you're all broken up inside just thinking about it, ain't you?"

Shea returned the man's glower. He was genuinely saddened by Tyree's death. He had tried not to like the man. He had not wanted anyone else involved with this mission for the very reason that he did not want anyone to be hurt. Now the agent was dead—and so young—and on his very first assignment. "Was he able to tell ya who he was?"

"Yeah. He showed us his badge."

"Then ya know what's goin' on with Bill Sharon?" At least now Shea would be able to get some help from another veteran.

"Mistah Sharon?" Bailey asked, curiosity marking his features. "He came fer his horse before good daylight this mornin'. He lit out for Shakespeare Rock up yonder in the mountains."

"You still here?" Gentry asked in an annoyed tone. "I thought I sent you for the—"

Bailey jumped. Though he appeared to be torn between loyalties, the black man hurried out of the barn.

"Known about Sharon for a while, now," Gentry said, returning his attention to Shea.

Shea became annoyed with the Pinkerton's game. "Then why're ya holdin' that hogleg down on me? Let's get goin'." He moved for the door.

"Not so fast, son." The older man stepped into Shea's path and pointed the pistol straight at Shea's chest. "Just cuz I'm after Bill Sharon and the doctor don't mean I'm apt to let you go."

Shea turned back to face the man. He frowned. "Ya mean Doc Jenkins?"

"Is there another doctor in Glenbrook?"

"But why?"

Gentry snorted. "Hell, son. Them two's yer bosses." He peered at Shea through a squint. "Didn't you even know who you were working for?"

Shea nodded. Apparently Cameron had not been able to tell the Pinkerton man everything before he died. "The governor of the state of Nevada."

Angus Gentry nearly choked on a hard chuckle. "You got one helluva imagination there, son. I'll give you that."

Shea stiffened. How was he going to prove that he was what he said he was? He had given his badge to Cameron. It had seemed the only thing to do, considering the situation. Now he wished he had kept it.

"Look, Gentry, I *am* a state agent workin' for the governor. My name's Shea Taggert. I've been with the company for about three years. I was assigned to this case about nine months ago, working undercover as a member of the gang ya caught up with this mornin'."

"Anybody could say that. Where's your badge?"

"Damn it!" Shea bolted to his feet.

Gentry jumped to face him off.

Seeing the seriousness of his situation, Shea finally

retook his seat. He could not afford to lose his temper. Chloe was in danger. She might even be killed—if she had not been already. He had to make this man understand. "Look," he began again, this time in a more subdued tone. "The bastards were already suspicious of me. I was afraid they might jump me in my sleep and find my shield. So, I kept it in my boot."

"Whip it out, son. I ain't unreasonable. If you can prove who you are, you can be on your way."

Frustrated, Shea shook his head. "I gave it to Cameron," he said, exhaling with a groan. He knew how it sounded.

"You expect me to swallow that one?" Gentry laughed.

"Look, he left his in his room at the hotel." This was not going to be easy. Damn it. He did not have time for all this. "This was Cameron's first assignment. He was afraid that they'd stumble on it and find out who he was."

"So when we came along, you being the senior agent, you did the only smart thing and gave him yours, right?" Gentry's pale eyes twinkled with laughter. He no more believed Shea than he would any of the other gang members. As far as the man was concerned, Shea was an outlaw.

And, unfortunately, Shea had no way to prove otherwise. He had to think of something quick. He had to find Chloe. "Look, if yer after Sharon, then ya know he's in up to his eyeballs with these robberies."

"Yeah, we suspected as much. He hooked up with Doctor Donovan Jenkins a couple of years ago, back in Chicago."

"I was under the impression that Doc Jenkins had lived out here most of his life."

"Nah." Gentry shook his head. "He was a reb doctor in the war. Killed about as many men at Belle Isle with bad medical practices and neglect as did the war itself, I'd say." He looked Shea in the eye, anger etching his features. "About a quarter of those were in the battalion under my command captured during the Seven Days' Battle near Richmond." He did not speak for a long moment. "I joined up with Allan Pinkerton a year later, and I've been after that butcher ever since."

Shea's heart went out to the older man, but he did not have time to waste on some old desire for vengeance. The war was over—had been for some thirteen years. The men that had been under Gentry's command during the war were dead. But Chloe might still have a chance. "Look, I don't know anything about the doc. But Sharon knows who *I* am. He's got my wife, Gentry. God only knows what he's got planned for her. Ya gotta let me go. I gotta find her before it's too late."

"I'd like to believe you, son, but—"

Out of the corner of his eye, Shea saw a shadow move up behind Gentry. It was an animal. Shea grinned. Satchel.

The cougar waltzed in, pretty as you please, and sat down only a couple of feet behind the Pinkerton man.

"Gentry, now I don't want to scare ya or nothin', but I wouldn't make any sudden moves if I was you."

Gentry appeared amused. "I'm the one holdin' the Colt, son. You threatening—"

Satchel let out a fiendish snarl.

The Pinkerton's eyes flew wide. He froze, his gaze riveted on Shea.

"Don't move," Shea commanded. Standing, he sidestepped slowly toward the cat. He was not at all sure Satchel would not attack. After all, the animal did not know the man, and if the cougar thought Shea's life was in danger the beast just might pounce on Gentry.

"What—what are you—"

"Shh." Shea bent down and retrieved the gun from the Pinkerton man.

Out of breath, Bailey ran inside. He slammed up against the door. His whole face split into a wide grin. "Mr. O'Dell done brung Satchel home yesterday. He said he can't handle that cat up yonder at the Lightnin' Tree. And when I hear ya tell that man here that yer new missus was in trouble, I went and fetched Satchel to help ya." He took a gulp of air.

"Ya did real good, Bailey."

"Don't do this, son. You'll only make things worse for yourself. We'll get somebody in here to collaborate your story. And when my men get here, we'll go after Sharon and that wife of yours."

"Sorry, Gentry." Shea raised the Colt, then brought it down on the back of the man's skull.

With a groan, the Pinkerton agent fell to the ground.

Shea shoved the man's gun in his own holster. "I can't wait that long."

By late afternoon, Shea, with Satchel tagging along, had reached the base of Shakespeare Rock, where Bailey had said Sharon was riding. It was a slim chance that *that* was where the bastard had taken her, seeing as how it was also where the outlaws usually met before a robbery. But it was the only starting place Shea had to go on.

He followed the foot of the sheer wall. There was something up a little farther. It looked like a body lying on the ground.

Satchel ran over to it and sniffed.

The air slammed hard in Shea's lungs. "Get outa there, Satchel!" No. Please, God, no. It could not be Chloe. He heeled his horse toward the sight. He jumped down even before the animal stopped. He pushed Satchel out of the way. Hesitantly, he rolled the body over.

It was a man. No—not a man—a boy. It was Jimmy Lee.

Relief washed over Shea, followed by curiosity.

The boy was part of the gang. One-Eyed John had said Jimmy Lee was on business for Bill Sharon. But where was Hank? The Indian had said the two were together.

He checked the rope cinched up tight around the boy's waist. It had been cut. Automatically, Shea peered up at the face of the cliff. What had happened? Had Hank severed the line? Was Chloe still up there somewhere with that old coot?

He jumped to his feet, then leapt atop the bay Bailey had given him and reined in toward the peak. He whistled for the cougar. If there was going to be trouble, he wanted the big cat with him.

Shea rushed up the mountainside. The boy had been dead less than a few hours, he guessed. Some of the blood on his face was still wet. Maybe there was still a chance for Chloe.

He wheeled his mount toward the gorge where he

and the outlaws had made their camp the previous night. There was no sign of anyone in the cave. But there was something—a noise—like whimpering.

He cocked his ear to the wind. Nothing. He paused another moment.

Satchel growled low in his throat.

"Shh, boy, quiet." He signaled the animal to come over to him.

But Satchel did not obey. Instead he moved to the natural stone path leading around the sheer face of the cliff.

"Somebody, please—please, help me." It was a woman's sob.

Fear gut-kicked Shea as soundly as if it had been a horse. He held his breath and listened again. Which way had it come from?

Satchel paced back and forth near the ledge.

Drawing his gun, Shea glanced around the wall as far as he could see. But the setting sun offered him little light with which to search out his quarry. He squinted at the shadow-covered stone, but saw nothing. He waited for another sound.

The forest grew quiet again.

Had he been so afraid for Chloe that he had imagined it? No. It had to be her. It was starting to get dark. He had to find her. He cupped a hand to his mouth. "Chloe!" he yelled. It did not matter if he drew attention from Hank. Shea had to find her. "Chloe!"

"Shea?" Another pause.

He had not imagined *that*. He leapt down from his saddle, and rushed toward the direction of the voice. "Chloe, where are you?"

"Here!" she yelled. "I'm here, oh God, Shea. I'm over here."

He ran past the mouth of the cave to the stone shelf. Pushing past Satchel, he inched around an outcropping of stone against the face of the cliff.

Something moved in the shadows.

Shea could not believe what he saw.

There Chloe was, appearing small and helpless, her back pressed flat against the sheer rock, sitting on a ledge barely wide enough for good footing. "It's her!" He patted the big cat's head. Pure joy shot through the entire length of his body, followed by a jolt of dread. How was he going to get her off of that mantel of stone? He could not let her see his concern. He smiled and waved back at her. "Where's Hank?"

She looked up to the edge of the cliff. "He's dead."

Shea exhaled. At least he did not have to worry about dealing with him. "Okay. I'm goin' topside. You sit still. I'll be right there to get you." He started to take a step, but stopped. "Chloe?"

"What?"

"I love you." He knew it was probably a dumb thing to say at the moment, but it felt important to him.

She smiled, a frightened-little-girl smile, and nodded. "Hurry."

Shea could not urge his horse up the mountainside fast enough. Even though he had found her, every minute counted. In her excitement, she could slip and fall. He had to be quick.

Reaching the top, he jumped down and grabbed the rope off of his saddle. He saw Hank's body crumpled on the ground, but he paid it little attention. Chloe was his only concern at the moment. Taking the coil of hemp, he secured it around the same tree as the boy had apparently used. The remains of a severed rope still hung fastened to the trunk.

Satchel ran over to him and pounced on the free end. He swiped it with his paws and rolled onto his back, chewing on it.

"No, boy. Not now." Shea yanked it out of the cat's grasp.

He tied a slipknot in the opposite end, then ran to the edge and tossed the line over the cliffside to the ledge below. "Chloe, do you see the rope?"

"Yes."

"Grab on and tie it around your waist."

Chloe shot him a fearful look. She shook her head. "I-I can't. I'll fall."

Curious as ever, Satchel joined Shea at the edge.

He gestured toward the setting sun. "It's gettin' dark. You've got to."

"I can't!" she screamed. "You come get me."

"Get up, Chloe."

She shook her head again. "I can't. I'm afraid."

"Do it, damn it! Get up and—" He cut off his words. Fear for her life had made him angry. He looked down at her, flattened so hard against the stone. He could tell she was crying. He had to calm himself if he was going to be of any help to her. He took a deep breath to clear his head. "I've got to stay up here to pull ya up, Button," he said in a soothing voice.

Eyes focused on him, she remained still.

"Ye've got to do this, Button, otherwise I can't help ya."

"You can come down for me," she said, her voice trembling.

"No, I can't. There's no one to pull us up." He looked away for a minute. He had to remain calm. He sucked in another gulp of air. "C'mon now, Button, ya can do this. I'll help ya all I can, but ya gotta do just this one part for me, okay?"

She appeared hesitant. Her gaze shot downward.

"No. Look up at me."

She did as he asked.

"Okay, now stand up."

She remained as she was a minute longer, then slowly she stood, her arms outstretched as if she were being crucified.

"Okay, Button, see the rope? It's only about a foot from yer hand."

She nodded.

"Good. Grab hold."

She inched her fingers across the stone wall until she touched the line.

The next part would be a little tricky. "Now," Shea continued. "Pull the slack up to you. Easy."

Her hands shook as she lifted the length of the hemp to the ledge.

"Okay, now pull it though the slipknot at the end." He swallowed hard. If she lost her balance, she would fall. He waited until she had accomplished that feat before he went on to the next. This would be the hardest for her to do. "Now, you've got to slide that lasso over yer head, and under yer arms. Can ya do that for me, Button?"

She appeared doubtful. Her gaze shot to the ground. Her balance wavered.

"Don't look down! Look at me!"

She glanced back up.

"Good, now slip it around ya just like I said."

With shaking hands she performed the deed.

He exhaled in a rush of breath. At least now she was secured and could not fall any farther than the length of the rope. "I'm goin' to pull ya up now, okay?"

"Please hurry, Shea. I'm scared."

He had no reply for her—no words of comfort escaped. She had sounded so afraid, like a very little girl. It made him feel helpless, and he could not afford to feel that way right now. He would need all his strength to hoist her up without dropping her.

He moved back a couple of yards. Then, after hitching his gloves tighter on his hands, he sat down. He braced his feet against a crag in the stone ground, took a deep breath, and gripped the rope.

Satchel padded up beside him. Apparently, the cat still thought Shea was playing. The mountain lion bumped the top of his head under Shea's chin.

"Not now, boy!" Shea railed. He shoved the animal away, then slowly, carefully, began to pull on the line.

It seemed like an eternity before he finally saw the top of her head. He strained with all his might to haul her up.

She gripped the rocks in front of him.

Satchel bristled, snarled, then relaxed. He must have realized who she was.

"Hold on, Button." Quick to move, Shea jumped up and raced to grab her. Grasping her hand, he heaved her up to him.

They fell back together.

Whimpering, she shuddered against him, maintaining a death lock around his neck.

His fear as great as hers had been, he clutched her tight. *Thank you, God*, he murmured over and over in his mind. He hugged her fiercely against him—held her and listened as she sobbed against his neck.

Satchel traipsed over to where they lay. He rubbed up against them, a loud purr reverberating through the entire length of his body.

Only after a very long time did Chloe's crying eventually subside into tiny sniffles. She raised her head and looked at the cat and smiled, her eyes red, and wet with tears. She ruffled his head. "You, too, boy?"

Shea frowned. What did she mean?

As if she had read his mind, she answered the question. "I knew you'd come for me, Shea," she whispered, her voice trembling. She swallowed a gulp of air. "I knew you'd find me, so I just sat tight and waited."

His heart constricted painfully against his chest. He pulled her close and kissed her mouth fully. He had come so close to losing her. Never would he allow that to happen again. But unlike the contact Shea had previously sought from his wife's embrace, no passion inflamed his tender touch. This time he desired only a gentle but insistent reclaiming of a love he had very nearly allowed to come to a careless end.

Fifteen

LYING ATOP SHEA, CHLOE SLIPPED HER ARMS AROUND HIS neck and held him in a fierce hug. She shuddered against him. She had come so close to losing him without ever fully giving herself to him.

He fitted his mouth to hers, his tongue warm and soft, gently defusing her fear.

She parted her lips, a welcoming whimper escaping. She had been so afraid of dying, of never seeing him again, of never getting the chance to show him how much she loved him. She had been so childish to hold herself away from him. She would not do so now.

Her body suddenly changed course from panic to passion. Her blood, still surging at a frantic pace, eddied, setting up a riotously sweet frisson of overpowering desire racing through her veins.

She had to get as close to him as she could. She deepened the kiss, probing the inside of his mouth with urgent strokes of her tongue. Gone was the shyness and resentment toward him. She had to feel him—know every inch of him. An anguished moan hovered in her throat, cutting off her air until it broke free in a hungry groan.

He pulled away from her, his expression puzzled. He stared at her for a long moment. His eyes darkened. "Are ya sure, Chloe? Are ya sure this is what ya want right now?"

Bracing her palms against the stone floor on either side of his head, she raised up, her golden hair draped around him. "I've never wanted anything so much in all my life," she murmured. She leaned down and nipped his bottom lip. "Make me your wife, Shea. Make love to me, here, now."

He did not seem to need any more convincing. In that same heartbeat, he clutched her to him and sat up.

Forced to straddle his hips, Chloe went weak with anticipation. She had waited a lifetime for this. She would deny it no longer.

He cupped her bottom and pulled her fully atop him.

She could feel his hardened manhood push through the layers of their clothing, felt it spring up against the vibrant, vulnerable part of her body. He could feel it, too. She could see it in the hungry look of his dark-lashed eyes. Lost within the realm of her own abandon, she leaned her head back.

He branded her throat with delicious, fiery kisses. Supporting her spine with one hand, he sought out the knot securing her blouse together with the other. He tugged it free, then cupped a breast. He squeezed a nipple.

She groaned, a soulful, blissful shuddering sound that sent a charge of excitement through the entire length of her being. She had never known such deep, pulsating longing. She softened against him, thrilling to the liquid warmth that lapped at the lower part of her body. She was burning up. The sweltering flames scalded her with sweet, scarlet heat, and she loved it.

Like a starving woman, she had to have more. She squirmed against him.

He pushed her shirt off her shoulders, letting it fall to the waistband of her pants.

Cool air rushed in around her.

She tensed, then shivered.

"Ya cold?" he asked, the husky texture of his voice betraying his emotion. His hands continued to roam her body. "I could build a fire."

She hesitated to answer. Gripping his upper arms, she dug her fingers into his muscles. She lifted her head a little and searched his features. How could he think of releasing her right now?

His questioning gaze shot a hot sensation through the very essence of her soul—searing her every nerve, muscle, and bone—nothing was left uncharred.

She saw the smoldering glow of eagerness in his eyes. Oh, yes, he knew exactly what he was doing. He was instilling more of a fever in her than any campfire ever could. The chill ebbed, giving way to the gentle insistence of his heated touch. Leaning back a little, she closed her eyes, and shook her head.

He pulled her torn camisole apart, exposing her breasts.

She held onto an expectant breath.

He claimed a nipple, sucking it wholly into his mouth.

A beautiful kind of pain, almost unbearably sweet, hit her senses. She gulped for air. Her lungs expanded, shoving the sensitive tip of her breast deeper into his mouth. Entwining her fingers in his hair, she pulled him tightly to her.

She seemed to have no control over what she was

doing. It was as though the lightning sensations bolting through her had come alive—an entity taking command. It dictated her every move, driving her forward. To what? She moved without thought, rocking her body against his.

He clutched her bottom, urging her hard upon him.

Pleasure shot through her like an alarm, but instead of resisting, as she had before, she answered it with a thrust of her pelvis. She was crazy with need. She pushed at his shirt. She had to get it off of him.

With a throaty groan, he released her. But just long enough to remove the garment. Heedless of the buttons, he yanked out the hem from his waistband and snatched it over his head.

She struggled to help him. She wanted to feel his heated nakedness against hers, put to memory every hill and plain of his body. Even before the shirt came off, she smoothed her palms over his shoulders, relishing the play of his corded muscles against the surface of her hands.

Satchel chose that particular moment to nudge them with his head. He purred loudly.

Chloe jumped. She had forgotten that the cougar was even there.

"Damn it, Satchel, not now!" Shea railed. He shoved the big cat a couple of feet away. He tossed his shirt in the mountain lion's face.

Satchel flinched. He scrunched his nose up with an indignant yowl.

"Go on, Satchel." Shea dismissed the animal with an angry wave of his hand. "Go play somewhere else."

Satchel hesitated, then finally trotted off into the woods.

Chloe bent over slightly, exploring the strength of his back with her nails. Her fingers tingled. She had a sudden incredible hunger to taste his skin. She trailed her tongue across his collarbone. Her mouth watered with the salty-sweet flavor of his fevered skin.

He clenched his eyes closed, groaned, and shivered. "Oh, God, Chloe!" he said in a rough whisper. Holding her a space apart from him, his gaze sought hers, turning desperately serious, almost savage. "I can't stand it any longer."

In frantic haste, he snatched off his holster, tossing it off to the side. Then, after unbuckling his belt and unfastening his pants, he leaned her back. His hands flew at the buttons on her britches. "Get up," he commanded harshly.

Chloe's heart pounded wildly as she did as he instructed. Was he angry with her? Shea was like an insatiable demon, and she, the earthly possession of his desire. Willingly, she gave herself up to him.

He jerked the garment down over her hips.

A sudden wave of embarrassment deterred her emotions. Never had anyone seen her nude. She moved to cover herself, turning away slightly.

"No, oh no, Chloe." Gently grasping her hands, Shea kissed her fingers, his enraptured gaze taking an upward trail over her body. "You're beautiful." Releasing his grasp, he palmed her bare buttocks and pulled her toward him. "C'mere."

Uncertain of what was expected of her, she held herself rigid, her hands suspended on either side of his head.

He snuggled close, caressing the downy mound shielding her womanhood with his cheek, then nuzzled her with his nose.

She could feel the warmth of his breath. It fanned the flame within her anew. She clutched his shoulders for support.

He tasted the sensitive bud hidden within her softness.

She jumped. A sharp, sweep pain rocked her. An anguished moan slipped from her throat. Desire flared, swiftly, uncontrollably.

His tongue, wet and hot, seared her flesh. The full span of his grip bit into her bottom.

With a gasp of sudden awareness, she moved against him. She could not help herself. Threading her fingers through his hair, she pulled him into her. So desperate was the longing inside her, she could not think of what was happening, she could only react.

Without words, he seemed to guide—no—*command* her responses.

And she willingly allowed it. Her blood was like molten lava, ebbing and flowing, hot from his touch, surging outward to every recess of her core. She pushed against him wantonly.

His tongue probed deeper, dancing along the sensitive walls of her womanly flesh.

Her stomach muscles tightened. Dizziness enveloped her. God in heaven! What was he doing to her? She swayed into him. Her emotions whipsawed from pleasure, to fear, to confusion. This was not natural. It was torrid and wonderful and recklessly wild. It could not be right. Nowhere had she found anything like this written in the romantic stories she had read. Yet she wanted it—oh God, she wanted it.

A sweet, blinding pain flashed through her limbs. Her heartbeat quickened. Sheened with perspiration, her nipples pulled taut against the cool evening air, her muscles tighter still. It frightened her, yet thrilled her even more. She dug her fingers into his scalp, and threw her head back in wild abandon.

With a sudden groan, Shea clamped his arms around her bottom, then pulled her to him, rolling them onto the ground.

Shocked, Chloe gasped at the bite of the chilled granite floor beneath her backside. If it were not for the devouring flames lapping at her insides, she might have lunged to her feet. But the aching need to feel him inside her held her prisoner atop the stone.

After tugging down his pants, he positioned himself above her. "Hold onto me!" He breathed out the words fiercely.

Lost in the rapture of the moment, a sudden urgency flared in Chloe. She wrapped her arms under his and clutched his waist. She felt the pressure of his swollen manhood press against her. She went languid and wet, clutching at him, drawing him inside.

Suddenly, like a lighted firecracker, a tiny pain shot through her. She gasped. Her eyes flew wide. Tensing, she pushed against him. "No—don't!"

"Relax for me, Button," he breathed against her ear. Moving slowly, inch by maddening inch, he penetrated her deeper. He balanced the fullness of his weight on his elbows. He stroked her temples. "It's all right now, just relax." Holding himself motionless, he kissed her again, soft and sweet, then pulled away and looked at her.

Chloe felt confused. She wanted him to make love to her, but the pain— She blinked. It was gone. Pleasure took its place. She smiled, a silent invitation.

He moved out, so slowly, then eased back inside, a tender assault.

Her body yielded a little at a time, until she took him completely. She felt liquid hot. Lightning bolted through her brain, building in a raging storm of powerful need. She could not stop herself. She wrapped her legs around his hips. Finding herself suddenly meeting his thrust, she basked in the glorious torture of his hard body pounding into her softness.

With an animallike growl, he plunged into her.

Her body convulsed. She arched against him, a shower of lights splintering her brain.

Shea rocked and thrust, the strain of his need contorting his features. He drove himself deeper and deeper, until the strength of his release finally shattered within her.

In the single naked moment that followed, Chloe heard an almost inhuman cry tear into the night air. She did not know who had made the tortured sound and cared even less. It seemed the proper ending, the final untamed delivery of one soul given unto the other.

The heat from their passion now spent, the evening chill closed in around them.

Lying on her side, her head pillowed on Shea's upper arm, Chloe wiggled closer into his body warmth.

"Ya sure you're all right?" he asked.

"Mmm-hmm." She pulled his hand across her bosom and shivered. "I'm just a little cold."

He kissed her shoulderblade. "Ya want me to build a fire now?" he asked, his tone teasing.

Her teeth started to chatter, she nodded. "Yes, I think I do."

He started to rise, then halted. He brushed his fingers across one nipple. "That's not what ya said a little while ago."

Only slightly embarrassed, Chloe grinned. "A little while ago, I was quite toasty."

"Yeah, I know," he said against her ear, a wealth of satisfied huskiness ringing in his voice. He hugged her close, then shuddered. "It is gettin' a bit nippy, though. Maybe I *ought* to see to that fire."

Once they were dressed again, and sitting in front of a roaring flame, Shea turned an earnest gaze of concern on her. "Ya know, I didn't mean for it to turn out like it did."

"What?"

"Our lovemaking," he answered with directness. Cuddled up next to her, he traced his fingertips up the inside of her arm. "I wanted our first time together to be slow and tender. I wanted it to be so good between us, something ya could thrill to a thousand times over in yer mind."

Chloe held herself to silence. She was so touched by his endearing words, she did not know what to say.

"I wanted it to happen in some big comfortable bed like the one at the Grand Central Hotel, not out here in the wilds on that cold stone ground." He nodded over his shoulder at the spot where they had made love.

Chloe swallowed the lump in her throat. He had just shown her the most extraordinary pleasure she had ever known and he was worried about the backdrop? "Look around you, Shea. Is God's own nature not the most splendid setting for such a loving act?" Releasing a small sigh, she looped her arms around his neck and laid her head on his shoulder. "Nothing could be more grand—not even the Grand Central itself."

"Ya don't understand." He hesitated. "This wasn't supposed to be this way. Ya weren't even supposed to come out here before this damned job was over."

Chloe raised her head and looked at him. She tensed. "You're sorry I'm here?"

"No—that's not what I meant." For the first time that Chloe could ever recall, Shea suddenly appeared uncertain of himself. "Damn it, Chloe, I'm so sorry for all of *this*." He gestured toward the cliffside.

Her bottom lip quivered. He *did* regret her coming to Glenbrook.

He shook his head. "I was so caught up in the excitement of my job, I didn't see the danger I had put ya in."

Relief coursed through her, and something more. She suddenly needed to hear the straight facts from him, once and for all. "Tell me the truth, Shea. I have to know if—"

"If I'm really a thief?"

She nodded.

"No, Button, I'm not." Cupping her chin, he lifted her face to his.

She nearly drowned in the naked truth of his woodsy stare.

"What I am is a special agent for the governor of Nevada."

She smiled, happy tears burning her eyes. She

should have listened to her own innate suspicions from the first.

"Lance got me in with the service. I loved it, the excitement, the danger—all of it. So much so, that I was willing to not only risk my own life, but put yers in jeopardy as well."

"Shh." She set a finger to his lips. "You don't have to say all of this."

"I want to." He stared off into the twinkling night. "It won't ever happen again, though." He paused, watching the black sky. "I've got to see this job through, but once it's done, I'm quittin'."

Chloe clamped her jaws together to keep from smiling. She knew what it had taken for him to make that decision, but she could not help but feel relieved.

"I don't know how yet, but I'm goin' to find a way to trap Bill Sharon and see him put behind bars."

Chloe tensed at the sound of the man's name. "He was the one that put me down there." Her gaze moved to the dark line marking the edge of the cliff. "He left me down there to die. He killed that boy, too."

Shea tightened his embrace around her. "I know."

Chloe's gaze slid back to him. "You do?"

Shea nodded. "The man at the livery told me he had seen him ride out this way. That's how I knew where to start lookin' for ya."

"Then we *can* see him brought to justice."

"We?" Shea's questioning stare moved back to her.

"Yes. Don't you see? *I* can testify against him."

Shea shook his head even before she finished. "Oh, no. I'm not takin' any more chances with yer life. Bill

Sharon's a cold-blooded killer. He'll find a way to get to ya."

"But we've got to try. It's the only way we can stop him."

He shook his head again. "No, Chloe. I'll find another way."

"But—"

"I said *no*! This is my problem. I don't want you involved any more than ye've already been. Once we get back to town, I'm sendin' ya home with Dudee."

Chloe tried to cut him off, but he would not let her.

"If yer pa gets mad when he hears about our marriage, ya can stay with Lance and Winter Magic at the Triple-T."

"My place is with you," she said firmly. She had no intention of going to either her father's ranch or Shea's family's.

But he did not listen. "Then once this's over, I'll come and get ya, okay?" He leaned into her line of vision.

She thought about disagreeing, but what good would it do? His mind was made up. "All right, Shea, darling."

He tipped his head to one side and stared at her, his eyes challenging her. "I mean it, Chloe. I want ya to do as I say this time."

Taking a deep breath, she nodded with an indulgent smile. She yawned, pretending to succumb. It would not do any good to argue with him tonight. At the moment he was too determined—but then, so was she.

She stroked his face, tracing the rough stubble on his chin with her fingers. "I'm suddenly very tired. We can talk about it tomorrow, all right?" Tomorrow was a different day. She would have at least three long hours of riding together to work on him. She thought about the last time they had ridden double, and of the passion they had just shared. She smiled a secret smile. Then again . . . it might not be quite so hard to coax him into going along with her plan after all.

Sixteen

JUST OUTSIDE GLENBROOK, SHEA CUT THROUGH THE FORest skirting the edge of town to the back of his and Chloe's house.

No one had seen them. Their approach to town had been easily concealed. Everyone was at the Fourth of July rally.

After tying the horse to the fence, Shea helped Chloe down, then ushered her quickly into the house. They could not afford to be spotted—not yet. Someone might accidentally mention to Bill Sharon that they had been seen.

Upstairs in their room, Shea lifted the curtains aside and peered out the window overlooking the main street. "There must be people from clear around the lake out there."

Removing her soiled, torn blouse, Chloe nodded. She poured an ample amount of water from the toilet pitcher into the basin, then leaned down and splashed the cool liquid into her face. "They've probably come to hear the doctor's speech."

"Ya know about that?" Shea turned toward her.

Chloe rubbed her hands with a bar of lavender-scented soap, then smoothed the lather onto her forehead, cheeks, and neck. "I met Doctor Jenkins on the steamer the other night." She splashed off the foam, then dabbed her face dry with a towel. It felt so good to be clean again. "I believe he's involved with Bill Sharon, Shea."

He nodded. "Yup, I know, but how do you?" Tucking the tail of a fresh shirt into his pants, he continued to shift his attention between Chloe and the street below.

Chloe swallowed. Would Shea be angry with her when he found out that it had been she that had informed the doctor of his endeavors with the outlaws? "I'm afraid I told Doctor Jenkins what you were up to."

Shea glanced at her, his expression unreadable.

After pausing another moment, she rushed on. "I was afraid for you, Shea. I needed someone's help, and when the doctor told me he was your friend, I—I—" Her hands shook. She could not bring herself to tell him any more. "I'm sorry. I guess I just didn't think. I was so frightened of what was happening to you."

Crossing the room, Shea came to stand in front of her. He grasped her by the elbows and pulled her into his embrace. "It's not yer fault, Button. I know ya were just tryin' to help me. I know ya must've been afraid." He kissed the tip of her nose. "I should've sent ya and Dudee to stay with yer pa as soon as ya got here. I should've never married ya the way I did."

Chloe leaned back a space and looked up at him. "You're not sorry you married me, are you?" *This* was one truth she was not certain she wanted to hear.

Chuckling, he smoothed his hands down the

length of her hair. "I wanted nothin' more. I just wished it hadn't happened the way it did."

A roar of cheers echoed up from the street outside.

Still holding her, he glanced toward the window. "I've got to go now."

"Shea, I really think it'd be better if I went with you."

"Look," he said leaning into her face, his nose almost touching hers, "we talked about this last night and again on the way here." Clasping his hands around her waist, he rocked her gently from side to side. "I doubt it's goin' to be a pretty scene down there when I accuse him and the doc of murder and conspiracy. I don't want either of those bastards to know yer here. Let 'em think yer still up on that ledge."

Chloe shivered at the memory of the dizzying height.

"Besides, somewhere down there, there's a Pinkerton agent ready to through my butt in jail."

"But surely he'll believe you when you tell him about what happened to me, and the two stage porters?"

Shea shrugged. "I'll have to take that risk. I hope so, but I hit him pretty hard. I don't think he's goin' to be too willin' to listen to anythin' I've got to say right off. I'm just hopin' my presence'll intimidate either the doctor or Sharon into makin' a mistake."

"So let me go with you." She had to try one more time. She did not want him to go out there without some kind of proof to back his story—and she was the best proof he had.

"I told ya no, so let's drop it." Pausing, he raised

his brows. "I'll try to find Dudee and send her back to stay with ya, okay?"

Reluctantly, Chloe nodded.

"Good. Now Satchel's lyin' down under the stairs. If anythin' happens—anything at all—you git him up here with ya, and ya lock the two of ya in this room. He'll see nobody hurts ya." He gave her a quick kiss then and left the room.

Once she heard the front door slam, she hurried to the window and watched as Shea made a clandestine path toward the crowd at the end of the street. She sighed heavily.

Even though she had not exercised her feminine wiles on him as she had planned the previous evening, she was not sorry. Their lovemaking had been so beautiful and special. And they had already suffered so much. She could not bring herself to cheapen their relationship by using such a deceitful ploy.

Still, whether he believed it or not, Shea needed her help. Neither Bill Sharon nor Donovan Jenkins was going to just stand still and let her husband arrest them. They were both influential men in this town. And though Shea was well-known and respected by the townsfolk, the wealthy owner of a lumber company and a doctor would more likely be believed than someone of Shea's status.

Even though he would eventually be able to establish the truth about the two men and give evidence of their crimes, Shea would first have to confirm himself as a special agent for the governor. That might take at least a couple of days. He had already told her that this Pinkerton man did not believe him. He did not have a badge, so he would have to wait for a telegram to vouch for him—probably from a jail cell, too.

Hurrying to her trunk in the other room, she opened the lid, looking for something to wear, but it was empty. What had happened to all of her things? Aunt Dudee must have unpacked them. Chloe glanced around the room she had slept in before her departure three days earlier. Except for the furnishings, the interior was void of anything personal. What had Dudee done with everything?

She dashed back to the big bedroom that was to be hers and Shea's. Sure enough, when she opened the huge oak bureau, there hung all of her dresses. How thoughtful of her aunt, and how wickedly sly, too.

Chloe chuckled as she chose one of her more simple, yet elegant gowns. The woman had counted on Chloe and Shea working out their differences. It was just like her aunt. The wise matron always *did* seem to know how a thing was going to work out, and if it did not suit her, she would work on the situation until it did.

Chloe laid the garment across the mattress, then retrieved a pair of her shoes from inside the wardrobe. She would have to hurry if she was going to be of any assistance to Shea. She could not simply sit around and wait for those two men to escape the law—no matter how unwavering Shea had been about her remaining home.

Sitting on the edge of the bed, she yanked off her jeans and socks, replacing them with a sheer pair of black stockings and pantaloons. Bill Sharon and the doctor might not be intimidated by Shea's appearance, but they most certainly would be daunted by *her* sudden arrival.

Once she was dressed in her demi-evening toilette and her hair was brushed to a glossy sheen, she pulled the golden mass to one side and tied a willow-green ribbon at the nape. Taking a step back, she studied herself in the mirrored chiffonier. She smoothed down the delicate pink-and-white flower print on her blouse. It was not the most fetching costume she had ever worn, but tasteful just the same.

She wanted to look her best, but this would have to do. She could not wait to see Bill Sharon's astonished expression when he saw her. After grabbing up a lace parasol, she all but flew down the stairs to the front door. She did not usually carry a sunshade, but today she wanted it for concealment.

She hit the landing and dashed for the door. Something snagged the hem of her dress. Caught off balance, she fell facedown on the vestibule floor. Her heart bolted.

An animal growled.

Even before she looked up, she knew what had happened. Rolling over, she sat up straight. "Satchel!" she said with a huff. "You naughty boy." She shook her head. What was it about her and dresses? Did he still think she was some kind of toy?

He ambled up beside her and bumped her chin with the top of his head.

"This isn't playtime. I've got to get out there to Shea. Understand?" She scratched his ear roughly, then grabbed the sides of his face and leaned toward him. "You know, Shea? Remember him?"

The big yellow puma snaked out his scratchy tongue and lapped a wet lick across her nose.

"No, boy, no," she sputtered. Grabbing hold of his collar, she pulled herself up to her feet. "I know you probably think nobody loves you anymore, but I can't play right now." Standing, she pointed toward his bed under the staircase. "You go take a nap. We'll play when I get—" Her eyes grew wider. She glanced down at the cougar. Shea had left the cat for her protection.

"Protection, hmm?" A plan forming in her mind, she grinned. "And so you shall," she said heading back up to her room for her belt. If Bill Sharon, the doctor, or even this Pinkerton man tried to thwart Shea before he could make his case, any or all of them were in for one very big surprise.

A loud volley of applause drew Chloe toward her target. So far, all had gone well. She had noticed a few familiar faces, but evidently her use of the small umbrella had worked. Even though she passed through the throng of onlookers with Satchel on his lead, none appeared to have realized her identity.

She edged as near as she dared to the podium where Donovan Jenkins, M.D., was concluding his magnanimous speech.

"You people have known me for many years," Doctor Jenkins stated in his smooth, rich voice. "I've watched Glenbrook and some of the other surrounding areas grow from a tiny trestle of iron to thriving lumber communities. After my wife passed away in seventy-three I didn't think I'd ever enjoy much of a life."

Chloe lifted the lace shading in front of her view. Where was Bill Sharon? She searched the many people thronging the speaker. She found him.

Off to the side of the platform stood the man himself. Dressed in a gray shadow-checked refined suit,

Bill Sharon looked out over the crowd. Hands behind his back, he smiled, though not too boldly.

Chloe gritted her teeth. She could feel the loathing building inside of her.

Satchel must have felt it, too. He growled, a low, deep sound that brought even the hairs on Chloe's neck to attention.

"Shh, boy." She patted him under his chin.

Doctor Jenkins raised his hands to the crowd and smiled. "I realize that the elections may seem like a long ways off to some of you, but let me tell you, November will be here before you know it. And if we're going to be able to reinstate the value of silver into our currency, then we must act now. Dick Bland needs every constituent he can get if we're to succeed in quashing the Act of Seventy-Three. If you elect me as your congressman, my voice will join his."

Chloe turned her attention toward the faces in the crowd. Where was Shea? Had something happened to him? Suddenly, she saw him.

Head down, hat at a tilt, he leaned against a beam on the front walkway of the Glen Brook House. His gaze was riveted on the two men at the podium.

Chloe could see the anger in his eyes and knew that he was about to make his move.

"Now, friends," the doctor's voice bellowed above the rush of murmurs sweeping the throng. "I set myself up for any questions that you would put to me."

"Yer words is good, Doc, but how can we trust that you'll vote like we want ya to?" a man called out. "This silver problem's important to most everybody's livelihood here. "One way or another we all need it."

"Dan Thompson," the doctor announced in a tolerant tone. "Didn't I deliver your son, Eton, three years ago?"

The man nodded. "Can't see what the hell that's got to do with my question, though."

"Well, Dan, as I recall," Donovan Jenkins said with a grin, rubbing his hands together, "you didn't have any money to pay me for my services."

Chloe watched the man called Dan turn red.

"Yessir, that's true, but—"

"And as I recall—" the doctor did not give way to an interruption. "I didn't ask you *how* you were going to pay me."

"No sir, ya didn't."

Doctor Jenkins gestured toward the man with a wink. "But you paid me, didn't you? You paid me, and I didn't even have to ask for it. I didn't ask you where it came from—it was just there. Some in small increments, but you got me paid back in full. I didn't poke my nose into your financial affairs. I just trusted you, and you got the job done."

Chloe frowned. Where was this grandiose speech leading?

"Well, Dan. That's the way it has to be with me. You have to trust me." He thumped his hands on his chest with dramatic flair. "If I'm voted to office, I promise, to the best of my ability, that I will do my utmost to make sure that the Bland–Allison Act is continually brought to the floor of Congress until it's passed. I know these mining communities could fold without the use of silver as currency. It's the silver mines that need your shoring beams. It's the silver mines that fill our children's mouths with food. It's—"

"And who is it that takes the money out of our pockets so that we can't feed our children?"

Chloe cringed. She knew that voice only too well. Shea had taken this opportunity to make himself known.

"Do I know you, sir?" the doctor asked.

Bill Sharon drew up taut.

All eyes turned Shea's way.

He tipped up his hat, exposing his face to view. "Ya should, Doc." He pointed at the man standing beside the speaker. "You and Sharon there conspired to murder my wife."

A flurry of loud whispers flew through the audience.

"Why, Shea, son," the doctor stuttered. "What are you doing here? I was under the impression that you had been taken to jail by the territorial marshal." His gaze flitted to Mr. Sharon.

"That a fact?" Shea moved in a little closer.

Chloe held her breath. Even though she did not know who to watch for, she shot a nervous look around the crowd. She was torn between not wanting the Pinkerton man Shea had told her about to show up and hoping he would. Shea might need some help.

"And why's that, Doc? Am I supposed to've done somethin' wrong?" Shea asked, his tone composed, taunting.

The doctor stiffened. His worried gaze moved over the people pressing in around him.

Bill Sharon hopped up on the platform beside his accomplice. He raised his hands. "Now, folks, listen. Just before his speech, the good doctor and I were informed of a terrible crime that this young man committed. We didn't think it necessary to upset all of you on such an auspicious day and all, but now that it's out, you might as well hear all of it."

"Tell us," somebody yelled.

"Well, now," Sharon drawled in a clear voice. "It seems Shea Taggert here killed a couple of men up on Shakespeare Rock." He pointed toward the mountain.

Shocked, Chloe blinked. What did this man hope to gain by such a lie?

A drone of angry, pity-filled groans came from the spectators.

"Now, folks, hold onto yourselves because it gets worse." Bill Sharon sucked in a deep breath. "You all know that Shea recently got married?"

Nods whipped up and down.

"And that he took his little bride to Tahoe City for a honeymoon?" He sighed dispiritedly. "Well, now, I'm sorry to inform all of you of this, but Mrs. Taggert has been reported missing. We fear she, too, has been killed by her husband."

Instantly the crowd pressed closer to Shea.

Chloe was torn. She had to protect her husband's life, but she had to stall until just the right moment to show herself so that she could ensure the demise of Bill Sharon and Donovan Jenkins. She held herself silent. She would wait a few more minutes.

"And why would I do that?" Shea did not sound quite so certain of himself anymore. He took a step backward, away from the crowd.

"Yes, Mr. Sharon." A gravelly voice rose up above the others. "Why would Special Agent Taggert do that?"

Chloe shifted her attention to a tall, stalwart man of about fifty.

Silver hair glistened beneath the brim of a brown Stetson.

Chloe blinked.

It was Mr. Gentry. The old gentleman she had ridden with on the stage. What was his part in all of this? And how did he know Shea?

"And you are?" Bill Sharon appeared suspicious—not to mention flustered.

Mr. Gentry held up a silver shield. "Pinkerton Agent Angus Gentry, Chicago Division."

Chloe gasped. Mr. Gentry was the Pinkerton man Shea had told her about?

"Now, if both you and the *good* doctor, as you call him, would step down off that platform and over to the sheriff's office, I believe we can set this matter to rights in no time."

Sharon jumped back. He reached inside his coat pocket.

Dropping her parasol, Chloe lunged forward. "Look out, Shea!" she screamed. She hiked up her skirts, shoving her way through the many people as she rushed toward him. "He's got a derringer!"

Like a wave in the ocean, the crowd moved with her.

A shot fired into the air.

The audience froze in a half-circle in front of the podium.

Only a few feet from Shea, Chloe flew to his side. Shot or no, she would not be kept apart from him.

He grabbed her, then pulled her next to him, a protective arm darting around her shoulders. "I thought I told you to stay home."

Chloe shrugged. She opened her mouth to reply, but Bill Sharon, who was pointing his gun, interrupted.

"You should've listened to him, ma'am."

"Hell, she ain't kilt," somebody hollered. "That's Shea's missus now."

The doctor moved up behind Bill Sharon.

Mr. Gentry eased his weapon from its holster.

"Uh-uh." Bill Sharon shook his head. "Toss it down, Pinkerton. Slow, now."

Mr. Gentry threw the Colt on the ground a few yards in front of the crowd.

"Now what?" Shea asked, glaring at Mr. Sharon. "Ya stole most of the payroll comin' into these folks. Ya murdered Jimmy Lee and Hank. Ya left Chloe to die up on that ledge—what's next?" He nodded toward the derringer. "Ya think ya can get the rest of us with that one shot?"

Out of the corner of her eye, Chloe saw Satchel move up from the rear of the platform. She had been so afraid for Shea, she had released the cat's leash, then forgotten about him. She cut Shea a knowing glance.

He followed her line of vision, then nodded. "Give it up, Sharon. You're outnumbered."

"Listen to him, Bill. We can still get out of this with our lives," the doctor pleaded in a shaky voice.

"Shut up, you old fool! They're only guessing. Nobody has any proof."

"Nobody did," Shea announced with a wry smile, "until ya made the mistake of leavin' Chloe alive." He hugged her to him. "She saw ya kill both Jimmy Lee and Hank."

"Jimmy Lee? The young stage porter? Hank?"

Their names were on the lips of everyone in the crowd.

"You know, I'm glad you pointed that out to me, Taggert." He gestured toward Chloe with a wave of his gun. "If you'll be so kind as to join me, Mrs. Taggert."

His politeness drove Chloe mad. She remained where she stood. She was not about to simply give herself over to the man a second time. "That's just how he spoke when he killed those two men."

"What?" Shea peered down at her. "Don't goad him on, Chloe. Save it for the trial."

"There isn't going to be any trial." Sharon stepped down from the podium and edged toward the front doors of the Glen Brook House. "At least, not with me."

"What about me, Sharon?" The doctor grabbed his sleeve.

"Let go of me!" Bill Sharon shoved the older man away, knocking him to the ground. "You're on your own." He took another step toward the hotel.

Satchel padded up behind him and snarled.

Sharon jumped.

Mr. Gentry dove for the weapon in the dirt.

The crowd moved forward.

Shielding Chloe with one arm, Shea whipped up his Colt.

Sharon turned. He must have seen Shea's move. He pointed the derringer in their direction.

Chloe screamed for Satchel.

The cougar lunged upward, attacking Sharon's arm. The small gun fired, the bullet aimed at Chloe.

Shea shoved her to the side.

She stumbled out of the way, but it was not quick enough.

Catching the full impact of the slug in Chloe's stead, Shea slammed into her back. The two of them fell to the ground in a flurry of dust, patriotic ribbon, and petticoats.

Chloe gathered Shea to her breast. She screamed in terror. *God in Heaven, no! Don't let him be dead.*

Angry shouts filled the air. "Catch him somebody! He's tryin' to get away!"

Chloe looked up just in time to see Bill Sharon dash inside the Glen Brook House.

Mr. Gentry grabbed the doctor.

She shifted her gaze from the confusion of the people to her blood-covered hand, then Shea's face. Fear nearly wrenched her apart.

His eyes were closed, and— Oh God! He did not move.

Sitting out on the porch swing in front of the house Shea had built especially for her, Chloe released a long pent-up breath. It had been nearly a week since the shooting and still no sign of Bill Sharon had been found. The doctor had been taken into custody by Mr. Gentry and the town had settled back into a semblance of normalcy.

Leaning her head back, Chloe closed her eyes and turned her face up to the early-morning sun. She rocked her feet back and forth from her toes to her heels. Shea had been right. She should have never run off from Boston like she did. Look at all the trouble she had caused by doing so.

Aunt Dudee had been hurt. She, herself, had been abducted. Tyree Cameron had been killed. Bill Sharon had murdered the two porters, and had gotten away with it. Many of the townspeople of Glenbrook and the surrounding area had lost money to the stage holdups Doctor Jenkins and Bill Sharon had instigated. And for what? Greed? Political votes? Power?

She sighed heavily. Oh, if she had not been so foolhardy and rushed out from the East to this wild and woolly place . . .

Footsteps sounded nearby. The front door opened.

Lifting her lashes, she looked up and smiled at the most alluring sight she could ever behold.

Arm draped across his chest in a sling, Shea beamed a smile down at her. He walked over to the swing and bent down. His mouth brushed hers in a soft, gentle kiss. "You're up early."

"Mmm." She nodded. "You, too. When I woke up to an empty bed, I hurried and got dressed. I thought we'd go for a walk by the lakeside, but Ushi told me you were in a meeting in your study." She patted the wood slats on the seat. "I decided to come out here and wait until you were finished."

Sitting beside her, Shea stretched his long legs out, then shifted his arm up tighter in the sling. "Angus Gentry came to see me."

"Really?" Chloe looked at her husband. "Did they find Sharon yet?"

"Nah, not yet. But Gentry's promised they won't stop searchin' for the bastard till they do."

"And the doctor? Did they ship him off to Chicago?"

"Yup. Gentry's takin' him, hisself." Shea turned to Chloe, a serious expression marking his features. He held up a folded piece of official-looking paper. "Brought me this before he left."

Chloe's interest peaked. "All right, Shea Taggert. Call me a trout. I'll bite. What is it?"

"It's a letter of commendation from the Pinkerton Agency—wired out all the way from Chicago, Illinois." He opened it. "It's addressed to the governor of Nevada."

Chloe brightened. It made her heart swell with pride to think that her husband had done such a wonderful job with his assignment. "Read it to me."

"Dear Sir," Shea began in a most dramatic voice. "This is to inform you that Special Agent Shea Taggert, currently of Glenbrook, Nevada, has performed above and beyond the call of duty. While seeing to the apprehension of known criminals, he put his life in danger on more than one occasion. He defied the overpowering odds at every turn and selflessly executed his responsibilities with the highest possible regard for the protection of the citizens of Glenbrook City, Lake Tahoe Territory, Nevada. He aided Pinkerton detectives in bringing a war criminal to justice, and was wounded while trying to save the life of a civilian. We at the Pinkerton Agency would like to bestow the highest recommendation on this outstanding agent. Signed: Allan Pinkerton, Commander in Chief, Pinkerton National Detective Agency, Chicago, Illinois."

"Oh, Shea, that's wonderful."

"Yup, it is kinda, ain't it?" He grinned. "Gentry said this'd probably get me any assignment I wanted, anywhere in the states."

Chloe's stomach tightened. She stared at Shea. What was he saying? He had promised her he was going to quit the agency as soon as this was all over. "You mean you're not going to quit?"

"Well, I said I would just as soon as I saw Bill Sharon put behind bars, didn't I?"

"Yes." Chloe swallowed. That *is* what he had told her. "But Sharon isn't behind bars. He's still out there, free somewhere."

"Well, then—" Shea leaned back and looked out over the lake.

Chloe cringed in expectation—she could not go through anything like this again. It was too dangerous. She had almost been killed and her husband had almost died trying to fulfill his commitment to this job. This career of his was not worth what it had almost cost them.

Shea's face slowly split into a wicked smile. "I guess you'll just have to call me a liar again."

Blinking, Chloe stared at him. "What?"

"You did say I was a liar, didn't ya?"

"Yes, but that was when I thought—"

"Seems to me I recall ya sayin' somethin' about me bein' a thief, too?" he asked in a teasing tone.

Exhaling a sigh of relief, she returned his smile. He was teasing her. "Yes, I'm afraid I did that, too."

"Well then, since I'm a liar, I guess I can't wait for Bill Sharon to be caught before I quit, now, can I? I guess I'll just have to *really* become that foreman I've been pretendin' to be for O'Dell."

Chloe beamed at him. "Really, Shea? You're goin' to quit? We're goin' to stay here in Glenbrook?"

He nodded. "Dudee sent my letter of resignation out yesterday." He slipped his good arm around her shoulders and drew her close. "But about this bein' a thief business . . ."

"Yes?" Chloe was so happy she was about to burst open from the inside out.

"Do you know a *dimwitted city doxy* that might have a little extra passion layin' around somewhere that she wouldn't mind me stealin'?"

Chloe drew back and stared at him. He had used her own words on her. He had learned to turn her own game around on her, and he was flaunting it in her face. "Is that what you're calling me, Shea Taggert?" She felt a bubble of laughter threaten to reveal her ruse of temper.

He bent nearer her mouth, his lips a kiss away. "That was *you* the other night that attacked me so wantonly, after I rescued ya off that ledge, was it not?"

Her gaze went limpid. She could almost feel his body warmth seeping into her breasts, yet he remained inches away. She nodded, a tingle of desire stirring her senses.

"And it was *you* who lay in my bed last night and flaunted her naked little body at me, was it not?"

"Shea!" She darted a gaze around, searching to see if anyone had overheard him.

He nipped at her lower lip. "Answer the question."

"Guilty," she whispered. "I did all those things."

"Mmm, then that must be what I'm callin' ya—ya mind?"

Eyes downcast, she smiled. She was helpless with desire when he spoke to her like this. He could have anything he wanted from her.

"Well then—" He ran his tongue across her lips.

At that moment, something bumped Chloe's knees. She flinched. But even before she turned her attention downward, she knew what it was. Giggling low in her throat, she turned her attention on Satchel.

The big cat butted her again. When she did not respond, he did the same to Shea.

"Not now, boy." Shea nudged him away. "Can't ya see I'm busy."

Satchel blinked. He peered at Chloe, a pathetic look of hope reigning in his expressive eyes.

She smiled sympathetically and bent toward him. "Poor baby," she said, reaching out for him. "Oh, look at him, Shea. You've hurt his feelings."

Shea pulled her closer. "You'll hurt my feelin's if ya don't pay attention here."

Satchel pushed on the swing with his head. It was only too apparent that he was not going to give up so readily.

"Go on, boy," Shea said with another gentle prod of his foot. "Go find somethin' else to play with."

Without further provocation, Satchel turned and ran around the side of the house toward the woods out back.

"Maybe you should go play with him a little, Shea. Since I've arrived you've hardly spent any time with him."

Shea grinned mischievously. "I got a better idea. How about we run upstairs and take a little nap right now."

"But we just got dressed." She knew what he wanted, and it thrilled her, yet she continued to play the game.

"We've got a lifetime to be dressed, Button. Maybe if we're lucky we can make Satchel a playmate while we're at it." He kissed her temple, fanning her ear with his warm breath. "Whaddya think?"

She shivered, reveling in the crazy excitement with which he was filling her. A child? What a wonderful idea. She had been so wrapped up in herself and the trouble with the robberies and Shea that she had not given even a single thought to the prospect of children right now. But, oh ... how wonderful it would be to have Shea's child. "It sounds like heaven." Her body warmed against his with another thought—a wildly wanton, hungry thought. She met his heated gaze head-on with hers. "And I've got all the passion you could want, Shea Taggert." She slid her arms around his neck and kissed him fully.

When he finally pulled away, his eyes had turned that wonderful shade of woodsy moss that signaled his assured arousal. Standing, he held out his hand to her. "Then let me whisk ya upstairs, Button. I've got another hankerin' to rob ya of a little more of that passion ye've been accusin' me of stealin'."

Chloe rose without further prompting. Yes, she probably should have stayed in Boston and waited for Shea to send for her. She should have acted like the proper young ladies did in all of those romance stories she had read.

But then, if she had, she might very well have remained a spectator of life. She might very well have missed meeting up with a very real romantic figure and the most loving thief any woman could ever have dreamed of encountering.

Dear Readers:

I am always delighted to hear from you and do so love receiving your comments about my stories. If you enjoyed *Tender Outlaw*, and would like to write to me, or would just like to be put on my mailing list, you can send letters to:

> P.O. Box 60631
> Bakersfield, CA
> 93386-0631

> —Deborah James

If you enjoyed this book, take advantage of this special offer. Subscribe now and...

Get a Historical

No Obligation

If you enjoy reading the very best in historical romantic fiction...romances that set back the hands of time to those bygone days with strong virile heros and passionate heroines...then you'll want to subscribe to the True Value Historical Romance Home Subscription Service. Now that you have read one of the best historical romances around today, we're sure you'll want more of the same fiery passion, intimate romance and historical settings that set these books apart from all others.

Each month the editors of True Value select the four *very best* novels from America's leading publishers of romantic fiction. We have made arrangements for you to preview them in your home *Free* for 10 days. And with the first four books you receive, we'll send you a FREE book as our introductory gift. No Obligation!

FREE HOME DELIVERY

We will send you the four best and newest historical romances as soon as they are published to preview FREE for 10 days (in many cases you may even get them before they arrive in the book stores). If for any reason you decide not to keep them, just return them and owe nothing. But if you like them as much as we think you will, you'll pay just $4.00 each and save at *least* $.50 each off the cover price. (Your savings are *guaranteed* to be at least $2.00 each month.) There is NO postage and handling—or other hidden charges. There are no minimum number of books to buy and you may cancel at any time.

FREE
Romance
(a $4.50 value)

Send in the Coupon Below

To get your FREE historical romance and start saving, fill out the coupon below and mail it today. As soon as we receive it we'll send you your FREE Book along with your first month's selections.

Mail To: **True Value Home Subscription Services, Inc.** P.O. Box 5235
120 Brighton Road, Clifton, New Jersey 07015-5235

YES! I want to start previewing the very best historical romances being published today. Send me my FREE book along with the first month's selections. I understand that I may look them over FREE for 10 days. If I'm not absolutely delighted I may return them and owe nothing. Otherwise I will pay the low price of just $4.00 each: a total $16.00 (at *least* an $18.00 value) and save at least $2.00. Then each month I will receive four brand new novels to preview as soon as they are published for the same low price. I can always return a shipment and I may cancel this subscription at any time with no obligation to buy even a single book. In any event the FREE book is mine to keep regardless.

Name _____

Street Address _____ Apt. No. _____

City _____ State _____ Zip Code _____

Telephone _____

Signature _____
(if under 18 parent or guardian must sign)

0043-3

Terms and prices subject to change. Orders subject
to acceptance by True Value Home Subscription
Services, Inc.

Diamond Wildflower Romance

A breathtaking new line of spectacular novels set in the untamed frontier of the American West. Every month, Diamond Wildflower brings you new adventures where passionate men and women dare to embrace their boldest dreams. Finally, romances that capture the very spirit and passion of the wild frontier.

__HOSTAGE HEART by Lisa Hendrix
  1-55773-974-9/$4.99
__FORBIDDEN FIRE by Bonnie K. Winn
  1-55773-979-X/$4.99
__WARRIOR'S TOUCH by Deborah James
  1-55773-988-9/$4.99
__RUNAWAY BRIDE by Ann Carberry
  0-7865-0002-6/$4.99
__TEXAS ANGEL by Linda Francis Lee
  0-7865-0007-7/$4.99
__FRONTIER HEAT by Peggy Stoks
  0-7865-0012-3/$4.99
__RECKLESS RIVER by Teresa Southwick
  0-7865-0018-2/$4.99
__LIGHTNING STRIKES by Jean Wilson
  0-7865-0024-7/$4.99
__TENDER OUTLAW by Deborah James
  0-7865-0043-3/$4.99
__MY DESPERADO by Lois Greiman
  0-7865-0048-4/$4.99 (October)

Payable in U.S. funds. No cash orders accepted. Postage & handling: $1.75 for one book, 75¢ for each additional. Maximum postage $5.50. Prices, postage and handling charges may change without notice. Visa, Amex, MasterCard call 1-800-788-6262, ext. 1, refer to ad # 406

Or, check above books Bill my: ☐ Visa ☐ MasterCard ☐ Amex	
and send this order form to:	(expires)
The Berkley Publishing Group Card#_____	
390 Murray Hill Pkwy., Dept. B	($15 minimum)
East Rutherford, NJ 07073 Signature_____	
Please allow 6 weeks for delivery. Or enclosed is my: ☐ check ☐ money order	
Name_____	Book Total $_____
Address_____	Postage & Handling $_____
City_____	Applicable Sales Tax $_____ (NY, NJ, PA, CA, GST Can.)
State/ZIP_____	Total Amount Due $_____